Of Milk and Honey

by

John Owens

I have come down to deliver them out of the hand of the Egyptians and to bring them up out of that land to a good and broad land, a land flowing with milk and honey. (Exodus 3:7-8)

Preface

If he had known there were so many of them, he would have headed for the high street rather than running into the estate. Once there it was easier for them to cut off escape routes and as he raced blindly down the passages between the tower blocks, they moved silently and with stealthy speed to block exits and pathways, all the time closing the net on him. It was on an outside stairwell that they finally caught up with him, a hand grabbing his ankle as it slipped on the metal stair. They didn't waste time with words but began to punch and kick and stab, and he became aware in a way he couldn't quite define that he was able to tell the difference between a blow that came from a knife and one struck with a fist. As the punches and kicks rained down on him his vision started to blur, and his body began to desensitize itself to the pain as his organs commenced the process of shutting down. And all the time there were no words, only the heavy breathing of people concentrating all their energies on hard physical work.

After a while, the rain of blows stopped, and he heard a voice saying, "Give me some space." He looked up and saw a blur of faces, a couple of them teenage - the hoodies and baseball caps failing to hide their pallid, pinched youthfulness - the others older. As the figures shimmered in front of him, he heard the voice again, this time ordering the people around him to move back and give him some room. The silhouettes melted away, revealing the pebble dashed wall of a tower block exterior, and then he heard the voice for a third time, and though he knew the words were being directed at him and although he focused all his attention on trying to decipher their meaning, he couldn't process them. A face danced in front of him and he saw its lips move and at last the jumble of sounds coalesced into a form of words he understood. "Jungle Bunny!"

He saw a baseball bat swing backwards in a smooth, lazy arc and then fill his vision as it accelerated towards him. A second later it connected with his head and there was a hollow popping sound - the noise a huge spoon might make cracking a giant egg - and his skull caved in and his head fell back and smashed against the concrete step, and in that moment, whatever the subsequent cardiograph might say to the contrary, conscious life left him. For a moment the figures stood in a semi-circle looking down at him while they recovered their breath and then they melted silently away into the darkness. Before they left one of them propped a small rectangle of cardboard against his leg: it was the size of a business card and was blank except for a red Cross of St George above which was superimposed the legend: YOU HAVE BEEN VISITED BY STORM FORCE 55.

He was nine years old.

Part One

If you wish the sympathy of the broad masses, you must tell them the crudest and most stupid things. (Adolf Hitler)

There is no crueller tyranny than that which is perpetuated under the shield of law and in the name of justice. (Baron de Montesquieu)

Nobody can build a wall like me. (Donald J Trump)

I

*If attending the English Rose meeting, turn right
and walk to the end of the corridor*, read the
message on the A4 sheet taped to the glass fronted
doorframe of a shabby looking office block in the
London district of Wembley. Taking a deep breath
and aware that his heart was thumping
uncomfortably against the cloth of his shirt and that
sweat was trickling down and pooling in the small
of his back, Frank Mason opened the door and
entered. Another A4 sheet sellotaped to a pillar in
the foyer read, ENGLISH ROSE MEETING: 7.30
CONFERENCE ROOM C, and inside Mason saw
other sheets taped to walls, and an arrow pointing
down a corridor. He took another deep breath,
followed the arrows down the corridor and found
himself in a room about the size of a school hall,
with chairs laid out in rows and a stage at the front.

A middle-aged lady in the doorway smiled
and handed him a leaflet. "Evening" she said, and
he found himself smiling back at her. The hall was
almost full, and he slid into a chair at the end of the
second row from the back. The seats were hard
backed and covered with dark blue cloth – the kind
of chairs used in hundreds of office and hotel
conference rooms up and down the country.
Looking around him Mason had to concede that the
audience looked disarmingly normal, there were no

shaved heads, tattoos or swastikas, in fact it looked for all the world like the kind of congregation one might see on an episode of *Songs of Praise*. He inspected the leaflet he was holding which was glossy and looked as if it had been professionally produced. It was entitled *English Rose: Reclaiming our Country*, and Mason began to read the text:

It is time that all Englishmen and women stood up to reclaim our heritage, the heritage of Henry V and John Bull, of buccaneers and best bitter, of cricket on the village green....

He glanced up and noticed that he was being observed by a middle-aged couple sitting a couple of seats along from him. He risked a tentative smile and the man returned it and said, "First time?"

"Does it show?" he said ruefully, and the man chuckled. "You remind me of how we felt the first time we came to a meeting. How long ago was that, Joan?"

"A year ago, last February," his companion answered promptly, "and we've been coming ever since."

"Always voted Tory, before," said the man, who wore a gaberdine zipper jacket and a pair of trousers that screamed Marks and Spencer elasticated waistband. "Always. Never thought we'd desert the party of Sir Winston and the Iron Lady, did we love?"

"And we wouldn't have," said Joan. "But we can't go on the way we've been going. Not with everything that's happened."

"Reg Brown," said the man, sticking out a hand. "Er… Frank Mason," replied Mason, returning the handshake.

"And this is my better half." Mason smiled dutifully and Joan smiled back at him and extended a hand in a gesture that was vaguely regal. As she moved, he caught a whiff of lavender and behind it, something fainter and sour.

"I mean, don't get us wrong," said Reg, "we've always been One Nation, always prepared to see the other side, always ready to listen to the other person's point of view. But we've got to do something, we can't go on the way we have been, otherwise… well, there'll be nothing left."

There was a stir in the hall and a huddle of figures moved through the crowd and ascended onto the platform. A man tapped the microphone on the table in front of him and said, "Good evening everybody and welcome to this English Rose open forum. If you've been here before, thanks for coming back and if this is your first time, we hope you'll hear enough to whet your appetite for more."

He was thirtyish and dressed in expensive looking jeans, Chelsea boots and a zip necked fleece, and he had the air of someone used to addressing crowds of people. "My name is Giles Farmer and I'm the Director of Communications for

11

English Rose, and I'm joined on the platform by regional secretary for north London, Mark Spencer and liaison officer, Kirsty Black." A burly, balding, middle-aged man and a slim, thirtyish woman with tinted brown hair acknowledged the introduction and the woman waved her arm briefly.

"I'm going to tell you a little about what English Rose stands for," said Farmer, "and then Mark will talk about how you can join up; if that is, we've managed to convince you that we're the party for you."

He smiled a disarming, boyish smile and ran his hand through a shock of straight brown hair that sprang instantly back into place. He had the look of a young man going places, a young man it would be hard to dislike, the kind of young man who gathered people and smiles around him wherever he went.

"As you know, English Rose as a political party has only been in existence for a short period of time, only a fraction of time compared to the parties we all grew up with. And I know many of you will have heard the disparaging comments in the media about the values we represent and about our ability to mount a challenge to the political establishment."

He paused. "And in normal times I would agree with those comments. New parties are 'fragile flowers' and many do wilt at the first sign of frost, but English Rose is different, and I'll tell you why, it's because we don't live in normal times any anymore, we live in extremely abnormal times. I don't need to tell you how much the catastrophic events of the last few years have changed the world we all took for granted."

He paused again. "You are here for the same reason we all are, because you know something needs to be done, and it needs to be done *now*, before the country we love disappears before our eyes." He paused a third time and smiled. "I have heard, as I am sure you all have, the accusations that our party is extremist. But look around you - look at the person sitting next to you…," there was a stir in the crowd and as Joan turned her head towards him Mason found himself staring into a pair of washed out, slightly vacant looking eyes.

"Look at the person sitting next to you," repeated Farmer. "Do you see an extremist? Do you see a yobbo?" Mason was forced to concede that he didn't. "No, of course you don't. All you see is the face of someone like yourself, a decent person, but a person so concerned by what they see around them they feel honour bound to try and do something about it."

Farmer stopped, ran his hand through his hair again and gazed out at his audience with an expression that was transparently honest and enthusiastic. "Across the country this meeting is being replicated in town halls, hotels, school halls, even in people's houses. Concerned citizens are meeting, not to cause trouble but out of a sense of civic pride, determined to do what they can to help our country in its hour of need."

He paused and his next words, when they came, were measured. "And determined that whatever needs to be done will be done with decency and dignity and a respect for the rights of others. We are not an extremist party, and if the extreme times we live in call on us to take radical steps, they will be taken with respect for every citizen of our country, regardless of race, creed or colour." He paused and an audible stir – of appreciation perhaps, or of relief – rippled through the audience.

As Farmer's words - soothing words, words designed to calm and reassure - filled the room, Mason's attention began to wander and before long, against his will, his thoughts drifted back to the terrible day that had set in train the chain of events that had led him to this time and place.

It had started with a knock on the door of the house he shared with Bianca and Matthew. Through the frosted pane, he saw two figures silhouetted against the late afternoon dusk with behind them a repeating flash of blue light, blurred and distorted by the thick glass. By the time he reached the door Bianca was beside him, her anxiety palpable. He opened the door and even before he saw the expressions on the faces of the two uniformed figures, one male, one female, he knew something seriously bad had happened.

Banca did as well and she called out, "Matthew... it's Matthew, isn't it?" in a quavering voice that turned into a wail when she saw the officers exchanging looks.

"It's Matthew, isn't it?" This time it emerged as a scream.

"Miss Lincoln?" said the female officer and as Bianca nodded dumbly her colleague, looking absurdly young in his crisply laundered white shirt, said to Mason, "Could we come in, sir?"

Mason's stomach lurched as he followed them into the living room. He put an arm around Bianca, but she shook it off and as the officers turned to face her, shouted, "Tell me... tell me what's happened to Mathew!"

The female officer said gently, "We just have to check, love. Can I ask, are you the mother of Matthew Lincoln?"

"Where is he... what's wrong...?" she screamed, the words emerging in a confused babble. "Tell me what's happened to him." She began to beat her fists on the chest of the policeman. "Tell me, you bastards!"

"Please sit down," said the female officer in the same gentle voice as before, and Mason, standing behind Bianca, put his arms around her. This time she did not resist, and he lowered her, sobbing, into a chair.

Eventually it was the female officer who spoke. "I'm afraid we've got some very bad news for you, Miss Lincoln," she said and, as he sat on the arm of her chair, Mason felt Bianca's body rack silently against his.

His thoughts were dragged back to the present by the emollient tones of Giles Farmer. "As I mentioned earlier," the Director of Communications was saying, "in a few minutes my colleagues and I will take questions, and after that," he smiled "there will be the opportunity to join our great movement, for those of you who would like to. Unlike other political parties we ask for no membership dues or for any other type of payment. We recognise that we live in exceptional times and we want to give concerned citizens, regardless of their income or personal circumstance, the opportunity to play their part in the great democratic movement we are launching. I'm now going to hand you over to liaison officer Kirsty Black who will tell you how you can join up."

"Good evening everyone," said the liaison officer with a smile. She was about Mason's age and wore a tailored suit under which lay the trim, firm contours of a body that worked out.

"I am happy to tell you that joining English Rose could not be easier. You can sign up online of course, or you can take a membership form home, but the easiest way to join is to simply go to the tables behind me where Karen and Dawn are sitting." At the back of the stage two pretty girls smiled and waved. "It only takes a few minutes and you can start going up while I talk if you like - we are not one of those tired, stuffy old parties that stand on ceremony."

A thin stream of people began to trickle towards the stage. "I'm going to hand you back to Giles now," she said, "but I'll be around until the end of the meeting and if you have any questions at all, no matter how silly they might seem to you, please don't hesitate to come and find me." She stepped back and this time there was a definite ripple of applause.

Farmer returned to the microphone and leant gently towards it, smoothing back his hair as he did so. "One of the things Kirsty said was that we are not like the tired, stale old parties you all grew up with, and I would like to emphasize that point. English Rose is a completely new political movement, unlike anything this country has seen before. We are a genuine party of the people and that's why we want to represent as many people as possible.

"Those of you who know your history will realise how difficult it is to challenge the established order, represented in our country by the two or three-party system that has dominated politics for hundreds of years. I would say two things in response to that. Firstly, the political scene has become much more volatile and things we once thought impossible are now, if not commonplace, at least conceivable. President Trump ran an insurgent campaign against the establishment when he was first elected, and around the same time Emanuel Macron came from nowhere to capture the presidency of France."

He paused. "Now I'm sure you have as little time for the politics of Macron as I do – they represent the failed policies that got the world into this mess – but what Macron tells us is that political movements *can* come from nowhere and capture power. He was an example of the political establishment mounting its own insurgency to capture power, and I think the people eventually saw if for what it was – a rebranding of the same tired old politics.

"But I want to ask you a question. If the political elites can start a new force that comes from nowhere to take power," he paused "why can't the people? Why can't the people cut out the middleman and do it themselves? Why can't we?" He paused for a moment. "Well, I'm here to tell you the answer to that question. We can! We can and there's nobody or nothing that can stop us!"

There was silence for a couple of seconds and then the applause started, scattered at first but steadily gaining momentum. There were shouts of encouragement and then people began to stand up and the applause got louder and the shouts merged into a roar, and at that point, Mason, conscious of why he was there, decided it would be a good idea if he stood up and joined in. He clapped mechanically but all the time he was looking around him, hoping to find something that would help him in the task he had set himself.

It had taken the year that followed Matthew's death for the anger that was slow burning in him to coalesce into white-hot rage, and a further two for it to cool and harden into an irreducible core of anger and resolve. And it was then that he made a covenant with himself, solemn and binding, that if it took him the rest of his days, he would hunt down the men who had beaten Matthew to death and terminate their lives with extreme prejudice.

II

Matt Rees crossed the street from Westminster Station and entered the Houses of Parliament through the Saint Steven's Gate entrance. He stopped in Central Hall to check his pigeonhole and then proceeded into the House of Commons chamber where the long-awaited debate on homeland security had begun. He paused as he went into the chamber which, unsurprisingly, for such an important debate, was full. In the old days one whole side of the chamber had been reserved for the official opposition, but with Labour's representation having been reduced to a rump of 97 M.P.'s at the last election, the arithmetic of the chamber had changed and conventions that had been adhered to for generations no longer applied.

These days there was often competition among the half dozen biggest opposition parties to get the best seats, the ones directly across the aisle from the government. With the thought that these were indeed strange times to be living in, Rees made his way to the back of the chamber and squeezed into a seat, nodding to a couple of colleagues as he did so. The Home Secretary was at the despatch box, smart in his blazer and slacks, Guard's tie prominently displayed.

"When planning this proposed change to the law," he drawled, enunciating the consonants clearly but strangling his vowels to the point of asphyxia, "we were conscious of the sensibilities of civil liberties groups and others for whom the idea of a national identity card scheme raised concerns. However, I would like to remind the House that Britain has twice operated a compulsory identity card scheme before, during the two great wars of the last century. Indeed," he looked at benches opposite, "the post war Labour government deemed the scheme so vital to the defence of our country that they retained it throughout their time in office and it wasn't until after the Conservatives were returned to power that Winston Churchill disbanded it in 1952."

There was a stirring in seats opposite and cries of, "Point of order, Mister Speaker," but the

Home Secretary refused to yield. "And of course, I don't need to remind the house that the currently identity card scheme came into being through legislation passed by a Labour government."

As he paused and ran a hand along the expanse of pate where hair had once flourished, there were cries of "shame" and a shout of, "that was a voluntary scheme" from across the aisle. "If members opposite would calm down," he went on smoothly, "I will explain why this legislation is so critically important in the changed world that we live in and why the scheme needs to be a compulsory one in order to give the authorities the powers they need to ensure our citizens are safeguarded and our borders are secure."

He gave way and fielded a couple of questions from Labour M.P.'s and one from Vinnie Groves, the leader of English Rose, the new kids on the block who had stunned the political establishment by winning 32 seats in the previous year's election. In contrast to the questions from Labour, which focused on civil liberties, Groves' intervention stressed the urgency of getting legislation through Parliament as quickly as possible to counter the growing threat to the country's security.

"I can assure the government that English Rose stands foursquare behind any measure that will protect the rights of this country's citizens, rights which are in danger of being damaged, if not destroyed altogether, in the dangerous climate we live in today." There was a chorus of "Hear hears" from the group of acolytes huddled around Groves, and then Rees saw the Speaker's eyes swivel and begin to travel in his direction and a moment later he heard his name being called.

"Thank you, Mister Speaker," said Rees. "I would like to ask the Home Secretary what form the ID card will take and what information will it contain, other than the holder's name, and I would also ask that he assure the House that the cost of the scheme, if it is successfully introduced, will not be borne by our constituents, many of whom already live from pay cheque to pay cheque?"

"Thank you to the Honourable Member for the question," said the Home Secretary smoothly. "As to cost, the precise details are yet to be determined, but naturally the government will do everything it can to ensure that our hardworking constituents are not overburdened financially. And in regard to the Honourable Member's other points, we envisage that the card will look something like the current driving license - a credit card sized ID card, with a photo and a serial number linked to a national database - and we will of course ensure that the design will incorporate the latest technology aimed at preventing counterfeiting. In terms of what information will be on the database, that has yet to be determined, but our security services do need the intelligence to enable them do their jobs properly, so it is likely it will contain employment and medical data specific to the individual, together with biometric information like fingerprints."

Rees stood up to ask a supplementary, but he knew that, representing a party seen as increasingly irrelevant in national terms, he was lucky to have been given a first chance. As the House listened in a desultory fashion to the Home Secretary batting away a series of follow-up questions, it knew that the current electoral arithmetic meant that passage of the bill was likely no matter what questions were asked.

At the previous year's general election, the Conservatives had fallen 15 seats short of the 326 needed to secure a majority but Labour itself had suffered its worst electoral result for over a hundred years. The nationalists in Scotland and Wales now held all but a handful of the hundred odd seats on the two principalities, while the Republicans and Loyalists had shared the spoils in Northern Ireland's eighteen constituencies.

What had changed was the emergence of English Rose, which had against all the odds secured 32 seats by targeting all its resources into seats in the North and the West Midlands where its intelligence had indicated that it had a chance of winning. There was also UKIP, which had redefined and reinvented itself for the umpteenth time, this time as the party of disgruntled Daily Express readers, and using the same tactics as

English Rose, had managed the not inconsiderable feat of winning 13 seats. On the other side of the political divide, the Green Party, responding to a growing realisation that climate change was the defining issue of our times, had won 25 seats. The Lib Dems had responded to the growing vacuum in the middle, by winning 45 seats, although there was much disappointment that the centre ground of British politics, from which the country had been governed for much of the previous two hundred years, was now so underrepresented.

How a voting system which has always favoured the established parties had yielded up such a mixed electoral bag was something the psephologists were still debating, but a consensus was beginning to emerge that social media and other new technologies may have allowed smaller parties to identify their potential voters more accurately and target resources on them with forensic precision. At any rate, the result was a House of Commons the like of which had never been seen before in terms of the number of parties with a significant representation of seats.

The Conservatives, although short of an overall majority, faced such a splintered and divided opposition that by tacking rightwards and utilising the support of English Rose and UKIP, they could ensure a majority for all but the most wet and wishy washy of their policies. A compulsory ID scheme certainly fell into the category of policies English

Rose and UKIP were likely to support, so Rees had few doubts that the upcoming second reading of the bill would garner the government enough votes to ensure the act would soon be on the statute book. He sat back in his seat and contemplated the upcoming legislative calendar with weary resignation.

***

In the end Mason had joined English Rose on that first evening, shuffling forward alongside Reg and Joan until they reached the table with the pretty girls. At the last moment, for reasons he wasn't fully able to articulate to himself, he had decided to join under an alias and had filled in the registration form under the name of Frank Brown. While they waited in line Reg and Joan had engaged him in the sort of small talk that people in queues have indulged in since the dawn of time. They vented about the weather and the state of council services, with Reg, who worked in insurance, especially scandalised by the reduction in bin collections and by the behaviour of the operatives who did the emptying. "Just leave the bloody bins all over the bloody road, they do; it's a symptom of the way the country's run these days, if you ask me."

Joan had expanded on their disillusion with the Conservatives and flirtation with the politics of the right. "We're not intolerant, we're absolutely not. I support a girl in Africa through *Save the Children,*" she said, "and Reg has worked with the Rotary Club for years, taking disabled kiddies to Thorpe Park. You should see it, lines of cars going around the M25 with balloons hanging off them and all those gormless little faces smiling out through the windows. One of your favourite days of the year, isn't it, Reg?"

Her husband acknowledged the tribute with a smile and she went on, "We're not troublemakers, we're ordinary decent people, but we can't go on the way we've been going, can we Reg? We just can't! We're as welcoming to foreigners as anyone, but we're full up - the country I mean - and we can't take any more. Our services can't cope with the people we've got, they just can't. And I'm not just talking about when we had the coronavirus or during the riots, I'm talking about normal day to day living; there just isn't enough to go around anymore. So, when English Rose says we need to start sending people back to where they came from, they're the only ones who are really addressing the problem."

"And" interjected Reg, "they've promised that repatriations will only be done following negotiation with the countries in question, with financial packages - very generous financial packages if you look at them - to ensure that the people returning to their homelands will have a good start to their new lives."

"Absolutely," agreed Joan, "I mean, we wouldn't want to be part of anything that was undemocratic, after all that's what this country was founded on – democracy."

Mason found his mind drifting again, back to the dreadful events that had altered the course of so many lives. He had met Bianca four years before Matthew's death and their relationship had quickly developed into something that he, at least, had not experienced before. And it wasn't just the sex, although that had been everything he could have wished for in terms of quality and quantity; it had also been the long lazy afternoons in the pub or at the cinema, the evenings curled up on the sofa in front of an old black and white film, the discussions of books and music which had often led to violent but good humoured disagreement, and most importantly, a shared world view, an agreed set of values and a common understanding of what was important in life and what wasn't.

Within a year of their meeting, Bianca had given up the flat in Neasden she shared with Matthew and they had moved as a family into a small semi just up the road. Bianca had been born in London, but her roots were in Trinidad, her mother coming to Britain to work in the NHS as part of the great influx that followed in the wake of the Windrush. Mason never ceased to be amazed that she had chosen him to be her life partner and he often gazed in wonder at her sleeping face as it lay on the pillow next to him. Her colouring was pale for someone of West Indian extraction, the product, she said, of illicit interactions between planters and slaves back in the old days.

Mathew was the product of a brief liaison she had had when she was twenty, and although Mason was not the boy's natural father, he had taken on the role of male mentor with a will, and quickly grew to love the bubbling, effervescent kid with the permanent smile and the inexhaustible zest for life. Matthew had the same rich, honey coloured skin as his mother, and like her his complexion was flawless. He was a bundle of enthusiasm, eager to learn, full of questions, soaking up information like a sponge, and blessed with so much energy that Mason referred to him a force of nature. He was also unmistakeably a child with a mixed racial heritage and that, ultimately, was what was to cost him his life.

The funeral had been a harrowing experience for all concerned, and Bianca had sobbed uncontrollably as the small beige coffin had been lowered into the ground. Mason himself had delivered the eulogy and although he had tried to capture something of Matthew's vitality and zest for life, the whole thing had been impossibly painful and he had been as relieved as anyone when his words had dried up and the tribute had limped its way into oblivion.

It is truly said that most relationships don't survive the loss of a child and although Mason had tried his hardest to generate a spark of life in Bianca's ravaged psyche, it had been an impossibility from the start. He knew, although she never formally charged him with it, that she blamed him for Matthew's death, because on that terrible day it had been he who had sent the boy down to the corner shop to get some milk. And although she never accused him outright, the looks of reproach he caught her giving him when she thought he wasn't looking were eloquent testimony to her thoughts.

It had taken six months for her to say, haltingly "I think we need to talk…" and the next day he had moved out and into the small flat he had lived in since. He had tried to keep in touch, had tried to help her in any way he could - in any way that she would accept - but she had become progressively more distant, her words sometimes slurring down the telephone line, and then one day she had stopped returning his calls. He had called round to try to see her twice and, on neither occasion had his knock produced an answer, although on the second one he could have sworn he'd seen a twitch of the curtains. He had looked around the neglected front garden for a final time, weeds now growing in the cracks she had once so lovingly tended. There was a rake leaning against the wall of the house and next to it a small trowel, a child's trowel, the one Matthew had used when he had squatted beside her, shadowing her every movement.

It was two years after Matthew's death, eighteen months after the spilt up, when he read a small paragraph in the local paper saying that Bianca had been found dead by a friend who, worried about her state of mind, had gone around to see her. The police had apparently said that there were no suspicious circumstances. Mason had attended the inquest, had in fact been called to give evidence about their time together and the tragedy of Mathew's death. In the end the jury had been unable to determine with certainty whether the cocktail of alcohol and prescription drugs that had killed her had been taken deliberately or whether her death had been a tragic accident. Mason knew though, and this second senseless death had hardened something in him and set his mind on a new track.

Hauling his thoughts back to the present he realized that someone was talking to him. "You didn't say what line of business, you're in, yourself, Frank?" Reg was asking.

"Sales," answered Mason, "but I'm taking a bit of gardening leave." This was true as far as it went but it didn't tell the whole story. His mother had died the previous year and left her only child the family house, a large four bedroomed semi in Crouch End. After death taxes and the sale of the property, Mason had been able to deposit just under a million pounds into his bank account, at which point he had spoken to his boss and secured himself an indefinite period of leave with the promise that his job would be there when he returned,"

"What are you going to do, Frank?" Jarvis had said over the pint they had shared in the pub near the office.

"Not sure, yet," Mason had replied.

"I'd travel if it was me, mate," his boss had said. "Never did travel when I was younger and," he grinned ruefully, "no chance of that for the foreseeable, not with three kids, a big mortgage and a wife who can spend for England."

Mason had answered non-committedly, not sharing the real reason for his decision, which was that he had decided to devote himself full time to finding the man who had used a blunt instrument to crush Matthew's head like an egg and, having found him, kill him in as painful a way as possible.

He calculated that with his inheritance in the bank, if he kept his spending within reasonable limits, he had up to twenty years to complete this task, and he promised himself that if it took every day of those two decades, he would have his moment of vengeance.

III

As Mason burrowed his way towards the centre of English Rose and what he hoped might lay beyond it, Matt Rees continued to represent his constituency in Parliament. The public perception of members of Parliament had never really recovered from the expenses scandal at the start of the century, but there were MPs like Rees - many MPs, if truth be told - whose daily practice gave the lie to the notion that those who choose to pursue a path in politics are venal, unprincipled, out for themselves, the tools of the special interests or a combination of all four. Rees had won his seat by a wafer-thin majority the first time he fought it – it hadn't been on the hit list of Labour's hopefuls – and then to universal surprise, had held it at the next election in the face of a significant national swing to the right.

He was a stocky bald man in his forties, and behind the thick rimmed spectacles he habitually wore were a pair of striking blue eyes that fixed piercingly and with disconcerting force on whoever he was talking to. A tightly coiled ball of restless energy, he had little time for small talk, preferring to get straight to the heart of whatever matter was at issue. His rather forbidding appearance was transformed when he smiled, and those who got to know him came to realize that the smile, which lit up his face, was not merely tactical - pasted on in pursuit of a particular end – but that it reflected the positive, decent nature of the man who wore it.

He was in fact an excellent constituency MP, an MP who worked virtually around the clock to represent everyone in his constituency, even the vulnerable ones who had little power or influence; in fact, especially the ones who had little power or influence. In a society where public confidence in members of parliament remained at an all-time low, where people viewed their MPs at worst as part of a huge conspiracy, or at best as anonymous cyphers entirely at the whim of national forces, Rees was a refreshing example of someone who, by dint of honesty, integrity and a phenomenal work ethic, *could* actually make a difference. It was almost certainly the reason why against all the odds he had unseated his diminutive, arrogant Conservative opponent in the first place, and why, to even greater general surprise, he had held the seat in the subsequent election.

The compulsory registration scheme he had spoken out against was duly rushed into law, and an apathetic public, seemingly indifferent to the loss of personal liberty which would ensue from compulsory identity cards, had received it with bovine indifference. Part of the reason for the public's apathy towards normal business at Westminster may have lay in the worsening weather patterns that had ensued as the pace of global warming accelerated. The melting of the polar ice caps was making habitation of low-lying areas in places everywhere from New Orleans to the Maldives increasingly unsustainable, and the disruption to the gulf stream caused by the warming of the sea had produced violent, unstable weather systems that were buffeting Europe with increasing frequency.

In addition, there had been a terrible drought in sub-Saharan North Africa and an equally terrible flood in Bangladesh, both resulting in severe regional disruption. The northerly flow of refugees had increased from a trickle to a torrent and there had been a full-scale battle in the Mediterranean between Italian coastguard forces on one side, and people traffickers on the other, resulting in a loss of life that was still impossible to quantify. Hungary had become the first European country to close its borders entirely to foreigners and had begun deporting foreign nationals back to their countries of origin. All over Europe the forces of the right were on the move and the continent was once more marching to the drumbeat of nationalism.

As Rees worked in the office he shared with his fellow MP, Bob Maxton, a TV in the corner was showing a live briefing from the press room at the White House. President Trump had been re-elected after four years out of office following a brutal, viciously fought campaign against Vice President Harris. Refusing to accept the result of the 2020 election, the outgoing president had started a new

TV station, Trump News, which gave a voice to groups like the American Freedom Party, the Ku Klux Klan and the Proud Boys, all of which had hitherto operated on the margins of American society. Armed militias had begun attacking Black Lives Matter protests and when the protesters had themselves taken up arms the scene was set for interracial violence not seen since the reconstruction years.

The growing number of refugees worldwide had increased pressure within developed countries for them to respond by simply running up their drawbridges and becoming fortress states. As the violence in the U.S. increased, calls for calm by Democrats and moderate Republicans had fallen on deaf ears and the 2024 election took place in a highly charged atmosphere. That the Democratic nominee was a woman of colour added to the toxicity of the campaign and Trump News was quick to christen her "Crooked Kam*al*a" (with the stress placed firmly on the second syllable of her name). Members of the self-styled Trump Militia, resplendent in green combat fatigues and red MAGA caps and exercising their first amendment right to carry arms, patrolled the streets around polling stations on election day, often, in contravention of local and national statutes, accompanying voters all the way to the polling booth to help them vote. Afterwards their leader thanked them for making the election the most transparent, open and honest in U.S. history.

Trump lost the popular vote for the third election in a row, but the margins were close in the swing states, and the election finally hinged on his adoptive home state, Florida, where Republican election officials apportioned Trump a wafer-thin majority and refused all calls for a recount. When the Supreme Court ratified this decision by 6 votes to 3, Trump was returned to power for a second term. His supporters were ecstatic, some celebrating wildly in bars and nightclubs, others going straight home to begin cutting holes in their sheets.

The President stood at a lectern with a pallid little man on one side and the Vice President on the other. The President began to speak, and as he did so the Vice President turned his head and gazed up at his leader with the kind of look that might have appeared on the face of Saint Bernadette at Lourdes, a look of love and reverence and veneration. ("Veneration, my arse," had been Maxton's response when Rees first shared this image with him. "It's exactly the kind of look my spaniel gives me when he knows I'm going to take him outside for a shit.")

The President looked out on the assembled press corps and said, "OK, I'll take questions. Yes… Mike?" He pointed towards the middle of the room where a reporter from Breitbart News had put his hand up. "Thank you, Mr President. We all know your administration has been at the cutting edge of the global response to climate change, and I wondered whether you had any thoughts you'd like to share with us?"

"Thank you, Mike," said the president, "That's a very good question. Not many people remember that I was the first world leader to talk about the dangers of global warming, but I was, and the scientists were amazed at how much I knew about the whole thing. They were genuinely amazed, they truly were, they said nobody had ever known as much about science as I did, with the possible exception…the possible exception… of Albert Epstein.

"And it was shortly afterwards that we decided to build the wall. We built the wall to protect us from rapists and thieves and murderers, but we also built it to protect us from climate change - to stop the climate change from swarming into our country and attacking our way of life. And the wall did that, but it didn't just protect us from rapists and thieves and murderers and global warming, it also protected us from the virus - the China virus - because the virus can't survive above a certain height, did you know that? When the virus gets above a certain height the air pressure kills it, *fries it*!" He made a pistol out of his finger, "*Zap!*" and blew onto the end of it. "And we built the wall at just the right height so the virus couldn't get over it.

"Of course, even though it was perfect, it was a perfect wall and it stopped Mexican rapists *and* global warming *and* the China virus, we didn't get any credit for that from the Lamestream Media. But that's OK. That's OK, because the people understand. They do. They truly do. Let me ask you a question. How many other countries built a wall to protect their women from getting raped and from climate change and from the China virus? You're right, Mike – nobody. Nobody else built a wall; no one else saw what was coming and built such a beautiful wall. And it *is* a beautiful wall, a very beautiful wall, don't you think it's a beautiful wall?

He pointed to a reporter in the second row and said, "Yes, You."

"Thank you, Mr President," said the reporter. "Jim Grady, Trump News. Mr President, on behalf of a grateful country, we would like to thank you for the wisdom and leadership you have displayed during these difficult times. Are there any announcements you would like to make or thoughts you would like to share with the nation at this time?"

"As you all know," said the President, having acknowledged the tribute with a curt nod, "border security is a priority for this administration, and with that in mind I announce today that we are locking down all entry and exit points in the country with immediate effect." He paused, gripped the lectern and leaned forward. "We have many, many people in this country who came here illegally, who do nothing to add to our wealth and who are a drain on our social security system, and because of that I am announcing today the creation of a brand-new agency, the Homeland Security Task Force.

"Its job will be to hunt down all the people who are in this country illegally," he paused, "and when we find them, we're going to deport them. We're going to send them back to the…" he put a finger and thumb in front of his lips… "countries they came from. I used a word to talk about those countries a while back and it got me into trouble so I'm not going to use it again. But you know what I mean. You know what I mean. We're going to find them and we're going to send every one of them back to the… countries they came from." There was a ripple of laughter around the room and some scattered applause.

"This force will be federally funded," went on the president, "and it will have powers to cross interstate lines in pursuit of these criminals. I am sending an emergency bill to congress this week and I am assured it will be passed with all due speed."

A hand went up and he nodded. "Will this force be similar to the FBI, Mister President?"

"It will actually be better than the FBI. As you know, the FBI has been plagued with people of low intelligence in recent years and we're going to make sure this new agency doesn't have those kinds of problems. It will have a higher quality of agent than the FBI and it will have a better uniform than the FBI has…" the pallid little man leaned across and whispered in his ear and the President continued without missing a beat, "… a better uniform than the FBI would have if it had one.

"The Homeland Security Task Force will report directly to the Acting Secretary of the Interior," he made a gesture towards the pallid little man, "who will report to me. Did you want to add anything to what I've said, Mister Acting Secretary?" He glared at the pallid little man and the pallid little man smiled nervously and shook his head and his Adam's apple bobbed up and down.

Rees stared at the TV screen for a moment and made a mental note to check whether there were any plans for the government to introduce a similar agency in the UK.

"What's he banging on about now?" asked Bob Maxton, who had come into the office with a couple of colleagues while Rees was watching.

Rees grunted. "Some new task force charged with hunting down aliens."

"Bloody country's gone mad," said Maxton. "Since Trump, I mean."

"The whole thing started before Trump, if you ask me," answered Rees. "Eight years before, to be precise, in January 2009."

Maxton turned to his companions, rolled his eyes and said in a stage whisper, "I think I can feel a sermon coming on."

"Because that's when Obama Walked into the White House for the first time," said Rees, undeterred by his colleague's words, "and that's when all the nonsense started, the abuse and the birtherism and Trump and all the rest of it."

"I suppose you're right."

"And if that *is* true," went on Rees, warming to his theme, "the question Americans need to ask themselves is whether the notion of a black man walking through the doors of the White House was too much for them to stomach? And whether the country has really moved on from the days of Bull Connor and Sheriff Jim Clark and Wallace and Ross Barnett and all the other racists who denied people their liberty in the name of states' rights?"

"I remember George Wallace," said Maxton, "Governor of Alabama, wasn't he, back in the civil rights era? But for those of us who don't share your in-depth knowledge of American politics, just remind us who the others were…"

"Bull Connor was the Commissioner for Public Safety in Birmingham who discharged his duties by turning water cannons on innocent black children, Sheriff Jim Clark ordered mounted troops to attack civil rights marchers on the bridge at Selma, and Barnett was the governor of Mississippi who did his best to out-nigger Wallace; arch segregationists the lot of them, however much they wrapped their bigotry and prejudice up in a lot of fancy packaging with states' rights written on it."

Maxton thought for a moment. "Well, in answer to your question, if you look at Trump's base, you'd think things haven't changed much."

"I agree, but there are millions of Republicans out there who supported Trump but who see themselves as decent, tolerant citizens and they're the ones who need to take a long hard look at themselves and ask themselves whether their country really has laid the ghosts of Wallace and Connor and all the other bigots or whether Jim Crow is alive and well but just went underground for a bit."

"Here endeth the lesson," intoned Maxton gravely. He looked at his companions. "Now, does anyone fancy a pint?"

IV

Meanwhile, Mason threw himself into his new life as a member of English Rose, attending meetings and volunteered for everything from dropping leaflets to manning phone lines in the hope of increasing his visibility. He also gave thought to how best he could create the kind of profile that the shadowy figures who lurked in the twilight world between constitutionality and extremism might find interesting.

For most of the year following Bianca's death he had been sunk in a bottomless pit of despair, consumed by self-pity, and angry at the way life had dumped on the people he had loved, and thus on him. But slowly he had come to a realisation that this reaction was epically self-indulgent, that Bianca and Matthew had suffered far more than he had, and that sitting around with his head metaphorically up his own arse would not respect their memory and might even be a betrayal of it. And the notion that he might be able to atone in some way for his feeling of culpability for their deaths had hardened into an implacable desire for vengeance against the perpetrators of Matthew's murder, especially the one who had struck the fatal blow. And even though he knew rage was a destructive force and that it was capable of eating away at him until it destroyed him, anything was preferable to the emptiness of the limbo he had existed in since Banca's death.

He had chosen English Rose as the instrument through which he would try to infiltrate the far right after some rather perfunctory research online. He knew that fringe organisations of the far right had been part of the political landscape as far back as the time of Mosley and his British Union of Fascists. The League of Empire Loyalists, The White Defence League, The British Movement, The

National Front, The British National Party and The English Defence League, had all participated to a greater or lesser degree in the mainstream of British politics, communicating with the public through advertising, direct mail and leaflet drop, and fielding candidates at national and local elections.

But it was in the murky quagmire that lay behind these organisations, where sinister groups, like Combat 18 and Blood and Honour lurked, that Mason hoped to strike gold. It was in this foetid swamp that he was sure Storm Force 55 existed, and it was this world he knew he must infiltrate if he was to find the men who had killed Matthew. He set himself the task of trying to find a way in and he told himself that if he was patient, one would come.

In the meantime, he kept his antennae tuned for others who might be scrutinizing English Rose for the same reason he was, as a vehicle to get access to what lay behind it. Mason's online research led him to the work of a blogger and anti-Nazi activist called Raj Kumar and it was in Kumar's writing that he first found a connection between the two groups. Kumar had written that researchers from the anti-Nazi group Unite Against Fascism had suggested that there might be an overlap in membership between English Rose and Storm Force 55.

Mason had exchanged emails with Kumar and, eager to glean as much about Storm Force as he could, had suggested they might meet. He had received a guarded email in return, suggesting that if Mason was to present himself at the seats outside the All Bar One restaurant on the mezzanine floor at Euston Station, Kumar might be willing to meet him. Having emailed Kumar a photo of himself in lieu of ID, Mason made his way to the appointed spot at the appointed time and, having nursed a coffee for half an hour, decided he was wasting his time and got up to leave.

He had gone down the escalator and was making his way across the main concourse when he heard a voice in his ear, "Mr. Mason?" He turned and recognised Kumar from the photograph on his website.

"Sorry I'm a little late," said the blogger, bestowing on Mason a smile of unusual warmth. "Shall we go back up to the restaurant?" he said and a moment later they were ascending the escalator. "Would you like another coffee, or something else? On me, for keeping you waiting."

"Hang on," said Mason, "if you've only just arrived, how do you know I've been drinking coffee?"

"I've been watching you Mr. Mason," said Kumar, speaking in a generic south of England accent, "and this particular location," they had now arrived back at the restaurant, "offers someone watching from below the opportunity to observe at leisure whether someone up here is alone or whether there are others in the vicinity."

Mason looked at him quizzically and Kumar smiled again as they took their seats. "One of the things I've learned in my field of work is that there are some very nasty people out there, people who would not hesitate to set up a meeting masquerading as allies and then seek to pursue their own agenda."

Mason looked at him. "Has anything like that happened to you?" he asked.

Kumar smiled. "I was once chased down the Old Kent Road by a very large man carrying a very large pair of garden shears, and the thought of how he was planning to use them has remained with me ever since."

"Bloody hell," said Mason, "I didn't realize things like that happened."

"I would advise you, Mr Mason," said Kumar, and there was a gravity in his voice that belied the twinkle in his eye, "not to underestimate the fanaticism of the far right. There are men and women out there who live and breathe racial hatred, and dream of the coming of the time when they can spend their days inflicting pain on people without having to face consequences themselves."

He allowed Mason to digest this and said, "Your texts said you were interested in finding out about Storm Force 55. Any particular reason why them in particular?"

Mason had been anticipating the question and had decided that he had nothing to lose in being candid. "Well," he took a deep breath and said, "three years ago my partner's son was murdered not far from here. They never found the person who killed him, although one man was sent to prison as an accessory after the fact."

As he spoke, his companion's mouth dropped open in a way that was quite comical, and he stopped, unsure whether to continue. Kumar stared at him intently for what seemed like a lifetime before eventually moistening his lips and breathing the words, "Mathew Lincoln."

Mason nodded and Kumar said, "I thought I knew you from somewhere. I remember seeing you on TV after the death." He regarded Mason keenly for a moment and then held out his hand, "What can I say except that I'm very sorry for your loss."

Mason took the proffered hand and nodded his thanks. "And you know that after Matthew's death his mother…" his voice trailed off.

"Yeah, I read about it in the papers," said Kumar, "What a tragedy."

"We'd split up by then of course," said Mason. "But still…"

Kumar looked at him until he was sure his eye contact was being reciprocated. "Anything I can do to help nail the bastards who killed that little boy will be an absolute pleasure. So, what *can* I do?"

"Well," said Mason, "if you remember, they weren't able to pin Matthew's murder on anyone, although there was one guy found guilty of being an accessory after the fact."

"I remember," said Kumar, "didn't they find something incriminating in his garden."

"They found a jumper with particles of blood on it that forensics proved came from Matthew," said Mason, "but the bloke – Danny Gates – had an unimpeachable alibi. At the time Mathew was being murdered, CCTV showed him in a shopping precinct five miles away, so he couldn't have done it."

"I remember," said Kumar again.

"His defence claimed that someone had thrown the jumper over the wall into his garden – although that would have been difficult, it was found folded and stuffed into a watering can – or that he had been fitted up in some other way. No one really believed them – Danny's been part of the pondlife lurking on the fringes of the far right for years - but they didn't have enough evidence to convict him of murder.

"In the end he was sent down for seven years for being an accessory after the fact and off he went. He's been interviewed by Special Branch on a number of occasions since and although they've offered him all sorts of inducements to give them names – they told me that themselves – he's refused to say a word."

"Sounds like he might be a bloke with a martyr complex," said Kumar.

"That or he's terrified of what might happen to him if he does talk," said Mason. "Either way, he's shut himself up as tight as a clam and won't say a word about nuffink to no one."

"So, you've come up against a bit of a brick wall, then," said Kumar.

"Exactly." Mason considered for a moment. "But I was thinking, if I could somehow find a way of, I don't now… infiltrating the far right, I might be able to get close enough to whoever did it to find out what happened." He shrugged. "Saying it out loud makes it sound a bit ridiculous, but… it's frustrating not being able to do anything, especially when the police seem to have run into a dead end themselves."

"I understand where you're coming from," agreed Kumar. "But can I suggest something before you go any farther? If you really want to get mixed up with these people, change your appearance straight away. Dye your hair, grow a beard, wear glasses: do all three if you think it's necessary."

"Yeah?" said Mason.

"I had a nagging feeling I'd seen you somewhere before," said Kumar, "and it's likely that whoever killed Matthew will have watched the subsequent investigation closely. And on that basis, I think you'd be mad not to change your appearance. It doesn't have to be anything fancy, just a bit of facial hair here or a pair of glasses there."

"It all seems a bit cloak and dagger," said Mason.

"Frank, you're trying to hunt people down who have committed murder," said Kumar. "And if they've killed once there's no reason to suggest they wouldn't do it again, if only to cover up the original crime."

Mason began to realize that he hadn't given this glaringly obvious fact proper consideration. In hunting the man who had killed Mathew, at some point he was likely to meet him face to face, in which case it was likely the man would recognise him, if only from watching the police investigation and coroner's inquest on TV.

"Right, I'll try and do something along those lines," he said

"Good man," said Kumar. "Better safe than sorry. Now, was it information about English Rose or Storm Force 55 that you wanted?"

"Well, both, really," said Mason. "Although at the end of the day it's the bastards who left the calling card on Matthew's body that I'm after."

"Sure," said Kumar. "Well, let's start with English Rose. I'm sure you know quite a bit about them already, now that you're a signed-up member. As you know, they arrived from nowhere on the back of the coronavirus, the drought in north Africa and the floods in Bangladesh and East Asia. Their platform is basically that the world is a changed place, that multiculturalism is the root of all modern evil, and that the only way forward is for communities and countries to draw in their horns, crawl back into their shells and run up the drawbridge…" he stopped for a moment, "…if that collection of mixed metaphors makes any sense."

Mason smiled and the blogger went on, "The fact that they've made such a big electoral splash is testament to the strange times we live in. They targeted all their resources on areas of the country where they thought their message might have a receptive audience, and… well, you saw what happened. They now have enough seats to hold the balance of power and they know it. The PM has sent out feelers to them so see if they're willing to vote tactically with the Tories on areas of mutual interest, but Groves is playing the game shrewdly, talking about needing to stay true to core principles."

"What do you know about Groves?" asked Mason.

"Vinnie Groves?" said Kumar, "Interesting case, didn't quite rise without trace, but something of a metamorphosis, nonetheless. Worked in the research department of the Conservative Party in his twenties; good looking bloke, charismatic, way with words, that kind of thing, and he was eventually selected to fight a marginal in the election before last. He was Vincent Ormsby-Groves then, upper middle-class background, private education, nothing remotely man of the people about him." He smiled. "Anyway, he lost the marginal and must have morphed into Vinnie at some point after that -

shortened his name, dropped a few aitches, talked a bit more estuary - wouldn't be the first time it's been done. So, in all likelihood he's just another chancer, but he's a plausible one, a chancer with charm and a gift for language and the ability to work a crowd."

"Interesting, his background being in mainstream politics," said Mason. "I always imagined the far right sitting around in bedsits wearing leather shorts."

"A lot of the foot soldiers are Billy-No-Mates types," said Kumar, "And some of the leadership are old style ideologues, but there are also blokes just out for the main chance who will jump on any bandwagon they think might take them to power. Oswald Moley was a rising star in both the Labour and Conservative parties before he led the British Union of Fascists."

"I didn't know that," admitted Mason.

"There's also been a shift in some of the strategies adopted by the far right in the last couple of decades," said Kumar. "Back in the sixties and seventies they seemed more interested in scaring the shit out of people than in actually gaining power. My dad said that John Tyndall, the leader of the National Front in those days, was a caricature right wing loony – a scary looking individual in a paramilitary uniform standing on a platform spewing out hate with a crew of knuckle scrapers lined up behind him. Same with that bloke Eugene

Terre Blanche and his crowd in South Africa: a load of big girls' blouses standing around in Eric Morecambe shorts waving silly flags and spouting racist claptrap - the whole thing would have been quite funny if what they were saying wasn't so vile.

"But in recent years the right's got a lot cuter and some of the groups have been setting out to portray themselves as sane and reasonable - look at the gains made by the National Front in France for example – hoping to gain power using the ballot box rather than the knuckleduster."

"Which is where English Rose comes in?" said Mason

"Which is precisely where English Rose comes in," agreed Kumar. "Now, as far as Storm Force 55 is concerned, they're a completely different kettle of fish; a proscribed organisation whose structure is wreathed in shadows and whose membership is unknown. What little I know about them is that they seem to have been inspired by an earlier paramilitary organisation, Combat 18, that they have a hard-line agenda of racial hatred, and that they see themselves as the foot soldiers of the radical right, the guys prepared to go in and do the dirty work their more scrupulous fellow travellers might turn their noses up at."

"Where do the names come from?" asked Mason

"Well, the '18' in Combat 18 apparently stemmed from the initials of Adolf Hitler being first and eighth in the alphabet," said Kumar, "but as far as Storm Force goes, because they are relatively new and so secretive, we don't have a definitive answer. There is a theory that the numbers 55 were chosen because they look like "SS" and there are others who say that the number is a celebration of the 55 million estimated to have died during the Second Word War."

"Nice bunch, if that's true," said Mason

"For sure. The truth is, nobody really knows, precisely because they are so secretive and because no one really knows what their membership is. And a word of warning to you on that front. Past evidence suggests that the organisations that are that secretive about who they are and what their agenda is are the really, really nasty ones – the ones with agendas so horrific that they don't want anyone knowing about them until it's too late."

"And what are the links between Storm Force 55 and English Rose?" asked Mason

"Very tenuous, if truth be told. A year or so ago I had a whisper from a source – I can't tell you who it is – that English Rose might be a front for Storm Force 55, or that Storm Force 55 might be the paramilitary wing of English Rose, whichever way around you want to put it."

Mason opened his mouth to speak but Kumar forestalled him with a smile. "I'm not saying the two organisations have formal links, but what I *am* saying is that there may be an overlap in membership, particularly at leadership level, and that they'll see themselves as being two prongs of the same spear - the Armalite and the Ballot Box, if you know your Irish republican history."

Mason opened his mouth again, but Kumar put a hand up to forestall him. "In fact, Northern Ireland during the Troubles might not be a bad place to start. As you know Sinn Fein represented the republican community – the Catholics - fighting elections, going on TV (when the authorities would allow them to), and making the case via the democratic process. And behind them, as everyone knew, was the Provisional IRA, engaged in what they saw as an armed struggle against the security services and the protestant paramilitaries.

"Now I'm not saying the two organisations were the same, or that they had a single, unified leadership, but what I *am* saying is that there was an overlap of membership, particularly at the top. Gerry Adams always denied he was a member of the IRA but there is strong anecdotal evidence that as well as being a Sinn Fein MP he was on the army council of the Provisionals, while Martin McGuiness, the other big beast of Irish nationalism, admitted that he'd been a brigade commander in the Derry IRA."

He paused and said, "With me so far?" and Mason nodded.

"And it wasn't just the republican organisations who had this overlap of membership," went on Kumar. "The other side - the Loyalists from the Protestant community - had exactly the same thing going on in their politics, although you'd rarely get the authorities in London to admit it."

Mason looked at him quizzically and he went on. "So, you had the Democratic Unionist Party, the one led by Ian Paisley, holding meetings and fighting elections and all that, while behind them was the UVF, the Ulster Volunteer Force, an illegal organisation that planted bombs and carried out sectarian assassinations. They weren't formally linked, they didn't hold joint meetings, but everyone knew that they had similar agendas and that there was an overlap in membership."

"I never knew that," said Mason.

"Don't get me started on Northern Irish history," said Kumar. "The British media let the Loyalists get away with calling Sinn Fein '*the political wing of the IRA*' or '*Sinn Fein / IRA*' without ever, with a few notable exceptions, pointing out that the same organisational overlap operated on the Protestant side. And the Republicans were always called '*terrorists*' while the Loyalists were '*paramilitaries.*' As I said, don't get me started on Ulster or we'll be here all night."

Mason grinned. "I won't. In the meantime, what you're telling me is that somewhere within the leadership of English Rose, there may be members of Storm Force."

"Exactly," said Kumar. "I'd be very surprised if Vinnie Groves doesn't know who the leaders of Storm Force are, even if he's not a member himself. My advice, if you want to find a way into Storm Force, is to get as close as you can to the leadership of English Rose. But be bloody careful mate, I don't need to tell you how dangerous these bastards are, so don't go blundering about like a bull in a china shop. They'll be on the lookout for anyone asking too many questions, and they'll know that in the past Special Branch have put sleepers into far-right organisations."

"I'll be careful," promised Mason.

"Have you worked out what you'll do if you find out who killed Matthew?" asked Kumar.

"Not really," said Mason. He had no agenda other than that of summary execution, and no thoughts as to what his own fate would be if he competed the task – life imprisonment he assumed – but he didn't want to make Kumar an accessory before the fact, so he kept his answer as non-committal as possible.

"Well, as I said, be bloody careful and tread carefully."

Mason was tempted to quote the aphorism, "walk softly and carry a big stick," but he didn't want to give any clue as to the murderous nature of his plans, so he forbore to comment.

"If at any time you need someone who you can bat ideas off," said Kumar, "I'll be glad to help," and Mason felt oddly comforted by his words. He had walked alone and held his own counsel for a long time and the thought of having someone on the outside he could confide in was an attractive one.

"I'd like that," he said simply.

"Here's my private email address," said Kumar, handing him a business card. "From now on don't post anything on any public platform. There are bastards out there who record every communication, however innocuous, and report it up the line."

They agreed to keep in touch and as they parted Mason felt that in Kumar, he had found an ally, an ally who might yet become a friend.

V

It was to be several months before Mason got his break and when it arrived, it did so in a rather unexpected manner. He had beavered away in his local English Rose chapter, volunteering for anything he thought might raise his profile and bring him to the attention of the leadership. He had also tried to get closer to Giles Farmer, the regional organiser who had spoken at the first meeting he had attended, recognising something in Farmer's poise and self-assurance that hinted he might have access to people that mattered.

Mason had done his best to create an image of himself as a simple, straightforward man who thought in straight lines and whose mind was not cluttered with political theory – and that part at least was true enough, he admitted to himself ruefully – someone happy to carry out actions dreamed up by minds more sophisticated than his own. He tried to hint at a willingness to engage in activities more specialized than stuffing envelopes and arranging chairs, but it was a difficult task. How, after all, did one create the impression that one was a violent thug without behaving like a violent thug?

Farmer had given him an opening one day during a meeting ahead of the upcoming local elections, in which English Rose was investing pretty much all its political capital.

"So, what's your story, Frank?" Farmer had asked. "I mean, what made you decide you'd had enough of business as usual and the metropolitan elite?"

Mason considered his answer and spoke slowly, almost haltingly, trying to create an impression of someone for whom the disclosing of personal information did not come easily.

"It just seemed to me," he said, "that everything's become geared up for outsiders, whether it's government grants or council housing or what's on TV, and that the... the native people, the English people, have been forgotten." He had heard variations on this theme since he had become involved with the party and it felt like a nice safe opening.

"Not sure what else to say really…" he tailed off and Kirsty Black, the organiser he had met at the same time as Farmer said, "More of the strong, silent type, our Frank, aren't you?"

The smile with which she accompanied the remark robbed it of any offence and he couldn't help smiling back at her. She was attractive in a quiet, understated way, the type of person who might have interested him in the days before his libido had been consigned to eternal cold storage by Bianca's death. As it was, occasional, half remembered stirrings, fragile and elusive, were all that connected the normal, healthy young man he had once been with the emotionally crippled wreck he had become.

He smiled back at her and said, "And what's your story, Kirsty?"

"Well," she said, and in an offer that included Farmer, added, "Buy me a pint and I'll tell you."

A few minutes later the three of them were comfortably ensconced in O'Neill's on Neasden High Street sipping their drinks.

"Thanks boys," said Kirsty as she savoured her pint of Peroni.

"I take it your suggestion that *we* buy *you* a drink was a rejection of the political correctness that pervades modern life?" enquired Farmer.

"Absolutely," she grinned back. "Nothing at all to do with the fact that I'm mean. Cheers!" She took a long pull from her glass and wiped the back of her hand across her mouth.

The banter continued and the atmosphere became increasingly convivial, and if Mason hadn't known the two were part of an outfit that was anathema to all he held dear, he would have thought them a decent, attractive pair, normal, witty and self-deprecating. The talk turned increasingly to the big speech that Vinnie Groves was scheduled to give ahead of the local elections. The hall they had hired had a six thousand seat capacity and the party had worked hard to publicize the speech, with digital press kits issued to the national dailies and the local media alerted.

The audience would be an invited one to ensure a positive, highly charged atmosphere, and supporters were being bussed in from outside the capital. Groves was going to lay out the core philosophy of English Rose and the speech was seen as a pivotal moment in the development of the movement and a chance for the party to crash through the glass ceiling which tradition and the electoral system had placed above those hoping to break into the big time.

"What's he like, Groves?" Mason asked, knowing that Farmer had worked closely with him

"All I can say is, once you've met him, you're never quite the same again. Would you agree, Kirsty?"

"He is very, very attractive to women," she answered, "and he knows it. And I would have written him off as just another predatory lounge lizard, except…" she paused… "there's something about the way he looks at you when he speaks, like a little lost boy but an incredibly sexy one, that makes you ready to walk over hot coals for him."

"And he really knows how to work a crowd," added Farmer. "Have you heard him speak?" Mason shook his head. "Well, you're in for a treat. He has this way of making what he says seem so blindingly obvious, makes you wonder why you haven't worked it out yourself ages ago. He starts quietly and then increases the pace and before you know it, he's got the crowd in the palm of his hand and he's making it laugh and then he's making it sad or angry or… anything he wants really."

"I look forward to hearing him," said Mason and in truth the prospect of being exposed to such oratory was intriguing.

"I'll make sure I introduce him to you," said Farmer. "We need people like you in the movement and he's always telling us to keep our eyes open for fresh talent."

Feeling that at last he was getting close to the acceptance that might offer him the opportunity he was looking for, Mason waited a moment and then said. "I've been thinking about how I could best help, and well… I'm never going to be one of the intellectuals of the movement…" he laughed off their protests "… but I do know my own mind and… well, I'm pretty handy with my fists, used to box when I was a teenager and… well, I was wondering whether the party had thought about security for its leaders and… security in general… I mean, we know we're going to face a lot of opposition… and well, we need to be prepared, and if the movement is looking for people who aren't afraid of putting their bodies on the line for something they believe in, well, I'm your man."

It had been the nearest thing to an impassioned speech he had made since he had joined English Rose, and he sat back and waited for a response.

Farmer looked at him for a moment and then said, "Funny you should say that Frank, but the whole idea of… security in its broader sense, is something that the leadership has been giving a lot of thought to. We're living in fast moving times, times when the political landscape is changing on an almost daily basis, and we know that some of the things we're advocating – things we know will benefit the country but that misguided people may oppose – will flush out some pretty heavy characters on the other side. And we need to be ready to meet them, to meet their physical force with our own physical force if that's what it takes."

"That's exactly what I mean," said Mason quickly.

Farmer looked at him appraisingly for a moment and then said, "I'll have a word with a few people and see whether there isn't a way we could better utilize your talents, Frank."

A week later Mason had his first meeting with Vinnie Groves. It was the day of the big speech and he had been helping deliver members of the audience to the venue, and as he was making his way through the hall, he heard his name being called out and saw Farmer coming towards him in the company of a group of men, among whom he recognised Groves.

"Frank, I wanted you to meet Vinnie Groves," said Farmer and Mason felt his hand being clasped in a firm grip. "Very pleased to meet you, Frank," said Groves. "Giles has told me about some of the skills you have that the party might be able to use – we're very lucky to have you on board."

Mason had been looking forward to observing Groves and trying to analyse what he had that seemed to inspire people, but he was nevertheless unprepared for his own reaction to the proximity of the other man. Groves radiated an energy that was tangible, and as Mason made eye contact, he found himself staring into the most unusual eyes he had ever seen. The pupils were black but around them were irises of a striking pale blue/grey that created an expression of incredible intensity. Mason's peripheral vision picked up a crinkling of the skin that suggested the other man was smiling and then he felt himself being enveloped in an aura of warmth and conviviality that was almost palpable.

He stammered something in response and then his hand was released, and the group swept away, leaving a vacuum occupying the space that had hitherto been taken up by an irresistible force. The meeting with Vinnie Groves left Mason shaken. If he, who harboured no illusions at all about the man, who regarded him as a reckless, perhaps criminally dangerous threat to the peace and security of the country, could be affected so viscerally, could feel an almost physical reaction to a meeting that had lasted only a few seconds, what might be the effect on those already predisposed to feel positive towards Groves and see him as the answer to their problems?

It was then that it dawned on him that the way of life that he and millions of people accepted unthinkingly as their birth right might be under an existential threat. He watched the group as it cut a swathe through the hall, leaving a visible wake behind it, with little knots of party workers and supporters who had been introduced to Groves engaged in huddled, excited discussion.

Two hours later the hall was full to bursting and loud music was being played to create an upbeat mood. A series of warm up men had been working the crowd into a state of arousal like ardent young lovers, and if they hadn't quite brought it to a climax, they had at least reduced it to an appropriate condition of quivering pliancy. Behind the stage was a screen on which was projected a large Tudor rose, with below it the inscription, *English Rose: Our Future Together,* picked out in bold letters.

As Groves entered the hall, lights flashed on and off and a floodlight began to quarter the room, eventually settling on his slight, upright figure as it moved through the auditorium. Pulsating music accompanied the light show and as Groves approached the front of the hall, the cheers rose to an ear-splitting crescendo. Then as he mounted the stage, the music died away, the floodlight was switched off and the disco lights stopped flashing, and all that remained was a slim, boyish figure who moved across to the centre of the stage and then stopped and waved an arm diffidently, almost shyly, at the crowd in front of him. The wave set off a great roar and he began to make calming motions with his hands and gradually the noise died down to something approaching silence.

"Thank you for that wonderful welcome," began Groves. "Please believe me when I say it is genuinely humbling and believe me also when I say that wherever this great journey takes us, I will always try to be worthy of the trust you have placed in me." A fresh round of applause erupted, and he made quietening gestures until there was once more something approaching silence.

"Men and women of England," he began again, "we are living through unprecedented times, and the decisions we take as a country in the weeks and months ahead will determine the nature of the society we live in for decades, maybe for centuries, perhaps for ever." He paused to let the words sink in. "And what I am going to say to you today is my attempt to plot a course that will help us navigate our way through these uncharted waters.

"Let me start by saying that some people listening to this speech may have picked up the wrong impression of what English Rose is all about. Now we all know how upright and honourable the mainstream print and broadcast media are," this produced scattered laughter and some booing, "but in case people have been misinformed, I want to say a few things about what we are and what we are not.

"Look behind me and you will see our emblem, the Tudor Rose. As many of you know, at the end of the Wars of the Roses, the new king, Henry VII, took the Red Rose of Lancaster and the White Rose of York and combined their designs to make a new rose, The Tudor Rose, that became a symbol of healing and allowed a disunited country to come together and move forward in harmony and unity.

"And that is exactly what, with your help, we at English Rose intend to do. So, for those who think we are a party of extremism, even a party of hate, I would like to read you some words of St Francis of Assisi that a leader from this country's past quoted when coming to power:

Where there is discord may we bring harmony. Where there is error, may we bring truth. Where there is doubt, may we bring faith. Where there is despair, may we bring hope.

"Men and women of England, I think those words are as true now as they were then. Yes, we have some hard choices ahead of us, yes, we are going to have to ask people to make tough decisions, but we are going to do those things with tolerance and humility, by consensus and by agreement, and above all," he paused "with respect for the rule of law, the same rule of law that has been the bedrock of our great country since Magna Carta was signed more than eight hundred years ago."

There was sustained applause at this, and Groves stopped, ran a hand through his hair and took a slip from his glass of water. "Now," he went on, "I want to take you on a journey, a journey that explains everything about what our country once was and what it has become. For those of you who like their history underpinned by intellectual rigour, I would point you to *Le Grande Remplacement* - in English, the Great Replacement - the seminal work by the great French thinker, Renaud Camus, which references some of the matters I am going to discuss and does so more eloquently than a simple man like me can ever hope to."

He paused and took another sip of water. "I'm going to start by asking you a question. How long have human beings walked the earth? How long would you say?" He let the question hang in the air. "Well, the archaeologists and anthropologists say that humans have been around for a couple of hundred thousand years but that they have existed in their present manifestation for about forty thousand of those years. That's a long time, a very long time. And those same scientists and anthropologists tell us that over the course of those forty thousand years, human behaviour has been consistent. Whether it was as hunter gatherers in the early days, or as permanent settlers following the first great agricultural revolution, humans lived and moved around in groups of others like themselves. And whether these groups were known as 'tribes' or later as 'farm communities' or 'city states' they were communities made up of people who looked the same, acted in the same way and talked the same language.

"The group provided warmth and comfort and companionship for its members, it allocated tasks and it made sure the young and old were looked after. But it provided something else as well. It provided safety. Safety from attack. When everyone in the group knew one another, the group was safe from attack by others. Outsiders were viewed with suspicion and seen as a threat, and upon meeting strangers, the group would take action to repel them. So, my friends, looking on someone who is different from yourself with suspicion and seeing them as a potential threat, is a perfectly natural thing, a healthy thing, something that for thousands of years has made people feel safer and, in all likelihood, prolonged their lives.

"And as humanity progressed and developed, that impulse became stronger, because if you know your Darwin, you'll know that any behaviour that protects the species *will* become more commonplace. The innate suspicion we feel towards people who are different to us has been essential to the way we operate for hundreds of thousands of years and is part of our collective DNA."

He paused to let the thought sink in. "Think about that. Really think about that for a moment. To view someone who is different from yourself with suspicion, with hostility, to see them as a threat and want to drive them away, is not something to be ashamed of. On the contrary, it is an impulse that has benefited humanity for hundreds of thousands of years and has enabled it to rise to its present position of pre-eminence in the natural world." So far Groves had been speaking in the calm, measured tones a vicar or a bank manager night have employed, and in the breathless silence that greeted his words, a pin could have been heard dropping in the huge auditorium.

"So, what am I saying?" he went on when he began to speak again. "What message can you take from what I have said? It is this: when you are walking along the street and you see someone who looks and dresses differently from you, who is a different colour to you and who speaks a different language to you, and you view that person with suspicion, there is nothing wrong with that, there is nothing to feel ashamed of, you are simply reacting the way your ancestors did for millennia.

"I am going to say that once more and this time I want you to really think about it." He allowed the silence to develop. "When you view someone who kooks different from you with suspicion there is nothing wrong with that; on the contrary, it is *natural,* it is *right,* and it is *good.*" A low rumble began and then it turned into a roar and people began to stand up and applaud. Groves let the wave run its course and when he spoke again it was once more in the calm tones with which he had started the meeting.

"So, let us recap. For forty thousand years humans have based their survival on a healthy distrust of those who are different from themselves and they have thrived as a result. It is only in the last few hundred years that, as a species, we have diverged from this way of life and started indiscriminately mixing, and only in the last half century that the process has increased so dramatically. To those of you who view this "multiculturalism" as the natural order of things, I would ask you to pause and reflect that it has been commonplace for only about seventy of those last forty thousand years, and that this represents less than 0.002 percent of mankind's history."

Groves had a showman's sense of when to pause and let the implications of a point strike home and he did exactly that now. "So, with that in mind," he looked out at the audience, "let us consider some of the consequences of so called "multiculturalism," let us look at how our lives have changed in the years since this indiscriminate mingling began. First, we had huge overcrowded ghettos in our cities, ghettos where any semblance of decency disappeared, where drugs were rife, and where sexual promiscuity destroyed the family unit that has sustained us for thousands of years. Then we had AIDS, a silent killer that worked its dark magic in the communities inhabiting those ghettos and among those who indulged in unnatural practices."

There was now utter silence in the hall and Groves enunciated his next words quietly. "I am pointing these things out, you understand, not to apportion blame to any particular group or community, but because these are things that need to be discussed before it is too late for all of us. We were given a warning with bird flu and the SARS virus and we chose to ignore them. And then we had the coronavirus, whose virulent spread was borne on the wings - literally on the wings - of an international transportation system that had millions of people whizzing all over the world for no other reason than that they could.

"I say to you, and I want you to think about this very carefully; the coronavirus pandemic would have been contained with ease if we did not live in a world where indiscriminate travel was available to people who have no business travelling indiscriminately. Consider whether all those deaths were worth it so that people could travel halfway around the globe to sit on bits of sand a few degrees warmer than the bits they've got at home. Well, one good thing did come out of the Coronavirus crisis and that is that governments took action to slow down the foolish, pointless intermingling of people that resulted from cheap air travel.

"And now, after all that, we have had the recent frightening acceleration in global warming, with all its attendant problems. In the past few years, rising sea levels have made certain parts of the world uninhabitable, and the warming of the sea is producing violent, unpredictable weather systems that are causing floods in some areas and droughts in others. We have seen the result of that; a teeming mass of diseased humanity swarming towards our country intent on destroying the way of life we love.

"I feel deeply sorry for those people, I really do, and I wish there was something I could do for them, but the sad answer is that there is nothing you or I can do for any of them. There are too many of them and their plight is too desperate. All we can do is protect our own –just like the hunter gatherers did for all those thousands of years.

"It is a crisis of truly biblical proportions; perhaps it is God's judgement on his erring children. If you believe in God – and I confess I do – you will remember the story of how he punished his children by sending a terrible flood down to destroy them, and you may reflect that perhaps the current apocalypse is God's judgement. And if you don't believe in God - and I know there are millions and millions of decent people who don't - consider whether what is happening is nature's warning to us, whether nature is telling us to step away from the things that have brought us to this place."

Groves stopped for a moment and sipped from a glass of water. He didn't look like a man cowed or made anxious by the importance of the occasion, in fact he looked like someone with absolute mastery of his brief.

"So far I have painted a bleak and devastating picture of a world spinning out of control," he went on, "and I make no apologies for that. It *is* a bleak and devastating picture. But I don't want you to lose hope, I don't want you to think that our future is so dark that there is no way forward. On the contrary, I am now going to talk you through a series of measures that we in English Rose are proposing in our new manifesto," he waved a booklet in the air, "a series of policies that will solve these terrible problems we are facing, secure our borders, and return this proud island nation to the broad sunlit uplands it once inhabited."

Behind him the Tudor Rose faded away, to be replaced by a picture of a pamphlet that said, *English Rose: Putting English Values First*. Groves held up the manifesto again.

"As I have said and as we all know, we live in dark, unprecedented times, times which demand unprecedented action. As a people and as a species we are now in the court of last resort. Let me tell you what will happen in the years to come. There will be hordes of people, literally millions of people trying to get from the hotter regions at the centre of the earth to the more temperate ones in the northern and southern hemispheres, bringing with them disease, disorder and pestilence.

"Our country and others like us will need to make border security a top priority: we know that the current government is implementing a national registration scheme and that is all very well, but my friends, we are going to have to do much better than that. We know how difficult it was to keep our borders secure in the good old days, how whatever measures the security forces put in place, the people traffickers found ways of getting around them. So, yes, compulsory ID for everyone is an absolute given, as is having our island literally ring fenced with physical security barriers that are the best that technology can offer."

He paused. "But that is not enough. You know it and I know it. Smugglers and forgers and people traffickers will find ways of smuggling and forging and trafficking people. They will swarm through our defensive measures offshore, and although our border security will keep a few of them back, many more will get through, bringing with them disease, disorder and chaos.

"But there's one thing that no one has been able to forge and that is the human face. Think about that. Think about the implications for security if the only faces people saw were faces that were the same as their own. Think about how easy it would be for the security services to find anyone who had slipped through the net. It wouldn't matter how sophisticated the forgery of papers or cards or iris recognition was, the interlopers would stand out like sore thumbs because, put simply, their thumbs, and of course, the rest of them, would be a different colour to everyone else.

"Think about that, Ladies and Gentlemen, think about the safety and security of having our borders forever inviolable, of knowing that outsiders would never again be able to get in. And those borders would be secure because…," he spread his hands, "… your face would be your ID. Your face would be your passport.

"Now I know what you are going to say. You will say that even if we didn't let a single person who is... different into the country for the rest of time, the ones who are already here will make the system I envisage unsustainable.

"And that is why..." he allowed another silence to develop "...English Rose is calling for the peaceful and orderly repatriation of all those currently living here who are not of Anglo Saxon, or Celtic, or European stock." There were outbreaks of cheering and of applause, but there was also something like shock and awe at the sheer scale of the proposal.

"Now let me make something quite clear," he went on after a few moments. "This repatriation must be carried out in an orderly manner, with packages of financial compensation for the individuals concerned, and for the countries they are returning to. It will be carried out with respect for the sensibilities of those who have been fortunate enough be able to share our way of life – and in some cases contribute to it - and it will be carried out in an orderly manner, even if that means it takes longer than we would ideally like.

"Whatever we have to do will be done in a way that respects the dignity of the individual and complies with the rule of law that has been the cornerstone of our way of life for so long." There was more sustained applause as the full import of what he was saying began to percolate through the ranks of the audience.

"And when we have to say goodbye to our friends from other lands, we will do so with a tear in our eye at the memory of the shared journey which, through no one's fault, has now reached a fork in the road. Men and Women of England, there are a couple of things I want to stress before I conclude this address. The first is to reiterate the point I made earlier, that this so called "multiculturalism" is not part of the natural order of things, it is an aberration and is neither natural nor desirable. The other thing concerns what I said about feeling no guilt when you feel hostility towards strangers."

He paused for a moment. "I'm going to go back to something I said earlier in the address and I want you to really think about it." He paused again and let the silence hang in the air. Then speaking slowly and enunciating each word distinctly, he said, "What I said was that when we view someone who looks different from us with suspicion, there is nothing wrong with that; on the contrary, it is *natural,* it is *right,* and it is *good.*"

There was applause and shouts of approval from around the arena.

He waited for the noise to abate a little before he spoke again. "I'm going to say it once more: when we view someone who is a different colour from us with suspicion, there is nothing wrong with that; on the contrary, it is *natural,* it is *right,* and it is *good.*"

This time the audience were on their feet joining in with the chant, and punching the air in time to the words, *natural, right, good,* like a football crowd

Groves went through the mantra four times more and each time the response got more rhythmic and more excited, like a crowd at a church or mosque responding to an incantation they knew would raise them to a state of exaltation. Eventually a sort of climax was reached and passed, and a shudder ran through the crowd then then it sank back, sated and exhausted. Groves ran a hand through his hair and took another drink and then addressed the auditorium once more, this time speaking quietly, almost wistfully.

"I want to finish by talking to you of the kind of England that once existed but that was destroyed by the creeping dark force of multiculturalism. I don't remember it myself because by the time I was born it was gone. But I know it existed because my grandfather told me about it."

He paused for a moment. "My grandfather grew up in the last century and in the great war against fascism he was a spitfire pilot based at Biggin Hill, in Kent. He was one of "the few," those brave young men – and how young most of them were - who took to the skies several times a day during the Battle of Britain.

"He never talked about the war - he was too modest for that - but he let me play with his medals and showed me some of the old photographs of himself and his friends. I asked him once why he had done it - why he and the others had put their lives in danger - and he told me that they were fighting for England. And when I asked him what he meant he told me about the England he was fighting for.

"He said it was an England of small towns and villages, where everyone knew everyone and had a cheery word of greeting for one another, where cricket was played on the village green and where you could watch the game from the beer garden of the Royal Oak with a pint of best bitter in your hand. An England where the shops were run by Englishmen – Bates the greengrocer, Sam Barnard the butcher, Grimes the grocer – and where those shopkeepers knew each other and had the same values. There was a church in the village, not a mosque, or a synagogue, or a *temple*, but a church, a church made of old English stone, a church that had stood on the same spot for centuries, where people from the same stock and with the same values had worshipped for centuries.

"Does that England sound familiar to any of you?"

There were shouts of "Yes."

"Well, it's an England that's gone, but…
maybe it's not gone for ever. With your help we can
restore that England."

He paused again and Mason could see that
the crowd were literally hanging on his words.
"Will you help me take this country from the
darkness of multiculturalism into the bright white
light of a new England, a new England that
represents the values of the old England we love?"
His words were almost drowned out by the noise
bouncing around the auditorium and he was forced
to make calming gestures before he could continue.
"My grandfather's favourite poem was *Jerusalem,*
and with your permission, I would like to read a few
words of it to you now:

And did those feet in ancient time,
Walk upon England's mountains green.
And was the holy Lamb of God,
On England's pleasant pastures seen.

"I'm sure you all know the last verse and I'm
going to read it to you now; please join in if you'd
like to." The words of the last verse were projected
onto the screen behind him and as he started to
speak, music began to play over the PA.

I will not cease from Mental Fight,

As he read the first line of the stanza,
audience members joined in and some of them
began to sing along to the music.

Nor shall my Sword sleep in my hand,

The singing increased in volume and intensity and for the final two lines the auditorium rocked with noise.

Till we have built Jerusalem,
In England's green and pleasant Land.

A couple of minutes later, when the cheering had died down, and something like order had been restored to the auditorium, Groves quieted the crowd and into the sudden pool of silence dripped the following quiet words.

"When he had finished composing the poem, Blake wrote underneath it a quotation from the bible,

Would to God that all the Lord's people were Prophets.

He waited a few seconds and said, "Will you be the prophets of a new England?" The crowd erupted and he went on, "Will you be those prophets and come with me on this great journey?"

Members of the audience were standing up and applauding, some were crying, some were singing *Jerusalem,* others were leaping up and down, and a few were giving Nazi salutes. In the midst of it all, Mason suddenly made out the figures of Reg and June, bouncing up and down like teenagers and applauding furiously, their upturned faces lit up with beatific smiles. A moment later Groves and his acolytes processed slowly down the central aisle and as they passed his row of seats,

Mason noticed that the party leader was literally drenched in sweat.

VI

Viewed in retrospect, the experience had had an almost out of body quality to it, with part of Mason observing everything with a detached, cynical air, and another part caught up in a very visceral way with the excitement and the noise and the passion as people projected their hopes and dreams or their hates and prejudices onto the blank white canvas that was Vinnie Groves.

It was certainly a night of triumph for English Rose and it was one of the defining moments in the surge that took it from a tiny, fringe party of the radical right, into the mainstream of British politics. Matt Rees watched the speech in a House of Commons bars with a couple of colleagues from the dwindling band of Labour members who viewed the world through eyes uncluttered by dogma, and the sense of a movement on the march was tangible.

"He's a clever bastard, all right, isn't he?" said Rees

"He certainly is," replied Barney Wilson, who represented a South Wales constituency. "He's talking about kicking several million people out of the country, some of whom will have lived here for generations, and yet he sounds for all the world like your friendly bank manager saying you've just got to reduce your overdraft a bit."

"He reminds me of one of those TV doctors, the ones on the breakfast shows," said Bob Maxton. "All smarm and charm and 'this is for your own good, you know it makes sense.'"

"He knows what he's doing, though," said Rees with grudging respect. "Did you notice how he used all these images, "dark," "black," "night," to talk about multiculturalism, and "white," "light," and "brightness," to talk about the brave new world he's proposing."

"Classic dog whistle stuff," said Wilson.

"So how are we going to stop him?"

"I don't know, Matt, how *are* we going to stop him. There's less than a hundred of us here and you know yourself the party's never been so weak at a local level."

"True," said Rees, "but we've got to do something, otherwise we might sleepwalk into the kind of society we've seen in other countries but have always said couldn't exist here because our institutions are too robust and our people have too much common sense." He paused and took a drink. "I'm not sure we can say that anymore, lads. What do you think?"

"I think I need another beer," said Maxton. "Same again, everyone?"

In fact, the surge English Rose got at the local elections following Groves' speech surpassed anything the party could have hoped for. By the impenetrable logic that local elections have always adhered to, some metropolitan areas were voting, while others weren't, and in the towns and shires the same thing was happening, but, when it was all over, when the votes were counted, amidst all the confusion the one unarguable outcome was that English Rose had emerged as the biggest single party.

Yes, these were merely local elections where voting turnout is usually lower than 30%, yes, the Conservatives were suffering the midterm blues that all governments have to deal with, yes, the erstwhile opposition had suffered a truly staggering decline and was now in critical care in terms of its status as a genuinely national party, and yes, those parties occupying the middle ground were still bickering and unable to find common cause.

But as true as these facts demonstrably were, what could not be denied was that English Rose had transformed itself from a tiny fringe party, barely registering on the electoral radar, to one that had won more seats than anyone else in an election where regions all over the country had voted. Suddenly its name was on everyone's lips, Vinnie Groves was asked to appear on the TV news and the breakfast shows, and there was even an invitation to appear on Radio Four's flagship morning news programme, *Today*.

For Frank Mason it was a challenging time; he knew he needed to appear to be sharing in the general excitement, even though he privately considered English Rose to be an organisation filled with dreamers and halfwits led by crooks and fraudsters. At the same time, he was aware that he needed to keep his eyes open and try to find some chink in the armour that was concealing Storm Force 55 from his gaze. He knew it was there in the background, tantalisingly close, knew that he might have colleagues who were secretly members of the paramilitary force, but he couldn't find a way in, and more than that he knew he couldn't be seen to be too obviously trying to find a way in.

In the end the break came a week later, on a cold, early Spring evening following yet another successful English Rose rally. Mason had been to a meeting in Bayswater in the company of Giles Farmer and North London Regional Director Mark Spencer. The meeting had gone well but it was now late and cold and they were returning to their cars, which they had left in a large NCP car park nearby.

Mason had got to know Spencer reasonably well in the past few months as they had worked together on the preparations for the rally that had propelled English Rose into the major league of British politics. The regional director was a burly middle-aged man who seemed forever on the point of bursting out of whatever clothing he happened to be wearing. He was taciturn almost to the point of rudeness and had no small talk whatsoever, appearing to operate on the principal that communication that wasn't purely functional had no purpose and, as such, was a waste of his time.

Mason had conceded ruefully to himself that, unlike Farmer and Groves, who were charismatic and friendly and didn't remotely fit the stereotype of white supremacists, Spencer could have come straight from central casting. There was something forbidding about him, something threatening, a barely concealed menace that seemed permanently on the point of exploding into the open.

"Cold out, tonight," Farmer said as they hurried along the street, through which a bitter north easterly wind was blowing.

"Sure is," agreed Mason, and Spencer grunted something unintelligible.

It was as they neared the entrance to the car park that they heard a voice behind them shouting, "Fascist bastards!"

An Asian man in a hoodie was approaching them from across the street, and there was something about the exaggerated care with which he moved that suggested he was under the influence of alcohol or drugs or both.

"Hold on, my friend," said Farmer, spreading his arms out in the universal gesture of conciliation. "Who says we're fascists?"

"*Who says we're fascists?*" mimicked the young man. "That English Rose rosette you're wearing for one thing, you Nazi cunt."

"Whoa, hang on a minute," said Farmer. "Let's try and sort this out, mate."

"I'm not your mate, you fascist wanker," replied the young man and although his face was concealed by the hoodie, the eyes half hidden by the cloth were wild with drugs or alcohol or something else, so wild they were actually rolling in his head.

The man made a sudden lunge towards Farmer and that was when Mason, who had been waiting for such a move, struck. He glided into the space between the two men and there was a glint of metal as his arm swept through the air and then the Asian man jumped back, clutching his shoulder.

"You've stabbed me," he screamed. "You've stabbed me, you fascist cunt." He staggered backwards and when he lifted his hand from his jacket, it was stained dark. "He's stabbed me!" he wailed. "He's stabbed me in the fucking arm!"

Mason crouched in front of him, the blade of the knife he held in the palm of his hand now in plain view. "And if you don't fuck off," he said in a quiet but menacing voice, "I'll stab you again, only this time I'll stab you where it really hurts." He lunged forward and the Asian man leapt back and

88

began to retreat in a half run, half stagger, whimpering, "Bastard stabbed me! Stabbed me in the fucking shoulder!"

Mason waited until he had disappeared around a corner and then looked down at the knife in his hand, which was short and thin with a wickedly sharp looking blade. Taking a handkerchief from his pocket, he wiped the handle and then, holding it by the tip, threw it towards a hedge that had some railings in front of it. The knife sailed over the hedge in a graceful parabola and landed in the bushes behind it with a soft thud.

Mason rubbed his hands with the handkerchief and turned to the others. "Probably best if we make ourselves scarce, gentlemen," he said. "He looks like the kind of saddo who'll crawl straight back to his bedsit and spend the night crying his eyes out, but it's just possible he might actually have friends, and if he came back with them, well..."

He left the rest unsaid and a couple of minutes later they had reached the multi storey car park and were approaching their cars, which were all parked on the same level.

"Wouldn't it have been better to have kept the knife?" said Spencer, speaking for the first time. "I mean, mightn't it be evidence or something?"

"Nothing to connect it to us," said Mason, "and on that basis much safer to dump it than keep it. I don't think he'll report it anyway - I think he'll probably wake up in the morning with a massive hangover and won't have a clue what happened to him. He looks more like a lone nutter than someone from a properly organised group."

"You're probably right," said Farmer.

"And I tell you what, gentlemen," went on Mason, "if they're recruiting blokes like him, we're going to have an easier time of it than we thought. And if it does set off some tit for tat action from the Pakis… well our boys will be ready for them; might even kill a few of the fuckers." He stopped and looked at the other two. "What?" He spread his hands. "It's where the whole thing's heading, isn't it," he paused for a moment and then went on, "so bring it on is what I say."

He had been watching Spencer covertly while he spoke and had noticed the regional director's brow furrowed in thought as he stared into space. Now Spencer looked across and Mason found himself the object of a cold, sustained, appraisal. He looked straight back and said, "What do you think, Mark?"

It was only after their cars had exited the car park and driven away that a figure emerged cautiously from the shadows and crossed to the little area of bushes where Mason had thrown the knife. The man, who appeared to be of Asian origin, searched in the bushes till he found the weapon, then took it over to one of the benches the council had thoughtfully provided for the public and sat down.

He held the knife up in front of him and regarded it thoughtfully, then he put a fingertip on the tip of the blade and pushed, and when the plastic shaft retracted smoothly into its handle, Raj Kumar smiled.

The whole thing had all gone off better than they had dared to hope, and he was quietly pleased at how adroitly he had managed to carry off the role of deranged lunatic. But more importantly than that, the incident had surely given Frank Mason's attempt to penetrate the inner circle of the radical right the kick start it needed.

Part Two

By means of shrewd lies, unremittingly repeated, it is possible to make people believe that heaven is hell - and hell heaven. The greater the lie, the more readily it will be believed. (Adolf Hitler)

'Emergencies' have always been the pretext on which the safeguards of individual liberty have been eroded. (Friedrich August von Hayek)

Why are we having all these people from shithole countries coming here? (Donald J. Trump)

VII

The chamber of the House of Commons was full as the Prime Minister emerged from his office behind the Speaker's chair and took his place at the despatch box. As he watched Alexander Cadogan move with practiced ease along the front bench, bestowing smiles on those whose eminence entitled them to such a gift, Matt Rees reflected, not for the first time, that the chamber was a mirror of the society it represented. According to his own father, a keen observer of the political scene in the seventies and eighties, most Tory MPs of the era fell into one of two categories, which he had designated the Tebbit Tendency and the Hurd Instinct.

The latter, named after old Etonian Douglas, was a dwindling but still statistically significant band of One Nation Tories, many of whom came from old money, others whose wealth was more recently acquired, but who all shared the values of a bygone age and the notion that service to the country was a calling in itself. Educated at the great public schools and at Oxbridge, some of them adhered to the values of *noblesse oblige* more successfully than others, but they were all in politics from a sense of duty and the idea of choosing to clamber up the greasy pole purely to further one's own ends was anathema to them.

The Tebbit Tendency, named in honour of the irascible and cantankerous Norman, who had famously snarled that his father hadn't sat around waiting for state handouts but had "got on his bike," was drawn mainly from the lower middle classes. They were self-made men, (and they were pretty nearly all men) with little time for tradition or the values of the old school, and like many self-made people, they had little sympathy for those not blessed with the life skills they themselves possessed. Rees had never forgotten one of their members on the awful election night of 1992, leering triumphantly at the camera from the count at Basildon as the result was announced, his teeth lined up like a set of piano keys. On the basis that one should know one's enemies, Rees had applied his father's test to succeeding generations of Tory MP's, and every time a new member ticked one of the boxes, he would offer a nod of acknowledgement to his long dead parent.

Then had come a new breed, epitomised by Cameron and Osborne and Johnson and their coterie of old Etonian followers. They had the veneer of the Hurd Instinct certainly, but there was something different about them. Their wealth hadn't come from old money - in Osborne's case it would have been dismissed as "trade" - and they didn't seem to share the sense of *noblesse oblige* that previous generations had brought to the way they went about their business. It was in fact hard to know exactly what their political principles were; even fellow Tories said that attempting to define what they stood or was like trying to eat custard with a knife and fork. But what they did have was the swagger and the sense of entitlement that money and Eton and Oxbridge gave to the children of the wealthy; the notion that they were different from everyone else, that the rules everyone else lived by didn't really apply to them.

In another age, when the product of such an upbringing might quickly have found himself a regional magistrate in imperial India with power of life and death over millions, imbuing people with a belief in their own innate superiority might have made some sense, but the wind of egalitarian change that had swept through not just the colonies, but the corridors of power in Westminster and the City of London as well, seemed to have made the public school experience less relevant in the modern world.

Or so it had seemed in the latter half of the twentieth century, as both parties experimented with cabinets drawn from the upwardly mobile middle cases; grammar school boys and girls most of them, the majority still Oxbridge graduates, but others educated at red brick universities or, in one notable case, no university at all. And then, with the advent of Cameron and Osborne and Johnson there had been a return to the old ways, except that the new lot no longer seemed to hold to those values of duty and service that had made their earlier counterparts possible to respect and, in some cases, even like.

It was particularly galling to hear the new breed of toffs refer to the exercise of politics as a game, as in *"it's all a game, really, isn't it?"* and Rees was one of many MP's who endorsed Bob Maxton's response, pithily delivered, that, *"it may be a game to them, but it fucking well isn't one to most of my constituents."* Having studied them over time, both inside and outside parliament, Rees had arrived at the conclusion that they were a collection of beautifully spoken, well mannered, charming grifters.

And in this respect Alexander Cadogan was a chip off the old block. Tall and handsome, with an effortless way of moving and talking, he had breezed his way through the party – intern, central office staffer, political adviser - until a safe seat had dropped as if by magic into his elegant lap at the moment of supreme opportunity. After that he had risen effortlessly through the ranks of the parliamentary party, acceding to the leadership at the tender age of forty-two.

One thing that distinguished Cadogan from his predecessors and that his acolytes made a big thing of was that he had been educated at Harrow rather than Eton. Quite why this should make such a difference Rees failed to understand - it was in his opinion rather like asking the electorate to choose which brand of ceremonial dagger it preferred to be shafted by - but he supposed it must have been of consequence to some. One of Cadogan's favourite aphorisms about his *alma mater* was the one about the three future prime ministers who'd been in the same form (imagine the bollocks that must have been talked in that class, Bob Maxton had said) and like his old Etonian predecessors, a praetorian guard of ex school chums operating in his private office and around the party served his every need.

Next to his leader on the front bench sat the Home Secretary, legs extended carelessly, his grey slacks pressed to a knife edge of sharpness. Although the matter at hand fell under his purview, there was something about the Home Secretary that had made the PM decide it might be better to take on the speech himself. The Home Secretary was loved by the Tory matrons of the home counties; he came from the same stock as them and they understood him, but his colleagues were aware of how little crossover appeal he had. It was something about the supercilious air he had, about the smoothness of his pate, about the half-smile that played on his face when he spoke, and the curl of the lip that told you that you were a twat of the first order but that, of course, he was far too well bred to tell you so to your face.

So Cadogan had taken on the responsibility for the speech and he now approached the despatch box and began to talk. "Mister Speaker," he began, "it has become customary to talk about us living in strange times, and were it not that we are indeed existing in times of unparalleled, unprecedented threat, I would not be standing before the house today asking it to pass this Emergency Powers Bill into law.

"I am as aware, as honourable members on all sides of the house are, just how unusual this request is so I would like to refer to those times in our past when it became necessary to introduce such legislation. In 1914, Parliament passed into law the Defence of the Realm Act, giving the government enhanced powers with which to prosecute the terrible war that had just begun. When the conflict was over the act was superseded by the Emergency Powers Act of 1920, and this in turn was upgraded by a new act in 1964, which remains on the statute book today.

"Over the course of the last hundred years, the act has been invoked as sparingly as possible, in all on only 11 occasions; during the general strike of 1926, for example, during a period of industrial unrest following the Second World War, and during the fuel crisis that led to the three-day week of the early nineteen seventies. The act, which justifies the declaration of a state of emergency where *'there have occurred, or are about to occur, events of such a nature as to disrupt the life of the community,'* has served this country well, but unfortunately it does not have the teeth necessary to meet the existential threat we face today. The original act was designed, and I quote, '*to make exceptional provisions for the protection of the community in case of emergency,*' and no one can doubt that we live in a genuine state of emergency now. But the current emergency is of an order undreamed of by the framers of the original act and that is why it needs new clauses to make it fit for purpose."

He paused for a moment and looked across the floor. "Let me explain why the current crisis is qualitatively different from the ones of the past. As we all know, global warming is causing the world to change before our very eyes in ways we could never have imagined. First, we had the terrible drought in sub-Saharan Africa and that was followed by Bangladesh flood and the great Atlantic storm of last year, and now, this year, we have had a monsoon catastrophe that has rendered large tracts of the Asian rainforest uninhabitable.

"Thousands, hundreds of thousands, maybe millions of people are on the move around the globe. As we speak, illegal transportation networks are being built all over Africa and Asia by pirates and people traffickers. There is a new generation of boat people in the Mediterranean and before long, they will be in the English Channel. They may even be there now.

"Of course, we want to help those people, of course we want to help everyone in the world who is suffering, but we can't do that if our country is overrun, *now,* by illegal immigrants.

101

"So, I am asking the house to strengthen our ability to protect our borders by placing in the new act a clause, which was originally included in the Prevention of Terrorism Act of 1974 to counter the threat of an IRA mainland bombing campaign. The clause gave the Home Secretary the power to exclude from Britain anyone he considered, on police evidence, to be involved in, and I quote again, the *'commission, preparation, or instigation of acts of terrorism'*. We propose to add to that last sentence so that it will read, 'commission, preparation, or instigation of acts of terrorism *or acts of illegal entry into the country.'*

"Mister Speaker, the current legislation allows for those arriving in our country, even those arriving illegally, to apply for asylum, requiring them to be housed until the application has gone through the courts, a process which can take months, if not years. That is simply unsustainable in the current world crisis. I do not wish to speak in apocalyptic terms, Mister Speaker, but unless the house passes this bill into law with the utmost despatch," he paused, "our country will be swamped by a tide of humanity that will render it uninhabitable."

A ripple of noise and movement spread across the assembled ranks and The Prime Minister allowed the chamber to settle. "When they vote on this bill, Mister Speaker, honourable and right honourable members will be voting for the lives and futures of their children and grandchildren; that is how high the stakes are. And so, Mister Speaker, I am calling on members to pass this bill into law for the sake of their children and grandchildren and for the sake of generations unborn. Consider, Mr Speaker, some of the times states of emergency have been called and compare them with our current crisis. Was this country really under more existential threat during the dockers strike of 1948, or the railwaymen's strike of 1955, or the miner's strike in 1972?" He allowed the House to digest this and there were calls of, "No!" and an isolated cry of, "Hear, hear."

"Another feature of the bill, Mister Speaker, is that it gives the government the power, and again I quote, to direct the armed forces into employment in *'agricultural work or in other work, being urgent work of national importance.'* We must enable our armed forces, Mr Speaker, to help us in our hour of need."

Matt Rees, sitting forlornly on the opposition benches, was acutely aware how precious civil liberties are and how easy it is for them to come under threat at times of stress. But as the tsunami of dubious assertions and paranoid half-truths washed over the House, he could feel its mood shifting, and with each plea from the Prime Minister working on the guilt, the fear and the vulnerability of its members, he could not doubt that the government would get its majority.

"Just before I yield, Mister Speaker," said the PM, "I would like to make a commitment on behalf of Her Majesty's government, to demonstrate to the world that the people displaced by these terrible events, wherever they may be, are in our thoughts. This government, Mister Speaker, here and now pledges that it will unilaterally increase its funding to the United Nations High Commission for Refugees by one percent, the increase to come into effect from the beginning of the new fiscal period, which will be in April next year."

A low growl of approval came from the government benches and in front of them the Home Secretary flicked an imaginary piece of fluff off his slacks and smirked. There then followed some desultory questioning in which the usual points were made. The Grand Old Man of the Conservative Party, a legendary figure whose words commanded the respect of the House in a way the Home Secretary's never would, made a measured contribution, reminding colleagues how liberty must not be allowed to atrophy through neglect, and Rees smiled at the irony of the Grand Old Man of the Conservative Party articulating exactly what the angry young men of Labour were thinking.

Cadogan praised the Grand Old Man for the wisdom of his contribution, telling the House how much his government valued the statesmanlike advice of the Father of the House. There was an approving murmur from behind him and on the front bench the Home Secretary smirked again.

Rees dragged himself wearily from the chamber and headed off to the tiny office he shared with Bob Maxton. Maxton was not there but a small TV was showing one of the huge rallies that the US President never seemed to tire of giving, whatever stage of the electoral cycle the country was in. The President was turning his ire on the press, those denizens of the fourth estate who half a century before had been hailed as the saviours of democracy when they exposed the corruption and criminality that lurked in the higher echelons of the Nixon administration.

But the world was now a very different place. Accreditation for the daily press briefings had been taken away from organisations hitherto regarded as at the core of the political process. CNN and MSNBC were no longer welcome and newspapers with whom the administration had taken umbrage found their accreditation abruptly terminated. The President's most stinging criticism was reserved for his twin *bêtes noires*, the Washington Post and the New York Times, and as a consequence of him continually calling them out at his rallies, their circulations had dwindled.

"And what about that great newspaper The Washington Post. What a great paper! And that other great paper The New York Times. Both printing lies about me since the day I came into office. Both printing fake news day after day, year after year." He held a copy of the Post between his finger and thumb and extended it towards the audience. "Know what I'd like to do with this? Know what I'd like to do? I'd like to cut the pages up into little squares and take them to the bathroom and… you know what I mean? But I can't. I'm a germophobe. You understand what I mean? I can't do what I'd like to do because I'm a germophobe."

The crowd began to whoop and holler. "But hey, did you see, Breitbart got hold of their subscription lists? Both papers. You see that? So now we know who they are. You believe that?" He shook his head and the cheers grew in intensity. "Can you believe these people? They have a list with all their own subscribers on it. They have a list and they've given it to us. We know who they are. Can you believe that? They've given us a list."

His showman's eye knowing unerringly where the main broadcast camera was positioned, he turned towards it. "We know who you are! We know who you are!" He looked around. "You believe that? They've put out a list – they've given us a list." He paused. "I probably shouldn't say this, I probably shouldn't say it, but if that list got into the wrong hands, it might be very dangerous for the people on it. It might be very dangerous for them." The crowd roared.

"You believe they'd do something like that?" He shook his head. "Put all their names on a list, I mean. You know what it's like? It's like turkeys voting for Christmas." He spread his arms in appeal. "Does anyone here think it's like turkeys voting for Christmas?" As the growl of approval slowly turned into a full-blooded roar, emails began to ping off in their hundreds and thousands towards New York and Washington cancelling subscriptions.

VIII

Mason waited a couple of weeks after the knife attack, hoping that in the retelling of the incident, ripples would spread far enough out to reach the people whose interest he was seeking to attract. But nothing happened. He spent most of the time working with Giles Farmer and Kirsty Black, engaging in the hundred and one jobs which needed to be done if a tiny regional party was to be turned into a great national one.

During the process he attended meetings, many of them, but all his antennae picked up was the normal cross section of opinions and views - some intelligent and interesting, others half formed and frankly flaky – that existed in the lower reached of a political party. Kirsty Black said something to this effect when, over a late drink with her and Giles at the Novotel Hotel in Hammersmith, he asked her what had first attracted her to English Rose.

"Funny you should ask that, Frank," she said, "I've done a lot of listening over the last couple of weeks and we've all got different reasons – for joining English Rose, I mean." She thought for a moment. "My family was always Labour and in normal times I was too. I liked the idea of the state as an enabler, as a force for good, stepping in when the market skewed things too much and created injustice.

"But when all this started – you know, deadly viruses, global warming, the whole thing – Labour seemed so out of touch, worried about not infringing this or that abstract right, or this or that minority group, when the whole house of cards was collapsing around us. I could have gone to the Conservatives but," she laughed, "my dad would have turned in his grave. And I've always seen them, the Tories, I mean, as having too many hang ups about the nature of government – about its needing to be small and not interfere in people's lives – when what the country actually needs is urgent action from the very centre of power." She shrugged. "And that left English Rose.

"I don't know," she shook her head, "three or four years ago, if someone had told me I'd be working full time for a party like ours, I'd have laughed in their face, but English Rose is exactly what we need; an activist movement, and one that's prepared to work the levers of power to make the sort of tough choices that will save our country and our way of life."

"Shame we couldn't have recorded that on film, Kirsty," smiled Farmer. "I've never heard the appeal of English Rose so eloquently articulated."

"Thank you, sir," she accompanied her words with an ironic bow. "Although, let's cut the crap and be brutally honest and admit that its main appeal is that its promising to drive the coons and Pakis who are turning us into a Mongrel race into the sea."

Mason, halfway through a swig, choked on his beer and even Farmer had the grace to look discomfited.

"I'm only saying out loud what everyone's thinking, Giles," she said demurely. "There's one other thing that attracted me to English Rose, though."

"It's generous expense accounts for full time officials?" said Farmer, who had by now recovered himself. "Speaking of which, anyone fancy another pint?"

He held up three fingers to a barman who was walking past and looked at Kirsty. "Go on then, what's the other thing?"

"Vinnie Groves," she answered. "When I listen to him half of me is thinking how good his policies are while the other half just wants to suck the face off him."

"Well," said Farmer, as he joined in with her laughter. "That bit might not make the party-political broadcast, but I wouldn't underestimate his appeal. Our leader is a very, very charismatic man."

"I'll second that," said Kirsty. "He can stamp my membership any time."

At that moment, Mark Spencer walked into the centre of the group and eased himself into a chair. They were the only people in the large, dimly lit room and in the soft glow of the hotel lighting, Mason hadn't been sure the figure approaching them was actually him.

Kirsty murmured a greeting and Farmer nodded, "Mark," as the big man sat down. There was something about the greetings that suggested to Mason that the arrival might not have been coincidental, might in fact have been expected by the others. When Spencer had ordered a drink and such pleasantries as he considered appropriate had been observed, there was a silence and, Mason, munching a peanut and trying not to look too eager, waited for someone to speak.

"I was telling Kirsty about what happened after the Bayswater meeting, with that bloke who tried to attack us," Spencer announced after what had seemed an interminable pause.

"It was certainly an impressive piece of work," said Farmer, and Kirsty added, "Sounds like you're not the sort of bloke to get on the wrong side of, Frank."

Mason shrugged and said between mouthfuls of peanut, "He started it and he got what he deserved."

"I looked for reports in the media and there was nothing," said Spencer. "And we know there was nothing reported to the local police because we have a… source there, so it looks like you were right about the guy being a lone nutter."

Mason said nothing and studiously continued to munch peanuts.

Spencer and Farmer exchanged glances and as if by unspoken agreement Farmer began to speak. "Do you remember when we were chatting a few weeks ago, Frank, and you talked about how best you might be able to help the movement?"

"In the pub that night?" asked Mason, and Farmer nodded.

"Do you remember what you said? You said, if my memory serves me correctly, that you weren't an intellectual, but that you'd done a lot of boxing as a boy and were handy with your fists." He enumerated the points on a finger. "You also said, and I'm going to quote you exactly, that if the movement was looking for people who weren't afraid of putting their bodies on the line, you were their man." After a short silence he went on, "Would you say that represents your position fairly accurately?"

"Very accurately," answered Mason.

"So…" Farmer paused, and it was Spencer who finally spoke.

"There are groups within the movement not many people know about, whose existence is… confidential."

"Inside English Rose?" asked Mason.

"Not exactly inside, rather elements with whom we have shared ideals and who want the same outcomes as us, but who are organised on different lines. Does that make sense?"

"Groups who are approaching this whole thing from the physical force end of the spectrum rather than the political one, you mean?"

Farmer and Kirsty grinned, and Spencer allowed the shadow of a smile to cross his face. "They said you were no fool. Yes. exactly that."

"So," said Farmer, "given what you are on record as saying about how you could help the movement, how would you feel - in general terms - about us opening up some lines of communication with some people who might be able to…"

Spencer grunted. "He's saying would you like us to put you in touch with others who think like you?"

"You mean some of those… elements who are at the physical force end of the spectrum?"

"Exactly."

"I would be very interested in exploring that avenue," said Mason after a moment.

The others exchanged glances and Farmer said, "The thing is, Frank, what we're going to tell you now is off the record and confidential and not for discussion with anyone else."

"We've been keeping an eye on you Frank," said Kirsty, "and to be honest, we've liked what we've seen. You look like you're made of the right stuff, the kind of stuff that we are going to need in the weeks and months ahead. But…" she paused.

"What she's trying to say, lad," Spencer cut in, "is that you'll be crossing a bridge and it's one you won't be able to cross back if you don't like what you see. Do I make myself clear?"

"Absolutely," said Mason, maintaining eye contact. "Bring it on."

"I told you he was all right, Mark," smiled Kirsty.

"Are you involved with these other groups then, Kirsty?" asked Mason

"We all are," Farmer answered for her. "Kirsty is responsible for keeping lines of communication open between the paramilitary people and the official party. And my job is to keep Vinnie up to speed with what's going on in the wider movement. It's all unofficial or course and every conversation we have is off the record and unattributable. As we all know, English Rose has deliberately positioned itself as a party of the mainstream that wants to work within the existing system. And that's one of its strengths – our rather nervous electorate has always been wary of supporting groups that pursue extra parliamentary agendas – which is why it's vital that there's nothing to connect the party with those organisations."

Spencer grunted and muttered something under his breath.

Kirsty smiled. "Mark is impatient for the next phase, when those in the wider movement will be able come out into the open."

Spencer grunted again. "At which point we won't have to worry about what the *electorate* thinks, because there won't fucking well be one anymore."

"It goes without saying," interjected Farmer with a smile, "that that particular aspiration doesn't appear in our current press releases. You can see why they employ me at the PR end of the movement and why Mark has got a more hands-on job."

In the brief pause that followed Mason looked across at Spencer. "So, what is your role, exactly, Mark?" he asked. "Other than the one you've got in English Rose?"

Spencer regarded him impassively and said, "I'm the leader of one of those other groups we've been talking about."

He took some peanuts from the bowl, munched then slowly, waited a few moments and added, "It's called Storm Force 55."

IX

In Mason's later recollection the silence that followed Spencer's disclosure seemed to last for ever, but the reality was that almost at once Kirsty had laughed and said, "Like we said, horses for courses."

Mason tried to maintain his equilibrium but the revelation, dropping without any warning out of a clear blue sky, had in fact shaken him considerably. He took a sip from his drink and scooped up a handful of peanuts, while all the time, welling up inside him was an irresistible urge to settle things there and then by reaching across the table and ripping Mark Spencer's head off its shoulders. He tried not to think of little Matthew, his precious life snuffed so casually out on the stairwell of a sink estate, tried not to think of Bianca's beautiful body lying cold and broken on a squalid bedroom floor, and summoning up all his willpower, he managed to find a way of putting the hatred for Spencer that was welling up inside him into a box, a box he promised himself he would throw open when the time was right.

Conscious of the need to act normally, he said, "What role do you see me playing, Mark?"

"Good question," answered Spencer. "At the moment, because of the need for security, Storm Force's organisation is a bit cloak and dagger."

"But soon," Farmer took up the story, "now that things are starting to move - you've seen that yourself – the time when the paramilitaries will be able to come out in the open is getting closer. And when that time comes, we're going to need a disciplined force, a force with a leadership and structure that people understand and know their place in, rather than a rabble of the discontented, the angry and the lawless."

"And that's where I come in," said Spencer.

"So," Kirsty took up the story, "we've formed a new organisation called Secure Your Neighbourhood; and if you think that's a dead boring name, don't worry, it's so by design. Its membership is by invitation only, all it's meetings will be closed, and it's stated aim is to organise 'citizen's support groups' to help communities who may come under threat from illegal immigration. We're going to bang on about the need for this force being most urgent in coastal regions but we're actually going to organise everywhere, and by this time next year we hope to have a paramilitary force ready to emerge from towns and villages all over the country when it's needed."

"That's a big ask in only a year," said Mason.

"You'd be surprised," answered Farmer. "There are groups all over the country who share our views – Sons of Albion, The League of Saint George, English Pride – so there's already a loose network out there and we've been quietly putting out feelers over the last couple of years. And the absolute game changer has been the rise of English Rose electorally. We've been able to convince these guys that if they unite behind English Rose there might be a pathway to power for them via the ballot box."

"And they're starting to see the logic of that approach," interjected Spencer. "After all we're only going to need the one chance."

"Is there a danger that it'll all be too visible?" asked Mason. "I mean, aren't the press supposed to on the lookout for private armies, or whatever they call them?"

"Ten or even five years ago, I would have agreed with you," said Farmer. "But these days there isn't the same public appetite for that type of story."

"Which is good for us," said Spencer.

"Which is very good for us."

"We've got half a million uniforms coming in from a wealthy donor," said Spencer. "They've been sitting in a warehouse in central Europe since the end of the Bosnian war. Blue camouflage, I think they are."

"The Two Tone Blueshirts," said Mason. "Not sure that's going to deliver quite the message we want."

Spencer glared at him. "This is a serious meeting about the future of our movement and the future of the country." His eyes remained locked onto Mason's. "So, we don't need any fucking comedians here, all right?"

Refusing to be stared down Mason returned the look with interest and said, "Tell you what, pal, you deliver me some heads to crack open and then we'll see how much of a fucking comedian I am."

He and Spencer continued to eyeball each other until Farmer broke in. "Now then, ladies, handbags down, we've got enough enemies without staring to fight among ourselves." In the end the party broke up with an agreement to meet at Spencer's house the next night to continue the discussion.

***

Spencer turned out to occupy a roomy third floor flat in a pleasant apartment block in Chiswick. Mason was met by Kirsty at the lift entrance, and they chatted about this and that on their way along the corridor. The door of the flat was opened by a young man with cropped hair in jeans and t shirt and as he led them in, he and Kirsty exchanged air kisses. "Tony, meet Frank, he's helping us organise London North West," Kirsty said as they shook hands. "Tony's been with us almost from the beginning."

Spencer and Giles Farmer were already there and the four took up where they had left off the previous evening, sitting at a table in the lounge, with Tony and a girl whose name Mason didn't hear moving unobtrusively in and out serving drinks or fetching documents for Spencer.

"The next big thing is the first meeting of the local Secure Your Neighbourhood group at the Milton Centre," said Farmer. "And because it's closed to the public there'll be security inside and outside to make sure no one who's not on the official list gets in."

"You're going to see a different kind of membership on Saturday, Frank," said Spencer. "And you're going to help me turn them into the kind of force we talked about last night. There'll be people there from London Storm Force, people I've known for years, the ones who are going to be the vanguard of the movement when it all kicks off, in at the sharp end doing the messy stuff."

"Salt of the earth," said Farmer, "but a bit rough around the edges, some of them, if you know what I mean."

"Nothing you can't handle, Frank, I'm sure," said Spencer with a faint smile and Mason thought he'd better respond to what appeared to be an olive branch. "I'll do my best, Mark."

"We're going to have to think about how best the groups might be organised," said Spencer. "Each county will have its own Secure Your

119

Neighbourhood Force and, in the end, each regional force will have a proper command structure, up to company or battalion level, depending on its size. They're also going to have uniforms, a knowledge and understanding of drilling, and access to weapons. Right now, we're allowing them some regional autonomy, just because we're so early in the process, but once we're organised, each group will be controlled from the centre, and every member will affirm his allegiance by swearing a personal oath of loyalty to Vinnie Groves.

"And that's why Vinnie will be addressing the meeting on Saturday. He wants to establish personal contact with as many of the guys as he can and because the London groups are likely to be the among the biggest in the country, he's coming down to press the flesh. And as we all know, Vinnie once met is never forgotten; he's our best weapon and by the time he's crisscrossed the country a few times we'll have an army ready and willing to lay down their lives for him."

Later, prior to leaving, Mason was in the bathroom, humming gently to himself as he washed his hands at the sink. Farmer and Kirsty were in the lounge and he could hear them making desultory conversation with the unnamed girl. Mason was drying his hands with a towel when his eye caught a movement in the mirror in front of him and he realized he must have left the door open a crack. Through the thin strip of light, he saw the half open door of the kitchen, and although it was hard to see exactly what the two male figures framed in the doorway were doing, Mason was sure he saw a hand glide across the blue of a pair of jeans and fondle a buttock. A moment later the door opened, and Mark Spencer padded silently and panther-like down the corridor in the direction of the lounge.

X

Arriving at the Milton Centre Mason sensed immediately that there was something different about this meeting. Tough looking individuals in Harrington jackets and leather blousons stood outside the building checking people's credentials, and the atmosphere was far more highly charged than the ones he'd experienced at English Rose events. Passing through security and taking his place in the hall, Mason had the sense of being in a qualitatively different environment.

Looking around him he noticed a gender imbalance that had not been evident at the party meetings; the audience was more male and looked younger and, well, *harder*. In addition to the denim and the bomber jackets, there were tattoos and big chains and chunky rings and here and there Doctor Marten boots. The few women who were there looked hard, too - the sort of women you'd think twice about making eye contact with at a late-night tube station or bus stop.

It was a bit like a football crowd, the kind of crowd that had existed before Sky TV gentrified the game until its clientele was barely distinguishable from the ones that frequented Twickenham or Lords; the kind of crowd from which bananas were thrown at the feet of speedy black wingers, where racial abuse of the crudest kind issued from the mouths of women who looked like your mum, and where anyone not immediately recognisable as stereotypically white, male and heterosexual, risked summary justice by way of a painful beating, swiftly, expertly and mercilessly applied.

Mason headed back outside for some fresh air and almost immediately noticed four middle aged men nearby gesturing silently to one another and pointing at a flamboyantly dressed young lad who was walking by. A moment later, without a single word being exchanged, the four surrounded the lad and began to punch him. The youth fell to the ground and the men gathered around him and, in total silence and with studied concentration, took turns to deliver a series of shuddering kicks into his prone, foetal form.

One of the skinheads on the door ambled across and got between the men and their victim. "All in good time, boys, all in good time," he said cheerfully, allowing the young lad to scramble to his feet and flee, at which point the four men dusted themselves off and returned to their conversation. Like many who had attended football matches before Sky Sports had changed the game for ever, Mason had pondered on what it was that drove middle-aged males, their youths long gone, to seek out complete strangers and inflict violence on them, and he had often wondered what these men now did on Saturday afternoons. He had a feeling he was about to find out.

"Right then, see you Saturday at the Milton Centre," had been Farmer's final words as they'd left Spencer's flat in Chiswick. "And remember, nothing at all about Vinnie addressing the meeting – it's still too early for him to be openly associated with that kind of thing."

Now Mark Spencer ascended the platform and there were scattered cheers from the crowd, whose number was hard to judge. Most were sitting but there were others standing at the back and around the sides and some of them were drinking from cans and bottles.

"Gentlemen," began Spencer. "And ladies," he added after a moment and there were ironic cheers. "Thank you for taking the time to come here tonight for the first London meeting of Secure Your Neighbourhood. Many of you in this room I know already, and I am looking forward to making the acquaintance of the rest of you later." There was scattered applause. "In a moment I'm going to introduce you to our main speaker, a man you know well, a man of vision and destiny, the leader of English Rose, Vinnie Groves."

The applause was now more sustained, and Mason heard a cry of "You tell 'em, Spence."

"But before I allow Vinnie to address you, I want to say a couple of things. Firstly, you are here by invitation, which means you have been personally singled out to be at the vanguard of this great movement, part of an elite corps, helping us bring about the changes that will make this country great again. Before long we will be an unstoppable tide, but right now we are at our moment of maximum danger. We have enemies everywhere, enemies who will do whatever they can to destroy us, twisting our words and impugning our motives, so I want to impress on you how vital, absolutely vital, it is that what we talk about tonight and at future meetings, does not go beyond these four walls."

He enunciated the final words slowly and distinctly and allowed a silence to follow them. "That means you don't tell anyone. Not your wives, not your girlfriends, not your mates down the pub. Nobody. And because, as I said earlier, our enemies are all around us, and because the need for security is so great, I don't want you just to watch what you're saying yourself, I want you to watch the person next to you.

"I know that goes against the grain. I know you see the person next to you as a comrade in this great struggle, and I respect you for that. But this country is battling for its very existence, and loose talk at a critical juncture like this could imperil everything we're working to achieve. So, if you see someone showing off to their mates or blabbing in the pub when they've had a drink, inform me or one of your local leaders. Remember this is not a game, it is deadly serious and if you have to harden your heart and report someone, you're doing it for the good of the movement and the good of the country."

Spencer picked up the papers he had placed on the lectern. "Thank you for listening to me and I'll be talking to some of you later about the command structure of Secure Your Neighbourhood. But now," he paused, "we are very lucky to have with us the leader of English Rose, the man sent by providence to lead our great movement, the man who with your help is going to lead this country out of the darkness and into a new light, Mister Vinnie Groves."

As Groves moved through the hall there was none of the glitz of the English Rose rallies, no rock music, no disco lights, no lone spotlight picking out his figure as he passed through the multitude, but in some way, this made him look more impressive, more authentic. As he moved, hands reached out to touch him and there was a growl of noise that increased in volume and intensity as he reached the front. He climbed onto the platform and the growl became a full-blooded roar and he had to stretch his hands out in an appeal for calm before it eventually died away and there was silence.

"Friends," he began, "thank you for giving me the opportunity to talk to you here tonight. And I use the word 'friends' deliberately, for this is not like other meetings I have addressed recently, meetings where I have tried to convince people of the rightness of our cause. You, my friends, don't need convincing, you are the ones whose wisdom and courage has marked them out for great things, and you are already marching at the front of the line.

"Many years ago, Ayn Rand wrote about the special ones, on whose coattails the rest of society rides, and before her Nietzsche talked about the Superman." He waited a moment. "When people look back on all this, my friends, when the history books are written and the medals are handed out, you the Supermen, the Atlases carrying the world on your shoulders, will be at the forefront of that history."

Mason hadn't been sure what he was going to hear, but as he looked around him, he couldn't but think that in all the bollocks he'd heard talked over the last few months, referring to the assembled collection of flotsam and jetsam as Supermen was in a league of its own. He couldn't deny the crowd was lapping it up though, and as the cheering continued Groves was forced to make calming motions again.

"When I give speeches at English Rose rallies," he went on, "I need to sugar coat things a bit - just for now, you understand - but you, the people in this room, don't need any of that, do you? You know that in the days ahead we are going to have to make difficult choices, and those choices are going to result in people having to carry out difficult… some might even say distasteful… actions for the greater good. And you have been handpicked because we know you will not shy away from carrying out those actions, however challenging you may find them.

"I'm going to remind you of something I said in my English Rose speech, something I say in all my speeches, which is that in the thousands of years humans have walked the earth, the fact that they've viewed those different from themselves with suspicion is not something to be ashamed of, on the contrary it is *natural,* it is *right,* and it is *good.*

"But now I'm going to say something I don't say in the speeches I deliver at English Rose meetings." He stopped for a moment and the silence grew around him. "The purity of our national DNA is being infected by a virus far deadlier than COVID 19. Our blood is impure, its cells are being destroyed by a deadly cancer, a racial leukaemia, and if we don't do something to purify our national body, it will die.

"So, I'm going to say it again and I want you to listen carefully." He waited until the silence was absolute. "When I walk along Piccadilly and I see a coon coming towards me and I want to stove his woolly head in with a piece of rock, there is nothing wrong with that; on the contrary, it is *natural,* it is *right* and it is *good.*"

There was a moment of stunned silence and then the room exploded. At the lectern, Groves leant back and folded his arms and his chin jutted out in a way that was reminiscent of Mussolini.

"Just in case you didn't hear me I'm going to say it again. When I walk along the Embankment, *our* Embankment and I see a Paki coming towards me and I want to castrate him with a Stanley knife, there is nothing wrong with that; on the contrary, it is *natural,* it is *right* and it is *good.*"

Groves waited for the roars to subside. "And when I walk through Soho and I see all those fucking restaurants and I want to burn them and the little yellow bastards inside them to the ground, there is nothing wrong with that; on the contrary, it is *natural,* it is *right* and it is *good.*"

By now the hall was blasting with noise and when Groves came to the words, *natural, right, good,* the crowd joined in with him. At the English Rose meeting it had sounded a bit like a football crowd, but now the incantation, booming, rhythmic and fanatical, had an almost religious quality to it.

"What did you say?" Groves cupped a hand in his ear as someone in the front row shouted up at him. "When I see a what? An Arab? Right, when I

128

walk through Green Park and I see a dirty, rag headed Arab…."

The roars got louder and soon suggestions were being shouted from all corners:

"When I see a Jew…"

"When I see a Turk…"

"When I see a queer…"

Groves rode the wave, working the crowd expertly by appealing to its patriotism or by plumbing the depths of its deepest, darkest impulses. By the time he had finished, the people who had come to hear him speak were no longer an audience, they'd become a baying mob, without individual consciousness or thought, no longer capable of exercising free will or engaging in rational thought.

Mason looked around and saw faces that were contorted by hatred, and others whose expressions suggested they were undergoing a religious experience, but what he didn't see were any that resembled Reg and Joan in the remotest of ways, and in that moment, he realised he had passed through some kind of portal into a very, very different place.

Before he finished, Groves had worked the audience into a frenzy. If a crowd of mostly male, middle aged, overweight and drunk racists could be said to possess a collective G-Spot, Vinnie Groves found it that night. And having worked the audience into a frenzy, he suddenly stopped and a moment later was gone. It took five minutes for the crowd to quieten sufficiently for Mark Spencer to be able to tell them that selected officers would be coming amongst them to tell them which local legion they would be in and where and when they would be meeting. This process took the best part of an hour and it was almost eleven o'clock before things started to break up.

A tall crew cut man in his thirties standing next to Mason had been providing those around him with a jocular, sometimes profane running commentary on the events of the evening.

"Good speech in the end though," he finished. "What did you think of it, mate?"

"Got the crowd going, all right, didn't it?" answered Mason

"Bit hard on the Chinkies though; I mean I like a bit of sweet and sour, myself." He winked lewdly and at that moment Spencer approached and the man called across to him. "Just saying, Spence, the boss was a bit tough on the Tiddly Winks."

Spencer smiled without mirth and said, "Can you hang on at the end, Frank? I want to talk to you about something."

"And of course," the man said, "you might have had an issue with some of the other things he said."

Spencer said nothing but gave the man a look that Mason was suddenly glad wasn't being directed at him.

"You know what I'm talking about, Spence." The man, leery, confident, drunk, had obviously not noticed - or chosen not to notice - the look. "You know, the bit about what he'd do to a queer… sorry, a *gay* person." He was swaying slightly, and the sweet aroma of stale beer hung in the air. "That's what I mean of course, a gay person… not a fucking turd burglar."

Spencer didn't move, and the man waited for a moment and then said, "Everyone knows, Spence."

Spencer finally spoke. "Everyone knows what?"

"About you, Spence; you know what I'm talking about." He minced a few steps, hand on hip. "Everyone knows you like a bit of chocolate on your lolly."

There was a snicker from somewhere but otherwise the people standing nearby were silent.

"It's not a problem." The man shrugged his shoulders elaborately. "I mean, I've always said, each to their…"

His words were cut off by the force of the punch that smashed into his mouth. There was a splintering sound and he cried out and then Spencer launched a two-handed assault of incredible speed and violence and a moment later the man's nose suddenly lost its shape

He crumpled to the floor in slow motion and Spencer went down after him, descending onto one

131

knee while continuing to rain blows onto his unprotected head and face. A middle-aged man tried to intervene, but one of the security guys blocked his path and after that nobody moved. The blows continued to rain down but now they had a wet, pulpy sound to them as they landed. Eventually the frequency and force of the punches began to diminish and then there was a final viscous, sucking compression and only then did Spencer stand up.

He was breathing heavily, and a fine spray of blood was spattered diagonally across his face. He looked slowly around him and, as he did so, dozens of eyes dropped floorward in a display of synchronized choreography Busby Berkeley himself would have been proud of.

"Just to make it quite clear, if anyone asks," he said, speaking between deep breaths and enunciating each word with terrible deliberation. "Mark Spencer is a heterosexual."

XI

With the electoral arithmetic making it increasingly difficult for progressives to summon up enthusiasm for the Mother of Parliaments, Matt Rees entered the Commons chamber in a huddle of Labour MPs whose footsteps were all, to a greater or lesser degree, lagging.

For a man leading a minority government, even his detractors were forced to admit that Cadogan was playing his cards shrewdly. He had made allies of English Rose and UKIP by ensuring his domestic agenda pandered to their wishes and this alone ensured him a working majority, and as he was alleged to have said himself, if either of those two fell by the wayside, he could always invite the Ulster Unionists around and get out the cookie jar.

The House was full because under discussion ahead of a vote on its second reading was the new Nationalities Bill. The Home Secretary had been entrusted with the job of leading off for the government but Cadogan himself would be making the final speech. In opposition, Labour's shadow home affairs spokesman would reply and, Rees, whose membership of the Home Affairs Select Committee gave him some seniority, was hoping for the opportunity to question aspects of the bill.

"Mister Speaker," began the Home Secretary, pulling down the cuffs of his blazer, "This is a bill that the government has had under consideration for a long time and, if I may speak frankly, it is a bill we bring to this house with some reluctance."

"Don't bloody well bring it here, then." A loud northern voice from near the aisle suggested the spirit of Dennis Skinner was alive and well.

The Home Secretary favoured this interruption with a smile of infinite condescension.

"I will be delighted to give way to members opposite, Mister Speaker," he said, "When, that is, they have something sensible to say… which may, of course, involve quite a long wait."

Behind him his colleagues chortled and harrumphed and waved their order papers and Rees felt his heart sinking at the prospect of the hours ahead.

"Mister Speaker," drawled the Home Secretary, his display of wit and repartee appearing to have improved his mood, "as I have said, it is with some sadness that Her Majesty's Government brings this piece of legislation to the house. We have, Mister Speaker, a long and proud record of inclusion in this country, going back to the time in our history when we reached out the hand of friendship to peoples around the world by opening up trading routes to their countries and bringing them under our protective wing. And later, when the day came that our chicks were ready to fly the nest, the friendships flourished and deepened under the aegis of the Commonwealth.

"But now, with great regret, we have to say that the relationship must change. At present, Mister Speaker, there are, as you know, millions of people with British citizenship who were not born in Britain themselves, and whose parents or grandparents were not either. And it is for these people that we are proposing a new type of citizenship."

There were growls of protest from the opposition benches and the Home Secretary waited for them to die down. "Before we go any further, I want to make it clear that the right of residence of the people in this new category will be guaranteed in perpetuity. I will come back to that point later, Mister Speaker but I am saying it now to allay fears, fears which I regret to say have been maliciously stoked by unscrupulous members on the other side of the house."

There was uproar at this, and the Home Secretary leaned on the despatch box with studied insouciance and examined his fingernails. When the noise finally died down, he began to speak again.

"We are proposing that the old rules of citizenship will still apply to people whose grandparents were born in Britain, and to people from certain countries or dependencies whose identities I will reveal later. For those who don't qualify for inclusion in this group, there will be a new category of citizenship, which we propose to call, Overseas Citizen Currently Domiciled, or OCCD."

He waited for the shouts and cries of "shame" to die down before he spoke. "As I said earlier Mister Speaker, I want to make it clear that we absolutely and unconditionally guarantee full rights of citizenship to everyone currently holding a British passport, including those who will move to OCCD status. The changes we are proposing will be put in place purely to ensure that no *future* claims, claims which may be spurious or fraudulent, will be considered.

"Mister Speaker, I do not need to enumerate the terrible events which in recent years have made border security an area of such vital importance, and I am confident that once this legislation is safely on the statute book it will ensure that our citizens, *all* our citizens, can look forward to a future of peace and prosperity. Mr Speaker, I commend the Bill to the house."

He sat down and the chorus of boos from across the aisle was drowned out by roars of approval from the government benches.

In the end Rees didn't get called to ask his question. The Shadow Home Secretary, whose career trajectory owed in equal parts to an ideological suppleness a circus contortionist would have been proud of and the fact that he was distantly related to a past Titan of the left, stumbled through a series of interventions which the Home Secretary fielded with studied distain. There was some desultory questioning from the Scottish and Welsh Nationalists, who clearly hadn't yet made up their minds which way to jump, and then the Grand Old Man was called and when he slowly rose from his seat, there was a stirring in the chamber, even Cadogan sitting up from the slouch he had allowed his body to fall into when the Home Secretary had begun speaking.

"Mister Speaker," began the Grand Old Man, "as someone who has sat on these benches for many years, and who has seen a welter of change over those years, I would like to sound a note of caution. No one is more aware than me of the unprecedented times we live in, and of the grave danger to all our futures posed by recent cataclysmic events. And as much as I agree that we must take firm, resolute action to protect our citizens and our way of life, the proposal before the house today is one that in my opinion, poses the gravest threat to civil liberties that I have seen in my lifetime. The House knows that I have expressed reservations about the recent changes to the Emergency Powers Act and the incorporation into it of features of the Prevention of Terrorism Act of 1974."

"History!" The call came from a couple of rows behind him

The Grand Old Man half turned. "History, yes, but I would remind my Honourable Friend that I sat in this chamber when those measures were being discussed and when they were passed into law. Mister Speaker, the Prevention of Terrorism Act of 1974 was passed as a knee jerk reaction to a bombing campaign and as such it was a mistake. Confessions were extracted under duress, the wrong people were given life sentences and our judicial system, the envy of the world, suffered a loss in public confidence that it took a generation to recover from. Mister Speaker…"

The Grand Old Man was forced to stop because at that moment the member for Romford East, who was sitting a few places to his left, suddenly blew, from behind his order paper, a thunderous raspberry. The was a short silence while necks were craned in the direction of the interruption, then a ripple of noise in which could be heard tutting, whispered words of censure, and at least one snigger.

"Order! Order!" called the Speaker in plaintive, quavering tones.

The member for Romford East got to his feet. "I apologise, Mister Speaker; an unfortunate accident." He turned, looked straight across at the Grand Old Man and said, "Wind!"

There was more tutting and a single cry of, "Shame!" but there were also barks of laughter and the member for Thanet East could be seen rocking with mirth and slapping his thigh. Across the aisle opposition members watched in silence, like embarrassed neighbours invited to a party, then forced to witness a family meltdown.

The Grand Old Man could be seen visibly gathering himself. "Mister Speaker, I have been too long in this chamber to be worried by insults. I have been insulted, frankly, by better people than my Honourable Friend. In fact, in relation to the Honourable Member for Romford East, all I would say is that if a man is to be judged by the quality of his enemies, then my life must be classed a failure."

The words were delivered with a *sangfroid* that even his political opponents found diverting, and Rees, watching from across the aisle, experienced an unexpected surge of affection for the Grand Old Man.

"Get on with it!" someone shouted from the government benches and someone else called out "Shush!" and there was more tutting.

"What I was going to say, Mister Speaker," drawled the Grand Old Man, now perfectly at ease, "and I won't let these rather ill-mannered interruptions prevent me from making the point, is that a society is judged by how its great institutions react, not when all is calm, but when they are under the greatest pressure, and we should let that lesson from history guide us as we move ahead."

The Grand Old Man sat down and as Cadogan stood up the speaker called out, "The Prime Minister."

"Thank you, Mr Speaker and I would like thank my Right Honourable Friend," Cadogan inclined his head graciously in the Grand Old Man's direction, "for his contribution. Now in terms, of the proposed implementation of this bill, I'm going to ask the Home Secretary to take you through the timeline..."

And that was it, thought Rees as the Home Secretary unwound himself and rose to his feet. At one time an intervention from the backbenches by Grand Old Man at such a critical stage in the passage of the bill would have been the main drama of the day; it would probably have led the evening news bulletins and would certainly have necessitated a response from the government. He had been many things, senior minister, prime ministerial candidate, back bench rebel, but whatever role he had occupied, he had always been *someone*, someone whose words carried weight, whose opinions were solicited and whose pronouncements shaped the thinking of others.

And now, after all that, after half a century of service in this place, he had become an irrelevance, his words received in a silence broken only by the flatulent intervention of a bastard offspring of the Tebbit Tendency from Essex. As the Grand Old Man settled back into his seat, Rees tried to remember who it was who had made that statement about all political careers ending in failure.

Rees never did get to ask his question, although he bobbed up and down every time the Speaker's eye roved around the room. He had wanted to question the Home Secretary about what the implications of the bill were for those who had, for example, three native born grandparents and one from the Commonwealth, and there were other questions, many questions, that Parliament needed to put if it was properly to do its job of scrutinising the government.

It was going to be down to the Home Affairs Select Committee to ask those questions, because it looked as if the House itself, judging by the performance he had just witnessed, no longer had the will or the stomach to carry out the role of holding the government accountable. Rees had recently re-established contact with a middle ranking official in the Home Office, a man named Archie Shore who he had met when they had served together in the Territorial Army. Shore was one of those dwindling band of civil servants with both brain and conscience, and over the course of a number of clandestine meetings among London's more unfashionable pubs and parks, he had told Rees of his concern at the way Home Office planning was developing. Rees determined it was time to get hold of Archie and try to find out what was really going on before the Home Secretary's scheduled meeting with the committee.

***

It was later that week and the Home Secretary was relaxing and enjoying the party arranged to celebrate the successful passage of the second reading of the Nationality Bill. The party, held in a large private house on the road between Cockfosters and the M25 where famous footballers were said to reside, was unofficial– extremely unofficial - in nature, the informal collection of MPs, senior civil servants and party donors who were there having attended similar events in the past.

That the house had a sufficiency of rooms upstairs the Home Secretary knew from experience – plenty of time for that later – but right now he was enjoying a glass of Armagnac and running a leisurely eye around the room. It was an eclectic mix, there was no doubt about that, and consisted in about equal parts of old, mostly overweight men (not Cadogan, he was reportedly fastidious about such things) and young - in some cases very young - boys and girls.

The Home Secretary sipped his Armagnac and ran his eye across the room. He was looking for the Nubile, as he called her; she had told him her name during one of their previous encounters, but he had forgotten it, and so to him, she would always be the Nubile. In the middle of the room there was a long table containing an array of edibles, at one end savoury finger foods - hors d'oeuvres, chicken pieces, quiche, cold meat – and at the other, desserts. Many of the younger guests were crowded around the dessert end of the table and the jelly seemed to be attracting a lot of attention.

Along one wall was an array of alcoholic and non-alcoholic drinks, while in a room next door, the Home Secretary knew, substances of a more esoteric nature were available for those who wished to avail themselves. As his gaze travelled around, it came to rest on the Nubile, who had entered the room and was looking around her. She saw him and smiled, and he smiled back and gestured towards the stairs with his eyes. He navigated his way around the huge bulk of the Chancellor of the Duchy of Lancaster, who was gorging himself on pork pie, and headed towards the door with a spring in his step.

Ten minutes later he was lying on a sofa bed upstairs with the Nubile standing above him. "Oh Humpty," she said, hooking a languorous finger onto her bottom lip and regarding him guilelessly from big baby blue eyes. "Oh Humpty, I've got a problem."

"Tell Humpty what the problem is, my dear and let's see if he can help you," he answered in avuncular tones.

"Well, Humpty, it's my little pussy." She was wearing a sarong-type garment that was little more than a square sheet of cloth with a knot tied in one corner. She shifted it and the Home Secretary saw that she wore nothing underneath it. "It's my little pussy, Humpty – it keeps crying."

"Well, my dear," he said, and the view as she twisted the sarong offered glistening confirmation that her words were true. "Well, my dear, if it keeps crying, Humpty will have to kiss it better."

"I was hoping you'd say that," she answered and began to straddle him. A few moments later she sighed and said, "The only problem is, Humpty, the more you kiss it the more it cries."

143

A little later, the Home Secretary lay on his back and looked down as a head moved rhythmically up and down. "Take your time, my dear," he said and stretched out luxuriously. Through the wall he could hear muffled voices, one of them unmistakeably the deep baritone of the Chancellor of the Duchy of Lancaster. The baritone spoke and a younger voice, male and adolescent answered. Then the chancellor of the Duchy of Lancaster spoke again and, although individual words could not be made out, there was a harsh note to his voice.

He heard the adolescent voice again and this time the words were distinguishable. "It won't…"

"Wider…" The Chancellor's baritone was unmistakeable and so was the urgency in his voice.

There was a shrill cry, quickly stifled and then the Chancellor's voice again. "That's better…"

The Home Secretary relaxed, determined to enjoy the fruits of his labour. It was rather like the R and R he used to partake in during those tours of Paddyland and Iraq. You had to make the most of it so that you were at the top of your game when you got back on the job – it really could mean the difference between life and death.

He reminded himself of the need to give the Nubile a decent tip. He knew she received payment from the organisers of the parties, she had told him herself, but he would top that up with twenty or thirty pounds from his wallet – forty if she really

144

put her mind to things. It was certainly more than she would get working in a supermarket on Saturdays, so it was a win-win really.

"A bit more oomph when you're ready my dear," he said to the head and it began to move faster. A little later his teeth bared in a rictus grin and his body jerked and there was a wet cough from below and the sound of a throat being cleared, and then a voice said playfully, "Who's been eating curry then?"

The Home Secretary cradled his head in his hands, stretched his body out to its full extent and gazed up at the ceiling. Ah well, to the victors the spoils.

XII

Two weeks after Vinnie Groves' speech Mason got a call from Mark Spencer, inviting him to a meeting at the North West London headquarters of English Rose in Wembley. "Don't share the details of this meeting with anyone," Spencer said. "It's by way of being confidential."

Mason arrived at the duly appointed time and noticed straight away that there was security on the door. A female English Rose volunteer who had come by to do some extra work was being turned away. "Not tonight love, come back in the morning," one of the security guys was saying to her as Mason approached and another one, recognising him, jerked his head towards the building in a signal for him to enter.

Once inside Mason saw that Spencer was there, together with Kirsty Black and about twenty others, mostly young, male and hard looking. He exchanged nods with Colin James, who he had met at previous meetings, and with a tough looking older man he had heard being referred to as 'Briggsy,' but apart from those two Mason didn't know any of the others, although he recognised some of their faces. Of the leery man who Spencer had beaten to pulp, there was no sign.

A few moments later the skinheads who had been guarding the entrance came in, locking the outer door behind them, and an atmosphere of expectation descended onto the group. "Sit down everyone," ordered Spencer and the security guys arranged plastic chairs in a rough horseshoe. Spencer waited at the front until till everyone had taken a seat and then began to speak.

"I've known most of you for a long time – years in some cases. We've done the same training, been on the same marches, sworn the same oaths, and some of us have taken part in what I shall call 'irregular activities' that we've had to be discreet about. We know things about one another that would put us in prison, but because of what we've been through together, because of the unbreakable bond that exists between us, we would die rather

146

than betray our friends or betray the movement. Am I right?" He looked around and there were nods and murmurs of agreement.

"I say all of us but that's not quite true. There's one person here who none of that applies to."

He let a silence grow. "And that person doesn't know what we do to people who betray us. What do we do to people who betray us, lads?"

There was a short silence and then Briggsy shrugged and said, "We kill 'em, Spence."

"We kill them. Liquidate them. Destroy them." Mason felt eyes boring into him and tried not to squirm, tried not to let the wave of panic he felt washing over him engulf him completely.

Spencer turned slowly towards him and said, "Frank," and Mason knew that everyone in the room was looking at him.

He took a deep breath and looked at Spencer. "Yes, Mark," he said, trying to invest in his words a confidence he did not remotely feel.

"Frank Brown," said Spencer, letting the words roll slowly around his slips. He looked at the others. "Some of you know Frank and some of you don't. And I've asked Frank to join us here today because I've been watching him carefully and I've found something out about him."

Mason wondered whether to bolt for the door but knew he wouldn't get halfway there.

"Do you know what I've found out?" Spencer went on remorselessly. "Shall I tell you?"

The silence seemed to last for an eternity and then he said, "I've found out he's one of us."

Mason tried to keep his expression neutral and not let the wave of relief that Spencer's words had caused to course through his body show too obviously. "A couple of weeks ago," Spencer went on, "and Kirsty will confirm this, we were walking back to the car park after a meeting and a Paki tried to attack us. Can you believe that, a fucking Paki tried to attack us?"

"Dirty black bastard," said someone.

"Well, as some of you know, I'm not a stranger to that kind of situation," said Spencer and a ripple of laughter ran around the room. "But before I had a chance to do anything, this bastard" he gestured at Mason, "this bastard here only whips out a knife, runs across the road and stabs the fucker. I don't know who was more surprised, me or the Paki?"

There was renewed laughter and a someone cheered. "Comes back cool as a cucumber, wiping the knife on his sleeve," went on Spencer, "and do you know what the fucker says? Says with a bit of luck the whole thing might kick off a race war."

A friendly punch landed on Mason's shoulder, and someone ruffled his hair.

"You can confirm this, can't you Kirsty?" said Spencer.

"I certainly can. Giles Farmer was there, and he said although he hasn't seen as much action as most of you have, he thought it was highly impressive."

"That sounds like Giles, all right," grunted Spencer dismissively. "Now, I've already told Frank something the authorities and the left-wing media would give their right arms to know. Do you remember asking me a question, Frank, about my role in the movement?"

"I do," answered Mason

"And what did I tell you?"

"You told me you were the leader of Storm Force 55."

"I told you I was the leader of Storm Force 55." Spencer repeated the words. "And now I'm going to tell you something else. I'm going to tell you that everyone in this room is in Storm Force as well."

Mason tried to absorb this information with an impassive face, but his mind was racing and his heart was thumping in his chest.

"Look around you, Frank," said Spencer. "This is the core of the movement - the London Chapter of Storm Force 55. And I'll be honest with you until very recently the London Chapter of Storm Force pretty much *was* Storm Force. Yeah, we've had an influx of people wanting to join in the past few months, and we'll let some of them in, but we know who the true believers are, the ones who joined up when the rest of the world was laughing at us. And they're the ones in this room, Frank, they're the ones sitting around you."

"So why are you telling me this, Mark… just as a matter of interest?" Mason tried to keep his words casual, his body language relaxed, but inside he was churning with a mixture of excitement and revulsion.

It was likely, more than that it was probable, that he was sitting in the company of the man or men who had killed Mathew. He tried to push the thought away, tried to focus on playing his part, tried to think how Frank Brown, racist thug, would react.

"Good question," said Spencer. "Kirsty?"

"We've been watching you, Frank." There was a different quality to Kirsty, something about the way she held herself, about the way she spoke, a *presence* he hadn't sensed before. "We've been watching you and we think you have some of the qualities we're going to need in the days ahead. When we achieve power, whether on the back of English Rose or by other means, we're going to have to do some… difficult things, and we're going to need strong people to do those things, people able to look beyond the actions themselves and see the benefits to society that will proceed from them."

"Kirsty is one of the intellectuals in the movement," said Spencer with a thin smile. "Her PhD examined how German special forces dispensed justice in the occupied territories during the war. Am I right, Kirsty?"

"More or less. Suffice to say, there's a lot we can learn about the future by looking at what they and others did in the past. But I digress. What we think we've seen in you, Frank, is someone who has the strength we're going to need when the weak people, the ones who talk a good fight but aren't up for actually doing anything, retire into their rabbit holes. Are you with me?"

"With you all the way so far," answered Mason.

"And what would you say if you were asked to do some of the things those special forces had to do?"

Mason shrugged. "I would say, 'lead me to it.'"

Colin slapped him on the back and down the line Mason heard someone say, "Top man."

"Very gratifying to hear, Frank," said Spencer, who had been watching with a sardonic smile on his face. "Although, of course it was never a question of you saying whether you were in or out – that was decided a while ago."

His eyes bored into Mason's. "You remember they used to talk about planes reaching 'the point of no return,' the point at which they didn't have enough fuel to turn back, but had to go on? Well, your plane passed that point about twenty minutes ago."

"I think Frank's worked that one out already, Mark," said Kirsty. "He's an intelligent man."

"Just spelling out the realities, Kirsty, just spelling out the realities. And I know you'll have

151

already worked out what I'm about to say, Frank, but I'm going to spell it out anyway. You join Storm Force 55, but you don't leave it. Nobody leaves it."

He paused for a moment. "Let me rephrase that, there is one way you can leave it. Whatever happened to that bloke who joined up with you, Colin? East End bloke, full of himself at the beginning but got cold feet and started talking about cutting a deal with the authorities. You remember him. Whatever happened to him?"

"Him?" said Colin. "Oh, you won't see him no more."

Mason could feel Spencer's eyes boring into him and knew others were watching him, looking for signs of what… Apprehension? Fear? Panic? He fought to keep his mind in control of his body and leaned back in his seat.

"I wouldn't be here if I wasn't on board, Mark, so you don't have to give me all the hard man stuff." His words were mild, but his eyes locked onto Spencer's and he could feel the other man responding in kind.

The others sensed the charged atmosphere and the antagonism, and there was no knowing what would have happened if Kirsty hadn't stepped between them and said, "Now, boys, let's keep all that testosterone bottled up for when we really need it." A ripple of relief went around the room and the sense of an atmosphere lightening was tangible.

"So, Kirsty" said Mason, realizing he was in danger of letting his loathing of Spencer and all he stood for show. "You talked about us needing to do things differently to the way they were done in the past."

"Yes. Let's not beat about the bush," she said and the it was clear she was including everyone in her words. "When our plans come to fruition, we're going to have thousands of people, millions maybe, who are of no use economically and whose presence… existence, undermines the security of our borders because it would allow others like them to hide in plain sight."

It was clear from the animation in her voice that this was something she'd given a lot of thought to. "OK we're all adults here and we all understand what's at stake. So, the question is, what are we going to do with all those people?"

"Repatriate them?" said Colin

"Yeah, some of them, definitely. But there are too many of them. Even if the countries we were sending them back to would take them, it would take years. And we haven't got years, we all know that."

"Put 'em in boats and launch 'em into the sea," said someone.

"How many boats would you need? And not good PR for Britain, although I've a feeling, moving ahead, that PR is something governments are going to be concerning themselves with less and less. No, we all know what's got to happen, we all know that when we've repatriated the ones who we can repatriate, there's still going to be millions of them left.

"There will be some…. natural wastage through spontaneous actions within local communities. That happened a lot in Germany, local communities acting independently to make themselves *judenrein,* Jew free. And it's a good model; individuals working together like antibodies to fight a deadly virus and purify the system - our propaganda people would have a field day with that. But that would still only account for a small percentage of the aliens. What are we going to do with the rest of them?"

There was a silence and then Briggsy spoke from his seat at the end. "We're going to have to waste the fuckers, aren't we, Kirst?"

She didn't answer him directly but said, "Has anyone here heard of the Einsatzgruppen?"

"Credit us with a bit of savvy, love," answered Colin. "We all have."

"Sorry," she smiled. "I know many of you will have researched these issues."

Researched the issues? More like sat in the bedroom of their Mum and Dad's, wanking over pictures of Nazis in shorts. Mason fought to keep his expression impassive as Kirsty continued.

"As most of us know, the Einsatzgruppen were the forces in the Third Reich charged with… removing deficient elements from the population. Although these days they're remembered more for the actions they carried out in Poland and the Soviet Union, their work began in Germany, identifying and disposing of undesirables, mainly Jews, but also homosexuals, criminals and the mentally feeble.

154

Their members were selected with great care, because the work they did required an ideological commitment to the movement as well as exceptional mental strength.

"Now, the reason I'm telling you all this is that I've been charged with organising something similar here, and as I look around this room what do I see? Ideological commitment – you've already proved that, all of you, by your actions - as well as bucketloads of mental strength. Gentlemen I'm proposing that we begin the process of creating our own Einsatzgruppen from among the people in this room."

"It'll to be a tough gig," broke in Spencer.

"Mark's right enough, so if any of you feel it isn't for you, no one will think the worse of you – there'll be plenty of other, less… specialized roles for people to play." She waited for a few moments, but no one spoke.

"And I've been thinking about how the leadership can support you better," said Spencer, breaking into the silence. "The German high command did recognise that the work was stressful and sent supportive messages to the guys out in the territories, but that was about it. The result was that many of them developed symptoms of PTSD afterwards, and some struggled with their mental health for the rest of their lives, which was unacceptable really, in view of the contribution they'd made. We're going to offer you better support than that lads, so there'll be counsellors available at the… workplace, together with regular opportunities for rest and relaxation at special holiday centres where a full range of services" (he winked) "will be available."

His final words produced a round of applause, and there were clenched fists at the end of crooked arms in that universal "give her one for me" gesture.

Spencer smiled. "Never let it be said that our movement doesn't concern itself enough with pastoral care," he said, and Mason, head metaphorically in his hands and unable quite to believe what he was hearing, couldn't be sure whether he was speaking from the heart or being deliberately ironic.

"We're going to call the group the Special Defence Force, or SDF" said Kirsty, "and it's brief will be to carry out 'such miscellaneous duties as are necessary to ensure the defence of the realm.'"

"Nice and vague, lads, nice and vague," said Spencer with a wink, and there was a ripple of laughter.

"Welcome aboard, Frank," said Colin, when the company had split into smaller groups.

"He's all right, is Frank." Briggsy ruffled Mason's hair. "And if he's not," he looked at the others, "'s all right, we'll just fucking kill 'im."

"Don't worry about Briggsy," said Colin. "Says whatever comes into his head without thinking first. Got no filter, have you, Briggs?"

"Naah." Briggsy scratched his head.

"How long you been involved then, Colin?" asked Mason

"Pretty much from the start, I suppose. Started with my Dad, he was a postman and then the Pakis started coming over and working all the overtime God gave. My Dad and his mates didn't bother with overtime - my Dad used to say no man should have to work double shifts to get a decent wage - and then, bugger me, didn't the Pakis start getting promoted over the white blokes. And before he knew it my dad was having to take orders from Pakis. Can you believe that? A white man taking orders from a wog! In England! And it was the same when I left school, all the Pakis going off to university and nothing left for the English blokes but stacking shelves at Tesco or the dole queue. Anyway, I looked around and I got talking to a few blokes in the pub and one thing led to another... well, here I am."

"I hear what you're saying," said Mason.

"It's like Vinnie Groves says; the whole country's gone to the dogs. Everything's geared up for coons and Pakis and Jews and queers. Do you know in some boroughs in London if you want to get a council house it's done by a points system and you get points for everything except being white English? My mate told me about a girl he knows who got a point because she's *Welsh*. Can you fucking believe it? I've been saying it for years, there's nothing left in this country for a white working-class man who's got red blood in his veins and likes shagging women."

He cracked the knuckles of one hand with the fingers of another. "Anyway, that's the reason I joined Storm Force, and do you know what, it was the proudest day of my fucking life."

At that moment Kirsty reappeared and one of the men called over to her, "What about sterilization, Kirsty?"

"Sorry?" she said, joining the group.

"As a way to sort out the problem?"

"For our surplus population, you mean?" she said. "Yeah, it would be one way."

"What, chemical castration?" said another man.

Kirsty looked at him. "Or actual," she shrugged, "I'm told it's very straightforward; all you need is a Stanley knife and a steady hand."

There was a lengthy silence which was eventually broken by a man called Ron. "You're well hard, you are, Kirst."

She stared at him. "I'll get one of our orderlies to practise on you if you like and afterwards you'll never be hard again." She waited a second and then added, "Not that it would make much difference, by the look of you."

There was laughter and someone cheered, but it had a forced element to it and as Kirsty continued to stare at Ron, he swallowed nervously.

Mason got through the rest of the evening somehow but although he drank a huge quantity of whiskey when he got home, he was unable to sleep and spent a restless night tossing and turning and dreaming weird dreams in which gas vans and lime pits featured heavily. The next morning, as he reviewed the previous months, it dawned on him exactly what he'd got himself into.

Part of him felt contaminated by having been exposed a world view that allowed people to talk in a matter-of-fact way, joke even, about castration and genocide. Part of him was frankly frightened because, although it was unlikely his cover would be blown, he had little doubt of what the consequences would be for him if it was. And part of him recognised how people like Colin must feel living in a society which they felt put the needs and wishes of newcomers ahead of their own.

He knew that London's past was the story of successive waves of immigrants - Dutch textile workers, French Huguenots, Jews, the Irish – who had all faced discrimination from the indigenous people on arrival, but who had survived, assimilated and eventually thrived. And yet there was something about the current sense of alienation within the native community that felt qualitatively different.

He eventually decided that he needed to expose his mind to some sunlight after its immersion in the dank, malodorous sewer that was Storm Force 55. Remembering how his last meeting with Raj Kumar had energised him, he sent a text to the secure email address and a little later received a reply suggesting a meeting on the mezzanine at Euston Station the following day. Kumar asked that instead of travelling direct to the station, Mason go via Kings Cross and walk down the Euston Road, and when Mason texted a question mark in response to this rather odd request, he received the reply "humour me."

XIII

Mason presented himself at the restaurant at the allotted time, ordered a coffee and sat in a place that commanded an excellent view of the station concourse. After twenty minutes he was starting to get restless when he felt a tap on his shoulder and turned to see the familiar features of Kumar.

"Bloody hell, Raj," where did you come from?" he said. "I thought I had the whole station covered."

"Let's just say I've been doing this kind of thing for a bit longer than you have," said the blogger with a grin. "Coffee?"

The drinks procured, Raj directed a keen look at his companion and said, "So how've you got on?"

Mason paused before he replied. Now that he was sitting in the reassuringly normal setting of Euston Station, rays of sunlight shafting through the opaque windows of the mezzanine, his paranoia of the night before felt a bit foolish.

"You look a bit wobbly, to be honest," added Kumar

"Does it show?" answered Mason ruefully.

"It does, and I'm not surprised. You've put yourself into a dangerous situation."

"I suppose I have."

"When you're trying to maintain a persona and having to stay continually in role, it's no big deal if your nerves get a bit frazzled from time to time. So anyway, how've you got on?" Kumar repeated his initial question.

"Well," said Mason. "I was going nowhere fast and then I had a stroke of luck - some Indian lunatic attacked me, and I had to stab the bastard."

Kumar laughed and Mason said, "It worked a treat, Raj; you should have seen the way Spencer looked at me afterwards."

"Mark Spencer," said Kumar. "A very, very nasty piece of work, so they say. Remember me telling you about the original National Front – all paramilitary parades and Nazi salutes – well he would have fitted right in with them. Wouldn't surprise me if he's connected to the modern-day paramilitaries."

"Funny you should say that," said Mason, "because I've found out that Mark Spencer is the leader of Storm Force 55."

"Bloody hell! How did you find that out?"

"He told me."

"He told you! Why did he do that?"

"As part of the process of inviting me to join them. To show me he trusted me with the information, but also to warn me I was so far in I wouldn't be able to back out even if I wanted to."

"Congratulations, Frank," said Kumar after a moment. "You're inside Storm Force 55! Wasn't that the object of the exercise?"

"I guess so."

"And have you got any closer to finding out who killed Mathew?"

"No. And that's where I'm a bit stuck, to be honest. I can't come right out and ask them, not without making them suspicious, and believe me, the last thing I want is for them to start getting suspicious."

"I suppose you've just got to keep playing your part and hope someone lets something slip when they've had a few drinks."

Mason filled Raj in on the people he'd met in Storm Force and when he'd finished the other man said, "I do agree with you about one thing and that's that some of them are more lost than evil."

"I'm not sure I'd call any of them 'lost,'" said Mason.

"Not even Colin and the other one, Briggsy? I think what we need to accept is that there are people in this country - and I'm not taking about thugs and the racists, I mean ordinary people - who think the whole multicultural thing has gone too far."

"Yeah?"

"I'm talking about ordinary people who feel that the world has changed, that no one asked them if they wanted it to change, and that the whole thing has moved too fast. It started with Brexit, or rather it started before that, but it was Brexit that told us there was a huge cohort of people out there who thought the whole thing – the European Union in particular and multiculturalism in general – had gone too far. And do you know what, they're entitled to their opinion and people like me, who aren't threatened by multiculturalism because of our own heritage, need to respect it.

"So, I'll be honest with you I've got some sympathy for blokes like your mate Colin. They've watched the world changing all around them, changing at a pace that frightens them, and they're scared, and one of the things they're crying out for is for people to start listening to them and respecting their opinion, and show them that 'the Establishment' does actually give a shit about them."

"You're saying they're victims?"

"I'm saying," said Kumar, "that if English Rose is a boil, and Storm Force is the pus on that boil, the infection that caused it is deep down under the surface and that's where we need to go if we're going to heal it."

"I was thinking along similar lines last night," said Mason.

"When we come out the other side of all this, we've got to listen to one another more. And that means the educated, well off, so-called metropolitan elite, has got to start listening to the likes of your mate Colin, addressing his concerns and asking him what he thinks instead of just doing things in his name. Anyway, I'd better get off my hobby horse or we'll be here all day."

"The one I can't put a finger on is Kirsty Black," mused Mason, changing the subject. "Sometimes she seems normal and decent and you could imagine her as a friend, and then out of the

163

blue she'll say something so disgusting it makes you feel physically sick."

"She's the one in English Rose I don't know much about," said Kumar.

"You'd think someone with a PhD would have more - I don't know - humanity."

"It's not always the case. You'd be amazed at how educated some of the Nazis were - one Einsatzgruppe squad had nine doctorates among a total of seventeen officers."

"That is a scary thought."

"There's no correlation between intelligence and decency, mate, some of the cleverest minds in history were also among the foulest. So, keep an eye on your Miss Black, she might turn out to be a female version of Goebbels or Himmler, spending her days writing memoranda condemning millions to death and then going home to play with the kids."

"I'll watch her like a hawk, after that."

"Your new friends do seem to resemble the Nazis in that respect; the ones with a bit of education in charge of planning and logistics…"

"While the likes of Colin and Briggsy go out and do the dirty work."

"Because when push comes to shove, how well-educated do you need to be to run an exhaust pipe into the back of a van or shoot someone lying in a ditch? Anyway, to get back to the current situation, what do you plan to do next?"

"Not sure, apart from making sure I tread bloody carefully. Sometimes I see Spencer watching me and it's almost like he's got a sixth sense something's wrong but can't quite put his finger on what it is."

"You think he's getting suspicious?"

"I don't know. I'm hoping he'll put whatever's nagging away at him down to a natural wariness about a new kid on the block. He's a clever bastard, though, I'll say that for him, and I don't know how long he'll buy it for."

"Be careful, Frank, he's a dangerous bastard."

Mason smiled. "It's funny, in some ways the whole thing grinds you down - having to pretend and be on your guard the whole time – but in others, the more you do it the easier it gets. It's just a shame the one person who could tell us what really happened to Mathew is going to remain banged up for at least another year."

"Danny Gates?"

"Yeah. Even though he couldn't have done it himself - we know that from the CCTV - he must know who killed Mathew. Just a shame he's well and truly out of reach.

Mason remembered Danny, how could he not, having spent five days at the trial watching his every move; remembered the pinched, grey face, the defiant jut of the jaw, the self-created image of a proud warrior going to the can to prove he wasn't a rat or a snitch or whatever they called it in the world he inhabited.

"Yeah, shame he's out of reach," echoed Kumar.

"Guess I'll just have to lie low and hope someone lets something slip."

"There's one thing I've been thinking about," mused Kumar as they prepared to leave.

"What's that?"

"The calling card; you know, the card that said, "You have been visited by Storm Force 55."

"What about it?"

"There was something niggling away in the back of my mind about it. I knew I'd heard about it somewhere - the leaving of cards on victims, I mean - I just couldn't think where. And then I remembered." He looked at Mason. "Any of the Storm Force boys West Ham fans?"

"West Ham fans?" Mason thought for a moment and shook his head. "I'm not sure, to be honest. Why are you asking?"

"Back in the day, when football hooliganism was a national sport, there was a group at West Ham who called themselves the Inter City Firm, or ICF. They used to travel by British Rail to get to their punch ups, hence the name; they wore Pringle jumpers and loafers rather than jeans and DM's and by all accounts they thought themselves a cut above. But here's the thing, they used to leave a little card on their victims that said, "You have been visited by the ICF."

Mason considered this new information.

"I knew I'd heard the phrase somewhere," said Kumar. "And there may be nothing in it…"

"True," said Mason. "On the other hand, the links between football hooligans and the far right go way back, don't they?"

"They certainly do. It might be worth keeping an eye out for someone who has a connection with West Ham or the ICF."

"Thanks, Raj, I'll file it away, said Mason and with that they parted, Kumar reiterating that he was available if there was anything he could do to help.

XIV

The TV sets around the Houses of Parliament were showing a press briefing being delivered by the President from the White House Press Room. The briefing had been trailed as an important one, so knots of MPs were gathered around the screens and there was an atmosphere of hushed anticipation as the President began to speak.

"I have called you here today because I have a very special announcement to make." The President was being presidential and wished to appear statesmanlike, and as always when he read from a prepared text, he spoke at a slightly higher pitch than normal, elongating the sounds of some words and finishing sentences with a rising intonation that produced an unusual, almost musical tone. He also had a habit of reading one sentence from the autocue to the right of the lectern and then swivelling to read the next one from the screen on his left. It made him look oddly like one of those rotund figures that emerge from certain brands of Swiss clock and trundle around in a stiff semicircle before disappearing back into the works.

"Today I announce a new programme that will offer many of our citizens the chance to return to the countries they came from," he intoned. "It will be fully funded and will be implemented by the Homeland Security Task Force, the body that has done such great work on our border security. The task force will report to the Acting Secretary of the Interior," he gestured to a short, fat, bald man standing to his right, "who will report direct to me. This measure will not only strengthen the security of our borders further, it will also give people the opportunity to return to their spiritual homes and embrace the cultures of their forefathers."

The President had evidently finished the portion of the presentation he was delivering via autocue because he stopped swivelling and when he asked for questions, the tuning-fork pitch had gone and he spoke in his usual voice.

"Yes, Mike," he nodded to the man from Breitbart

"Mr President," said the man from Breitbart. "Could you give us some information about the families who will be taking part in the programme?"

"That's a good question, Mike. I would like to introduce you to the..." an aide whispered in his ear, "... the Clays, one of the first families selected for this great programme."

168

An attractive black man, his attractive wife and their two attractive children were shepherded forward, smiling nervously.

"These fine people," the president gestured in the family's direction, "will be pathfinders in this great project. They're going to return to their African home and pave the way for others to follow. And we'll be sending some very good people out there to help them. Very good people!" He pointed at a reporter. "Yes?"

"Thank you, Mr President. Can you tell us which country in Africa the Clays will be returning to?"

"Yes, they will be returning to…" an aide whispered in his ear, "… to… Guinea." He looked at the aide, "… really, that's a…? OK."

He shrugged. "They'll be returning to Guinea and we've liaised with the Gui…. with the Guin… with the government there, and they're going to give them whatever help they need."

Behind the President was a board with the words, *The Homecoming*, picked out in huge letters, under which was a picture of the Clay family, while at the bottom was a quote from Marcus Garvey, who had led the Back to Africa movement in the nineteen twenties: *"A people without the knowledge of their past history, origin and culture is like a tree without roots. Look to Africa."*

"Mr President" The man from Trump News had his hand up. "Could I ask how long you envisage it taking for this program to be implemented?"

"Well, we're working on it. We're working on it like you wouldn't believe. We're talking to the government of Africa..." the aide whispered in his ear again, "...to governments *in* Africa, to get this done as quickly as we can. And look at the pay off - we get better border security, and people get to return to their ancestral homelands. I mean it's a real win-win."

"And presumably you endorse the words of Marcus Garvey?" a reporter asked, gesturing towards the board.

"I do. Very much so. I don't know him, I haven't met him personally, but I've heard he's a good person and I know he's said very good things about me."

"And what do you say to the people who may not want to go back to Africa?" asked a lone voice from the back of the room.

"Well, I haven't heard of anyone not wanting to go back. Have you heard of anyone?" He appealed to the room. "I mean why would anyone not want to go live in Africa. All that sunshine... and the dancing! Have you ever seen so much dancing? Africa's a very beautiful country..." the aide whispered in his ear, "...a very beautiful continent. You get a chance to go travel to a beautiful country... continent... like Africa, all expenses paid, with all that dancing, who wouldn't want to do that?"

"But what if people don't want to go?" persisted the voice.

The President glared at the owner of the voice. "My Justice Department is overseeing the implementation of the programme and they haven't identified one family who doesn't want to take part. And of course," he spread his hands out, "if a final adjudication is needed, my Supreme Court will be there to deliver one. After all, we must, as custodians of democracy, respect due process and the rule of law."

(That evening the President tweeted, *"How many people want to go to Africa as part of my new programme? A LOT!!"* adding a few minutes later, *"And how much do they want to go? BIGLY!!"*)

Rees shook his head as he gathered his papers.

"I don't know how he gets away with it." said Bob Maxton.

"I do," said Rees. "You can't blame him, really. His base doesn't care what he says, and he knows the public only listens to what politicians say with half an ear."

"He still shouldn't be allowed to get away with it."

"I agree, but it's too late now. He's been getting away with it for so long that he's forgotten what the truth is, if he ever knew in the first place. And do you know when the whole thing started, it started on his very first day in office, when he claimed that more people had been to his inauguration than any one in history. And when the press produced those aerial photos showing that there'd only been half as many people at his inauguration as there'd been at Obama's, what did he do? He sent his press secretary - remember that bloke Sean Spicer; face like a pug with haemorrhoids – out the next day to insist that he'd been right. Unbelievable! And then on the Sunday he sent Kellyanne Conway onto Meet the Press and when Chuck Todd questioned Trump's version of events, what did she say? She said that the president was putting out *'alternative facts.'* Can you believe that? 'Alternative facts!'

"And what did Todd do - he looked sceptical and raised an eyebrow and rolled his eyes! Instead of laughing in her face or asking her if she was familiar with the work of George Orwell, he rolled his eyes! On his first day in office the president told a lie so ludicrous, so pathetic, so easily disprovable that a five-year-old wouldn't believe it, and what happened, he got away with it. Sure, Todd and the other panellists shook their heads and threw their eyes up to heaven, but so what, Trump doesn't care what those people think anyway.

"What *should* have happened was that Spicer should have been called out by the guys in the press room and Conway should have been called out by Todd, and then on the Monday when Spicer went back in to brief the press, he should have been called out again. *'Mister Spicer, to return to the statement you made at the weekend...' 'Mister Spicer would you like to compare these two photographs I have in my hand...'* on and on, day after day if necessary, to the exclusion of all other business, until the administration was forced to admit it'd been talking bollocks.

"But the press didn't do that, they let Trump off the hook, and the message he took from it was that if you can say something so ridiculous on your first day and get away with it, you can say anything."

"Have you quite finished?" said Maxton, who had been trying in vain to get a word in.

"Yes, I bloody have, and do you know what, I feel better now that I've got that off my chest.

Rees dragged his thoughts away from the gatekeeper of western civilization and tried instead to focus them on the committee meeting scheduled for the following day. The constitutional role of a select committee is to scrutinise the work of whichever department it is linked to and it has the power to question ministers and civil servants and call on experts from the world of industry and commerce, or even members of the public, to testify. The Home Affairs Select Committee, on which Rees served, was comprised of eleven members, and by the time it was ready to take evidence the following morning, Rees had spent several hours working on the questions with which he hoped to probe the inner workings of the new Nationality Act.

The official being interrogated was the deputy permanent secretary, Horace (soon to be, or so rumour had it, Sir Horace) Carstairs, and Rees wanted to question him about some of the proposed changes in the act, particularly what the implications were for those who didn't have the requisite number of home-born grandparents. Members of select committees were drawn from the back benches and there were those M.P.'s who, through thwarted ambition or in order to showboat their own talents, used the platform as a bully pulpit to harass witnesses. Over the years there had been numerous unsavoury occasions where members had ripped witnesses to shreds, safe in the knowledge that parliamentary privilege protected them from retribution via the legal system.

The chair of this committee though, was a Shire Tory of the old school, the very embodiment of the Hurd Instinct, a decent man who took his duties seriously and saw his job as protecting the rights of the country's citizens. Select committees often met in the mornings so it was just after eleven thirty when Rees got the opportunity to ask the questions he had prepared. Carstairs, who had arrived with a coterie of advisers including, Rees noted, Archie Shore, sat at the front of the room with a horseshoe of members curling around him in a threatening arc.

"Mr. Carstairs," said Rees when it came to his turn. "I'd like to try to shed some light on the new citizenship status, the Overseas Citizen Currently Domiciled, or OCCD."

Carstairs crossed one elegantly trousered leg over the other, flicked a piece of fluff off his jacket, straightened a cuff and waited.

"Can you confirm that for a person to qualify for full citizenship, not only will they have to have been born in the UK, but their parents and grandparents will as well?"

"That is broadly correct."

"And even that may not give everyone automatic right of citizenship?"

"In a limited number of cases during very specific time periods – during the expulsions from Uganda in the seventies, for example, and at other times in Hong Kong - the citizenships granted were subsequently deemed... unsafe."

"Unsafe?" said Rees. There was no response. "Would you care to elaborate on that?"

"Only that we believe it to be a relatively small number of people and that the Minister will be writing to those concerned."

"And are you able to tell us what those letters will say?"

Carstairs looked at him. "Are you suggesting I broadcast the content of private communications between the government and its citizens *on television*," he managed to imbue the words with a distaste that only a thousand years of breeding can bring. "I mean, broadcast the contents to all and sundry before the recipients have had a chance to read them themselves? I *can* tell you that the Home Office will shortly be publishing a set of guidelines that will make clear what the exceptions to full citizenship, as outlined in the new legislation, are."

"In terms of the new categories, then," asked Rees, trying a different tack, "what right of appeal will those who fail to qualify for full citizenship have?"

"There will be an independent body set up, under the direction of the appropriate Ombudsman, which will liaise with the Home Office and appoint tribunals to hear appeals."

"When you say this body will be independent, who will appoint its members?"

Carstairs turned for a moment and consulted a sleek young man who had appeared as if by magic at his shoulder. "The composition of the body has not yet been determined," he flicked another imaginary speck of fluff off his jacket, "but I can say that the Prime Minister and the Home Secretary will be consulting with the relative authorities and that its membership will be fully representative of the population at large."

"And will those whose appeals fail have the right of appeal to a higher court?"

"Again, discussions have not yet reached a stage where the government is able to lay down a precise framework for appeals. However, I would like to reassure the committee that, as the Home Secretary stressed when he introduced the legislation," he paused to give the next words authority, "this new category of citizenship will not affect the right of residency of anyone already living here. The legislation is on the statute book purely and simply to discourage *future* applications for citizenship from outside the UK, while the current crisis endures."

Rees and his colleagues tried by various methods to probe for further information, but each attempt was rebuffed with silky condescension, and in the end, Rees was forced to concede that the deputy permanent secretary had given a perfect lesson in the art of communicating without conveying meaning. As Bob Maxton said afterwards, it was a master class in the dissemination of bullshit, and once Carstairs had exited with his adolescent advisers in tow, Rees and Maxton sat and scratched their heads.

"Thank you for giving us as much time as we needed, Ian," Rees said to the chairman as he was gathering his bits together.

"Not at all, Matt. Only sorry we weren't able, any of us, to get much out of him." He picked his pipe up and as he headed towards the door, he sighed, "I don't know whether it's just me, but I sometimes wonder whether the country's creeping towards authoritarianism?"

"Creeping?" Maxton watched the chairman's departing back. "Fucking galloping, more like!"

It was later that evening that Rees caught up with Archie Shore. They had agreed to have a pint in the Buckingham Arms near Victoria Station, where they were unlikely to be recognised.

"How's it going, Archie?" asked Rees as they sat down with their pints of Stella.

"Could be worse." Shore took a long pull from his glass. "You didn't get much out of my lord and master, then?"

"Much!" Rees grunted. "Anything would have been nice."

Shore chuckled. "I've said it before and I'll say it again, there's no one who uses more words to say less than Horace Carstairs."

"He's a slippery old bastard and no mistake," said Rees. "We both know the whole OCCD thing is a device to exclude millions of people from full citizenship, which will impact on those whose origins are in the old Commonwealth, while giving the government powers to lift selected people out of the new category."

"People from nice middle-class white countries like Australia and Canada?"

"That's what the cynics say, and God knows there's no shortage of them." Rees stared into space for a moment and went on, "They're as clever and cynical a bunch of bastards as ever I've come across, Archie. Remember the Nuremberg Decrees in Germany? Well, the critical piece of legislation was the one that re-categorized Jews as "subjects" of the Reich rather than full citizens, and everything that followed subsequently flowed from passage of that one crucial law.

"And they're doing exactly the same thing here – creating a new category of citizenship, an inferior one for those "overseas citizens" who happen to be "currently domiciled" here." He rubbed his eyes. "And into that category will fall millions of people who were born here and have lived their whole lives here but whose origins are in the Commonwealth. And guess what, they'll all be people of colour. And even though our masters claim that they're only doing it to protect the country against future immigration and that all current OCCD's will retain full citizenship in perpetuity, we only have their word for that. All they need to do is bring another bill to the House revoking those rights and there'll be nothing anyone can do about it."

He stared into space again. "Wasn't it Martin Luther King who said, 'Never forget that everything that Hitler did was legal?'"

Rees suddenly looked tired and defeated. "Can I ask you a favour, Archie? Will you keep me up to date on the timeline for that appeals process. This whole bloody thing needs proper scrutiny."

"Of course," answered Shore, "although it's getting harder and harder to find out what's really going on at the Home Office. I get the feeling that I'm falling out of favour with the powers that be. I can't quite put my finger on it but I'm not being invited to meetings I used to attend as a matter of routine, and…," he pulled a face, "… I think there are other ones going on that I don't know about."

"Have you talked to anyone about it?" asked Rees. "I mean, presumably you still have colleagues you trust?"

"There are still people I trust," answered Shore, "though their number is dwindling, and yes, I have talked to them. But it's almost as if there's a new, inner brotherhood at the Home Office that has access to things the rest of us don't know about, and…" he paused, "… on top of that there's been this influx of staff transferred in from the MOD –

they keep to themselves and no one's quite sure what they're supposed to be doing."

"Are we being paranoid?" asked Rees. "Or are the bastards really out to get us?

"Bit of both," laughed Shore. "Actually, on the subject of paranoia, there is something that's been bugging me over the last day or so."

Rees looked at him enquiringly and he hesitated, as if he was unsure what to say next. "Tell you what," he said eventually, "I won't say anything yet."

"You've got me thoroughly interested now, Archie," said Rees. "Not like you at all to be reluctant to express yourself."

Shore thought for a moment. "All I'll say is that there's going to be a major crime story all over TV and the tabloids tomorrow, an assault case that's going to lead every news broadcast..."

"And...?"

"Well, I did a bit of digging and I've discovered something that, well, on the face of it, simply can't be."

"How do you mean?"

"I mean, it's impossible." He paused and scratched his head. "Well, when I say it's impossible…" his voice trailed off.

"You're really confusing me now, Archie."

"It's something that I found, or rather didn't find." Shore hesitated again. "Something to do with the identities of some of the people involved. Something that would mean…," his voice trailed off again. "I'll be able to explain it better once the story's out. We're meeting again on Friday, aren't we? We can chat about it then."

"You're being very mysterious about it all, Archie. Are you sure you don't want to share it with me now?"

Shore shook his head.

"How about another pint, then? You never know, it might loosen your tongue a bit."

Shore grinned and looked more like his usual self. "Well, it's the civil service's job to carry out the will of Parliament isn't it, so if Parliament is paying, who am I to refuse?"

XV

"Right," said Mark Spencer, holding a squat, short barrelled rifle above his head. "Who can tell me which country this little beauty comes from?"

Gathered around him in the hall of a big house in Highgate were perhaps thirty men, the ranks of those who had met earlier in the week having been swollen by a dozen or so new faces.

The man next to Mason subjected the gun to a silent scrutiny and said, "China?"

"Not bad," conceded Spencer. "No bad at all. It's actually North Korean."

"*North Korean*! Fucking hell," someone said.

"Gentlemen," announced Spencer, twirling the weapon in his hand. "I would like to introduce you to the Type 88 assault rifle. It's used by the military in North Korea and it packs a nice little punch."

There was a murmur of voices and he went on, "Don't fucking ask how it got here; all I'll say is that international arms dealers swim in murky waters."

He twirled the gun in front of him and Mason found his eyes following it as it moved.

"It's the North Korean version of the Chinese T81, a gun itself influenced by the Russian AK74, and while it's not up there with the weaponry that NATO uses, it nevertheless remains a very nice little gun." He ran a cupped hand along the thick barrel in a way that was faintly masturbatory. "Capable of firing a hundred rounds a minute, with an effective range of 500 metres, it uses a 30-round capacity steel magazine and although it lacks the penetration of the typical NATO round," he smiled thinly, "that isn't really going to matter where we're going to be using it."

"Who wants to have a feel?" Willing hands reached out and as the gun was passed around, he continued, "We're hoping that before long we'll be deploying the weapons our own armed forces use, but in the meantime, this will do nicely. How does it feel boys?"

There were murmurs of approval as the weapon was passed from hand to hand.

"One of its best features is that it's easy to use and to maintain. In fact, it can be field stripped in one minute without the use of tools, and that gentlemen, is what you will be doing tonight, learning how to strip, clean and reassemble a Type 88 until you're so good at it that you can do it in the dark. A large number…a very large number, of these weapons are on their way to us or already in the country, and before you leave the building tonight you will all be proficient in maintaining one. Any questions?"

"Any idea when we'll be able to fire the fuckers, Spence?" asked a burly skinhead amid laughter.

Spencer smiled without warmth. "All in good time, Lennie, all in good time. We're trying to find premises in a more… remote location, where you'll have the opportunity to use the weapons in practical situations. But in the meantime, learning how to strip and reassemble the weapon is vitally important, in fact, as those of you who have served in the military will know, that knowledge could save your life."

At his signal long, wooden packing cases were brought in, and over the next two hours Mason and the others learned to strip the weapons down, to clean them and to reassemble them. Mason was no expert, but he couldn't help thinking that Storm Force had chosen wisely because the weapon turned out to be extremely straightforward to take apart and reassemble.

As he stripped and cleaned and polished the gun, Mason couldn't help recalling that the last time he'd been in Highgate, it had been with Bianca and Matthew. They'd taken a picnic to Waterlow Park on one of those endless late summer London afternoons and he'd watched Mathew, relentlessly energetic, charging around with a football at his feet, doing keepie-uppies, practising Cruyff turns and Rabonas and dribbling mazily in and out of the picnic area. Eventually, temporarily worn out, the boy had thrown himself down between them and grabbed a leg of cold chicken.

"How long left - of the holiday, I mean?" he asked, his words rendered indistinct by a combination of meat and bone.

"Another couple of weeks, darling," Bianca had laughed. "No need to panic!"

"It's not that, it'll be good to get back and see my friends, it's just I'm enjoying the holiday."

"You're happy wherever you are, aren't you, mate?" Mason ruffled his hair.

"Why wouldn't I be?" answered Matthew. "Got a lot to be happy about, haven't I?" He began to check items off on his fingers. "Got my birthday coming up," he turned a pair of mock serious eyes on his mother, "I've already started my list, and when we get back to school," he paused to add drama to his next words, "Mr Grant says I've got a good chance of being captain of the football team now I'm in Year Six. Got my mates, got my games, got the park…" He shrugged. "What is there not to be happy about?"

"When you put in like that, nothing," said Mason and turned to Bianca. "We need to pick up a few bits at the Seven Eleven on the way home."

"Oh, God, I hate the old bat in there," said Bianca. "She's got a permanent frown on her face and she scowls at me whenever I come in."

"I'll get the shopping," volunteered Matthew.

"Don't you mind her being so miserable?" said his mother.

"Well, she usually looks grumpy when I go in, but when I talk to her, she perks up."

Mason laughed. "It's that million-dollar smile of yours, Matt."

"I don't know why people don't smile at one another more," he answered. "I mean, it doesn't cost anything, does it?" He grabbed another piece of chicken, jumped up and chipped the ball neatly into his mother's picnic basket.

"You're supposed to be oiling that gun, Frank, not staring at it." Colin's voice broke into Mason's reverie and he immediately got back to work with his rag.

When they'd all had a go at cleaning and reassembling the guns, they took their places on a horseshoe of seats that had been placed at the front end of the hall and Spencer ran through the maintenance procedures a final time with a weapon on the floor in front of him.

"Right, I think we've got that sorted," he said finally. "Now, to the next item on the agenda."

At a signal from him two men, the same two who'd barred the door the night Mason had been inducted into the movement, went and stood by the doors that led into the hallway, while another blocked the exit at the far end of the room. Mason

185

was not the only one to notice this; the buzz of conversation died away and there was a perceptible cooling of the atmosphere, as if a window had been opened letting in a chill breeze.

Spencer stepped back so that everyone sitting in the horseshoe could see him. He didn't speak and as time passed and the silence grew the tension in the room became palpable.

"What did I say last time?" he eventually growled.

The silence was now invested with real menace. No one dared look at Spencer or make eye contact with their neighbour.

"What did I say at the last meeting?" he repeated and looked around. "Briggsy?"

Briggsy scratched his head in an elaborate pantomime suggestive of deep thought, but otherwise forbore to comment.

"Colin? Any thoughts as to what I said?"

"As far as I can remember, you said quite a few things, Spence" said Colin in what was clearly an attempt at humour.

"Don't get clever with me, you cunt!" The words cut through the air like a whiplash and Colin, eyes now pointing firmly downwards, made no further comment.

Spencer moved down the line until he was standing right in front of Mason. Mason didn't say anything and after a moment Spencer said, "Frank. Any thoughts?"

Mason looked into Spencer's eyes. "Well, Mark…," he had determined long before not to use the sobriquet, 'Spence,' "…Well, Mark, I agree with Colin that you did say quite a few things last time, so if you could point me in the right direction…?" He smiled to rob the words of offence and waited.

Spencer walked to the end of the horseshoe without speaking. If he was attempting to crank up the atmosphere, he was succeeding, because by the time he stopped and turned, the dropping of the proverbial pin would have sounded like the crack of doom.

"Security!" He finally spoke, spitting out the word. "What did I say about security?" He looked around. "Anyone?"

There was a silence that seemed to last a lifetime and then a small voice quavered, "You said people should be careful, Spence… that there should be no loose talk."

"Thank you." Spencer was still walking. "I thought I'd been fucking talking to myself all these months. I said, 'No loose talk.' And I said more than that, I said loose talk could threaten everything we've been working for all these years.

"And what do I find?" His voice rose. "What do I fucking find? I find that someone in this room has been going around shooting their mouth off and putting the whole thing in jeopardy. You been shouting your mouth off, Roy?" He addressed the man who had answered his question.

"Not me, Spence."

"What about you, Colin?" Mason could hear Spencer's footsteps approaching.

"No way, Spence."

The footsteps moved on. "Lenny?"

"On my life, Spence…"

Mason waited for the footsteps to move on, but they didn't. Eventually Spencer spoke in a voice so quiet and menacing it chilled the bones of everyone in the room. "That's not what I've heard, Lenny."

"Honest, Spence, I don't know what you're talking about…"

"I'll tell you what I'm talking about, Lenny." Spencer was now standing right in front of the skinhead. "I'll tell you what I've heard. I've heard you've been blabbing all over Wapping about what a big man you are." His voice was quiet, but every word could be heard in the stillness of the room. "I've heard you were in the Van and Horses last Saturday night, giving it large to some little slag whose knickers you were trying to get into, about what a big man you are."

He looked at the others. "He even mentioned this place! Can you fucking believe it? He's been going around shooting his mouth off, putting everything we're doing at risk just to try and get into SOME SLAG'S KNICKERS!" He roared out the last words.

"Honest, Spence, on my life, I never…" Lenny was babbling incontinently.

Spencer went around to the back of the horseshoe and stood behind him. "So, Lenny," he spoke quietly. "We've got to decide what we're going to do."

188

Lenny's head swivelled around in a desperate search for his tormentor. "Spence, listen…"

"EYES FRONT!" The words came out as a scream. "EYES FRONT, YOU CUNT!"

Lenny's head snapped forwards and he sat, frozen into immobility, like a mouse that is aware of the proximity of the cat but is so paralysed by fear it can't move.

Spencer's hand came out of his pocket with something bunched in his fist, something that glinted in the harsh glare of the overhead strip light. His arm rose smoothly until it was above his head and then descended in a lazy arc, landing with a soft concussion on the top of Lenny's head. A moment later the fingers uncurled, leaving something long and thin pointing upwards.

Mason saw an expression of surprise cross Lenny's face and a moment later a long shudder passed through his body and then he let out a groan or a sigh and one of his arms jerked and his body slid slowly from the chair and came to rest on the floor, still in a sitting position. There was a moment of stunned silence and then Lenny's body twitched several times and a second later a long, slow, wet, bubbling fart escaped him as wind passed through his body for the final time. An overpowering smell drifted into the centre of the room and several people gagged.

Mason looked at Lenny's head and saw that a thin bone handle, perhaps four or five inches long, was sticking up from the centre of his skull.

There was an awful silence and then Spencer leaned over the dead body, for that was assuredly what it now was, and grasped the bone handle. He pulled and it slid smoothly out, revealing a long, thin pointed blade, a bit like a screwdriver, only finer and sharper.

Spencer held it up so that everyone could see it and said, "Oriental ice pick. Not one of those European ones that look like little pickaxes, they're fucking useless. Japanese. Slides in smooth as you like and there's hardly any blood. Best weapon in the world for close quarter fighting, as I'll demonstrate when we do unarmed combat next week. And how much did it cost? Go on, have a guess. All right, I'll tell you, fifteen quid. Fifteen fucking quid from eBay. I mean you couldn't make it up, could you?"

XVI

The lead item on the following morning's TV news was a story about the abduction, rape and murder of a twelve-year-old girl by a gang of five Pakistani men. A photo of a pretty girl in school uniform was shown and she was named as Lorraine Byrne. The newsreader went on to say that police believed the men had lured Lorraine into a park in Hanwell, West London and then subjected her to a horrific series of attacks before killing her.

The acts perpetrated on the girl were considered too depraved to be broadcast, and the newscaster confined himself to naming the five suspects as their photos appeared on the screen. He went on to say that the men were currently being held at Cannon Row police station. "The police officer in charge of the investigation, Detective Superintendent Trevor Ross, made the following statement earlier today."

The shot cut to a burly man in a suit. "These men," he said, using the formal, stilted tones policemen everywhere seem to reserve for these occasions, "carried out a series of brutal sex acts on this innocent young girl, acts so vile that I am unable to give details of them, before murdering her in cold blood. Since they have been arrested," he continued, "the men have shown no remorse whatsoever. In fact," he looked into the eye of the camera, "such is the depth of their depravity that they have actually been heard laughing in their cells."

The camera cut back to the newsreader who said, "It is understood that all five men have pleaded guilty to the attack. Earlier this morning the solicitor acting for Lorraine's family read out a statement on the family's behalf."

The shot cut to a middle-aged man who read from a script:

These monsters have taken away our darling girl and ruined our lives for ever. It is a national disgrace that the animals who committed these acts will be kept in comfort at the taxpayers' expense and then be released to commit more crimes. We are calling for a national debate on whether the

191

death penalty should be restored so that other innocent young girls won't have to go through the same ordeal as our daughter. We will never forget our darling Lorraine and we thank everyone who has offered support and sent their condolences but now we want to be left alone to grieve in peace.

"The Prime Minister is expected to make a statement in the House of Commons this afternoon," said the newsreader gravely. "And now, over to our home affairs correspondent at Westminster for the latest on the story…"

The Sun carried a photo of a plump, middle-aged man in a *kurta pajama*, above which was a banner headline that said: FACE OF EVIL. Inside were photos of the four other defendants and an editorial which began:

The Sun today calls for a referendum on the restoration of the death penalty. We ask our readers to complete the coupon below asking the Prime Minister to introduce legislation calling for a referendum as a matter of urgency. The Sun also demands that the result of the referendum be back dated so that the callous monsters who brutalised and murdered little Lorraine Byrne can meet the fate they deserve. We are calling the legislation Lorraine's Law and we ask all our readers to get behind the Sun's campaign to bring to Lorraine's family the justice that Lorraine herself was denied.

Two days later, the Prime Minister stood up, moved to the despatch box and began to speak. "Mister Speaker, this government has been considering whether the penalties that society exacts on those who commit the most serious of crimes are appropriate and whether they remain fit for purpose in the world we live in today. Now, following the tragic death of Lorraine Byrne, we feel that it is time our citizens had a say in how society punishes such crimes.

"Mister Speaker, this government has always been committed to putting the people of our country first and that is why we are today introducing emergency legislation that will enable the people to decide, through a referendum, whether capital punishment should be restored in the case of certain very serious crimes. Personally, I have always felt that half a century ago, when Parliament voted to abolish capital punishment without consulting the electorate, it was guilty of an arrogant disregard for the voice of the people. Our citizens were not consulted then, so it is only right that we redress that wrong by consulting them now. This government will not allow the people's voice to be silenced at this pivotal moment in our history."

Behind him there were shouts and cheers and order papers were waved, and across the floor Matt Rees and Bob Maxton exchanged looks in which despair battled with resignation.

***

Two days later Mason was back in the house in Highgate. The same people were there as before but it was clear that recent events were weighing

193

heavily on those present because there were no jokes, no one larked about, and everyone avoided one another's eyes.

After cleaning the ice pick Spencer had directed the guys guarding the doors to take Lenny's body away. "There's a furnace down in the cellar," he said, cleaning the blood off his hands. "Quite convenient, really."

And once the body had been dragged away, he addressed the room once more, only this time in the regretful tones of a dutiful house master forced to break up a midnight feast.

"You see, lads, how important security is. You do see that, don't you? We are *so* close to achieving everything we've dreamed of. So close. And when that day comes, all of us, and by that, I mean everyone in this room, will be able to wear our beliefs as a badge of honour rather than having to hide them like we do now.

"And then there'll be a reckoning. Then there'll be an accounting." He looked slowly around, nodding his head as he did so. "Oh yes, my friends, then there'll be a reckoning, and on that day, we'll take care of all outstanding business and when it's all over, the people of this country will respect you and they will fear you and you'll never have to hide your beliefs again."

"Fucking don't mind admitting the whole thing scared the shit out of me," said Colin, when the conversation had turned to Lenny's demise. "I thought he was going to stop in front of me, Spence I mean."

"That Lenny was a bit of a wanker, though, wasn't he?" the guy next to Mason said to him.

"I didn't really know him."

"Always giving it the big 'I am' – trying a bit too hard, if you know what I mean."

"I suppose so."

"I mean, we've got to have discipline, haven't we? And Spence *had* made people promise not to go around blabbing about what we're doing."

"Couldn't have spelt it out any clearer, could he?" said Briggsy.

"So, he got what was coming to him, did Lenny, if you ask me. Anyway, I wouldn't lose any sleep over him. There's going to be a lot more of that kind of stuff before we're done, that's what Spence says."

"Do you reckon he's going to be leader of the whole thing?" asked a burly man. "Spence, I mean?"

"It'll be between him and Vinnie Groves, I reckon," answered his mate.

"What about the Chameleon?" asked Colin Smith.

"The Chameleon?" Mason hadn't heard the name before.

"Yeah, there's supposed to be this mysterious bloke who no one knows about, but who goes all the way back with Spence and Vinnie, right back to the beginning. Nobody knows who he is or what his name is, that's why they call him the Chameleon. Spence is always going on about him, isn't he, Ron?"

"He's supposed to be working undercover, no one knows where, making sure there are no traitors in the movement and reporting back to Vinnie on what he sees."

"Yeah, they reckon you could be sitting next to him at a meeting and you wouldn't know."

"Fucking hell!"

One of the skinheads made a show of looking around. "You're not the Chameleon by any chance, are you, Briggsy?"

There were snorts of laughter and Mason heard a voice saying, "Not even the Chameleon could disguise himself that well."

"Anyway, don't go losing any sleep over Lenny Vance," said the hard-looking bloke who Mason remembered was called Ron. "Well rid, if you ask me."

"I agree with you, mate," said Briggsy. "We got to do what we got to do, ain't we?"

Colin and Ron wandered off and Briggsy turned to Mason and said, "Be a few more casualties before this is all done, mate." He had the heightened colouring of the heavy drinker and there were patches of greying stubble on his chin and his neck where the razor had failed to find its mark.

He leaned towards Mason and said confidentially, "You know what done if for me, don't you? Got me into Storm Force, I mean?"

Mason shook his head and did his best to appear interested.

Briggsy leaned closer and said, "The Harlem Globetrotters."

"The Harlem Globetrotters?"

Briggsy nodded and tapped a knowing finger on his nose. "That was the final straw for me; what got me into the movement. You know who they are, don't you? The Harlem Globetrotters, I mean."

"American basketball team?" said Mason, wondering where this was heading.

"That's right. Anyway, that's when I decided to get involved," said Briggsy. "I used to watch them on the telly, and when they kept on winning year after year, I thought I'd try and get a bet on the other team, the white blokes – law of averages, like. Bloody bookie laughed in my face."

He looked around him, leaned towards Mason and said quietly, "You know the whole fucking thing was fixed, don't you?" As he spoke, Mason noticed that his face was curiously lacking in expression and that his eyes had a dead quality to them, like windows at the front of an empty house.

Mason was wondering how best he might respond when Briggsy spoke again. "Those basketball games; you know they was all fixed?"

Aware that the other man was watching him intently, Mason considered for a moment before saying carefully, "I thought perhaps they might have been."

"It was when I found out the whole thing was fixed," said Briggsy, "that's what done it for me." A vein on his temple had begun to pulse rhythmically. "I mean, all those games on the BBC, year after year, and every time they played, *every* time, the coons beat the white blokes. And all the time it was fixed!"

His words having failed to elicit the hoped-for response, he went on, "I mean, on the BBC! On the fucking BBC! Can you believe it? That's when I realized how big the conspiracy was." He shook his head again, clambered to his feet and shuffled off in the direction of the kitchen, absent-mindedly rubbing the pulsing vein.

Colin, who had meanwhile arrived from a different part of the room, watched him go and then asked, "Was he telling you about the Harlem Globetrotters? Briggsy, I mean?"

"He was."

"Don't worry, he does it to everyone. Bit of an obsession with him, to be honest, but if he's telling you about the Harlem Globetrotters it means he's accepted you into the group."

He looked at the door his friend had gone through and said, "One thing I'll tell you about Briggsy, Frank; he may not have been at the front of the queue when they handed out the brains, but you wouldn't want anyone else next to you in a ruck. And that's exactly what we're going to need when this fucking thing goes off – blokes like Briggsy."

At that moment Mason looked up and saw Briggsy returning from the kitchen in the company of someone he couldn't see properly but who looked vaguely familiar.

"Hey, look who I've found," Briggsy called out and there were shouts of surprise and words of greeting for the new entrant, who was still half hidden by the bulk of his companion.

Then Briggsy moved to one side and Mason found himself looking straight into a face he knew he recognised from somewhere.

For a millisecond he couldn't identify it, even though an alarm bell had started ringing somewhere in his mind the moment the man had entered the room.

Then, in a blinding flash, he realized who it was.

It was Danny Gates, the man who'd been imprisoned as an accessory to Mathew's murder and someone he'd sat not ten feet away from for the entire week of the subsequent trial.

Part Three

The most effective way to destroy people is to deny and obliterate their own understanding of their history. (George Orwell)

A single death is a tragedy, a million deaths is a statistic. (Joseph Stalin)

We should have more people from Norway. (Donald J Trump)

XVII

Matt Rees and Archie Shore were back in the Buckingham Arms, this time sipping from bottles of Becks that Shore had ordered instead of pints in deference to his expanding waistline.

"Did you see Vinnie Groves in the Commons yesterday?" asked Rees and Shore nodded.

Groves had had twenty-four hours to consider his response to the PM's call for a referendum on the death penalty, and Conservative whips, mindful of the part English Rose's votes played in their Commons majority, had nervously awaited his contribution. But his first words had set their minds at rest.

"Mister Speaker, English Rose fully supports the proposed legislation under the Emergency Powers Act." He paused to allow a wave of approval to harrumph its way across the government benches.

"I would like to assure the House that, of course, the government can count on the support of English Rose in this matter. I do, however, want to make an appeal to the Prime Minister on behalf of the people of our country. Mister Speaker, this legislation *must* carry in it the capacity for retrospective application, particularly in regard to the sub-humans who carried out the terrible acts in west London this week. If it doesn't, we run the risk of our communities feeling so betrayed by the judicial process that they decide to apply summary justice themselves.

"Of course, we ask our citizens to exercise restraint, although equally we understand that when feelings run so high this may be difficult for them. The notion of "restorative justice," Mister Speaker, is something that we are all familiar with, but today I would like to offer the House a new interpretation."

He read from a sheet of paper in front of him. "The Oxford English Dictionary defines restorative justice as: *an approach to justice in which one of the responses to a crime is to organize a meeting between the victim and the offender, sometimes with representatives of the wider community*."

"Mister Speaker, the family of Lorraine Byrne would be only too happy to *organize a meeting* with the animals who murdered her. All over the country, Mister Speaker, *representatives of the wider community* are itching to visit the neighbourhoods that spawned these monsters and apply their own version of restorative justice."

His voice had grown louder and his tone more emotional, and then, like the master showman he was, he suddenly lowered the volume.

"Mister Speaker, it is vital the government allows this legislation to be applied retrospectively. Otherwise, our communities may appoint representatives to apply restorative justice in their names. And of course, Mister Speaker, while we urge restraint, we also recognise how high feelings are running at this critical time in our national story. Of course, we ask our communities to exercise restraint, but equally, Mister Speaker, we understand that…," he paused, "*…they may not be able to help themselves!"*

That night there had been outbreaks of rioting all over the country; a mosque had been burned down in Bradford, parts of Birmingham had become no go areas, and Southall in West London had witnessed scenes reminiscent of the disorder of the nineteen seventies. An uneasy calm had descended on the country the following morning but now with nightfall approaching again, Rees and Shore, like millions of their fellow citizens, awaited developments with a sense of deep foreboding.

"We certainly live in unusual times," said Shore as he sipped from his bottle.

"By the way, what was it you were going to tell me about the big crime story you mentioned?" asked Rees. "By which I assume you meant the Lorraine Byrne attack; you said there was something bugging you about it."

Instead of answering, Shore looked around, and only after making sure no one was within earshot did he moisten his lips and begin to speak.

"Well, it was nothing much at first, but we got a request – at the Home Office I mean – for information about Isaaf Aqbul, one of the men in the Lorraine Byrne case, and the odd thing was how quickly it came, within an hour of the attack happening. I mean, if the police had got there straight away and arrested the men on the spot, it was just about possible, but it set a little alarm bell going so I decided to dig a little."

"Go on." Rees, interest now thoroughly aroused, took a sip from his bottle.

"Well, the first thing I did was look up the names of the five men on the national database."

"The one in the Office for National Statistics?"

"Yep."

"But isn't that restricted these days – since the Emergency Powers Act?"

"Yep again. Access to the Office for National Statistics database is now restricted, God knows why. Restricted to…" he thought for a moment, "…I'm not actually sure, to be honest, but it's way above my pay grade."

"So how did you access it?"

"Well, I've got this colleague who's an absolute IT genius, he can ghost his way in and out of any system without anyone knowing he's been there. Anyway, he hacked me into the births, deaths and marriages database, and…"

"Go on."

"I found details of the five men, all right."

"So, what's the problem?"

"Well, on a whim, I decided to put Lorraine Byrne, the victim's name and date of birth in. And…" he stopped.

"And what?"

"There was nothing there."

"What do you mean, there was nothing there?"

"I mean there was nothing there. Nothing on the database. According to the register of births, deaths and marriages, Lorraine Byrne doesn't exist and never has done."

***

When Mason looked into the eyes of Danny Gates, the urge to walk across the room, grab him by the throat and punch his lights out was almost overwhelming. At the same time, a different part of his brain, the bit that senses danger, was screaming at him to simply stop whatever it was he was doing, drop everything and run for his life. He managed to do neither of those things, however, instead contriving somehow to turn on the other man the kind of blank, incurious gaze one bored stranger might visit on another.

He watched as Danny's eyes rested on his and then passed onwards. After a second, though, they stopped, moved back and fixing themselves onto Mason, and as they did so, an expression appeared on his face - the look of someone thinking, *I've seen that face before, just give me a minute and I'll remember where it was, I saw it.*

And, of course, it was a face that Danny *had* seen before, many times before, because it had spent the entire five days of the trial sitting not ten feet away from him, examining him with an unblinking stare. Given all that, Mason couldn't help but think that it was only a matter of time before a shutter in Danny's memory clicked and he remembered why the face looked so familiar.

Was it without conscious thought that he then spoke, or was it the result of a lightning quick, almost subliminal, recognition that he needed to do something to short circuit a process that would inevitably lead to capture and death? Afterwards he was never quite sure, but all he *could* be sure of was that when he heard his own voice uttering the words, "What are you looking at, you weaselly little fuck?" in a menacing undertone, it was with mild surprise.

The expression on Danny's face – surprise combined with blank terror – was indicative of his confusion, and Mason decided to press home his advantage. "I'm talking to you, cunt face," he said, moving threateningly towards Gates as he spoke.

"Whoa, hold up, Frank…" said Briggsy and Mason heard other voices raised in protest.

Colin moved between them and said, "Hang on, Frank, he's a friend."

"Yeah?" said Mason, his eyes still locked onto Danny's. "Well, he's not fucking well acting like one."

"What?" Danny, hands outstretched, looked around for support. "What did I do?" he asked in a voice that had suddenly gone up several octaves.

"Calm down, Frank, I'm telling you he's all right." This was Colin again.

"Well, he shouldn't walk into a room and start eyeballing people, that's all I'm saying." Mason couldn't think of anything to do other than to shrug and look sheepish and appear mollified by the other man's words.

"That's all right then," said Colin with a grin. "Frank Brown, Danny Gates."

As he performed the introductions and the two men shook hands, Danny refused to make any kind of eye contact and Mason took satisfaction from the thought that if the other man couldn't even bring himself to look at him, there was at least a chance he wouldn't recognise him straight way.

"What are you doing here anyway, Danny?" asked Briggsy. "I didn't think you were due out until next year."

"General amnesty," said Danny. "Anyone with less than eighteen months to serve's being released - something about there being a national emergency. That's the official version anyway, but a screw told me they'd been told to free up prison space for illegals."

Listening to the conversation with half an ear, Mason applied his mind to the urgent matter of what he ought to do, something he was aware might be critical to his chances of surviving the hours ahead. Although he had managed to reduce Danny to a condition of abject fear, he knew from his reaction when their eyes had met that his face had set an alarm bell off somewhere in the other man's memory. Could he really rely on Danny – admittedly not the sharpest tool in the box – being dumb enough not to eventually recognise him as Mathew Lincoln's stepfather? He was realistic enough to know what his fate would be if Danny did remember who he was; after all, hadn't Spencer recently executed a man in cold blood for being a bit indiscreet with some bird down the pub.

It was, all things considered, a conundrum. He had made a promise to what was left of his broken self to try to avenge Mathew and Bianca's deaths, and he was now standing only inches away from a man who almost certainly knew what had happened to Matthew. On the other hand, he knew that at any moment something, anything, might jog Danny's memory, and if that happened, he had few illusions about what it would mean for him - he has seen Mark Spencer in action enough for that to be clear.

So, as he stood and chatted and pretended to listen, his mind was racing as he tried to decide what to do for the best. *Stay or go. Stay or go. Stay or go.*

He was jerked out of his reverie by a voice saying, "So, you weren't on the estate yourself that night, Danny?"

An expression of cunning passed across Danny's face. "Not saying I was, not saying I wasn't." He was clearly enjoying being the centre of attention.

"Everyone was proud of you, you know, Dan," a big man said." I mean, taking the rap and doing the bird and all that."

Danny swelled visibly. "Yeah, well you can't be a rat, can you?" he said. "I mean, 's the way you're brought up, innit?"

"So, what did happen that night, Dan," said the big man, "just between friends. Unless, of course you don't know yourself."

Danny preened. "Oh, I know what happened all right, don't you worry about that…"

He took a breath and opened his mouth to speak and at that precise moment the door behind him swung open and Mark Spencer and Kirsty Black walked into the room. Mason sat on his hands and looked at the floor and fought with every inch of his being not to scream out his rage and frustration.

"All right, everyone?" said Spencer. "Just give us a few minutes to set up and we'll be with you. Turn the TV on, someone," he added. "Be interesting to see whether our streets are a bit quieter tonight."

The TV was turned on and the face of Vinnie Groves, who was being interviewed by someone at the BBC, filled the screen.

"What we have seen over the last couple of nights," Groves was saying, "is the natural frustration in our communities at the government's painfully slow response to recent events. And of course, while we appeal for calm, we cannot condemn our citizens for wishing to protect their vulnerable members."

He had not been idle over the previous twenty-four hours, tweeting, "LIBERATE SOUTHALL!!", then "LIBERATE BRADFORD!!", and finally, "LIBERATE ALL OUR INNER CITIES!!"

"Mister Groves," the voice of Laura Kuenssberg asked, "do you think your deliberate misuse of the term 'restorative justice' has contributed towards the disorder?"

"Absolutely not," answered Groves. "On the contrary, reports we've been getting suggest that the violence we're seeing has been deliberately stoked from within the communities that produced the animals who murdered little Lorraine, in order to distract attention from the bestial nature of those crimes."

He reached out a hand and touched her elbow. "Laura, you know that English Rose is committed to the democratic process, you've heard me say so in speech after speech, and of course, I appeal for people to exercise restraint until the passage of Lorraine's Law allows our communities to deliver the justice people are crying out for. But equally, I'm sure you can understand how frightened our communities are in the current climate, how under threat they feel. Surely it is not a crime for our citizens to want to safeguard their children and do what they can to prevent them from meeting the same fate as little Lorraine?"

Back in the studio the newscaster reported that there had been further violence in Bradford, in Birmingham, and in the London suburbs of Southall and Hounslow, while there had also been disturbances in Brixton and Willesden, two London districts with an Afro Caribbean rather than Asian flavour to them. The report finished with a live outside broadcast in which a correspondent stood on a darkened street and said to camera, "On the evidence of the light in the sky you can see behind me, it appears that the centre of Bradford may be on fire."

Spencer, who had been listening to the broadcast with half an ear, chuckled. "There's your *judenrein*, Kirst," he said over his shoulder. "Much more of this and there won't be anything left for our lads to clean up."

"It's all there in the history books, Spence, much as I'd like to take the credit." She smiled and turned to the others. "We need to get the projector screen set up next door and we're good to go."

"Five minutes, lads," said Spencer and followed her out.

Left with the others, Mason's mind was in turmoil. He had come within an inch of discovering who had killed Mathew only to have the knowledge snatched away from him by Spencer and Kirsty's entrance, and now he wasn't sure what to do for the best. That he was risking his life on a random throw of the dice that were rolling around in the otherwise empty vessel that was Danny's brain, he could not deny. He knew his real identity was locked away somewhere in Danny's memory, like a forgotten document in the recesses of a dodgy, barely used hard drive. And he knew how close that document had come to being opened - he had seen it written plainly on Danny's face as his brain had strained to match the image in front of him with the one in its memory.

And yet, having come *that* close to finding out what happened the night Mathew had died, he also knew that if he hung around and tried to find a way to revisit the conversation in a way that wouldn't arouse suspicion, he might still strike gold.

At that moment Danny, sitting a little to the front and right of him, turned his head and looked around and Mason's blood froze as he realized that the configuration of their chairs was exactly as it had been in court, meaning that Danny would have the same view of him as he'd had during the trial. It was too late to move, however, and Mason could only watch in horrified slow motion as Danny's vacant gaze moved slowly along the line and eventually came to rest on his face.

Nothing happened for a second and then Danny's eyes narrowed and he frowned with the effort of thinking and then his face started to clear and an expression of satisfaction, almost of triumph, dawned on it as he realized his brain was about to solve the problem that had been bugging it. For half a second Danny's face in repose had an almost childlike quality to it and then a little light seemed to go pop somewhere as it dawned on him exactly where he'd seen Mason before.

And then, as the implications of this piece of deduction began to reveal themselves to him, a succession of expressions - triumph, certainty, doubt, fear – began to race across his face.

At precisely the moment Mason saw Danny start to scan the room in search of an authority

214

figure - any authority figure – he leaned forward and said quietly but distinctly, "You eyeballing me again, fuck face?"

Danny gulped and looked wildly around, and Mason congratulated himself on the psychological mastery he had achieved, because if the other man had simply stood up and denounced him there and then, it would have been all over. And yet he couldn't quite bring himself to do it.

Mason could see uncertainty – panic perhaps - writ large on Danny's face as he tried to decide what to do for the best. He *knew* this was the bloke who had sat watching him in court for five days. He was sure. Or was he? Was he quite sure? Was he absolutely one hundred percent certain?

Mason could see the succession of thoughts racing across Danny's face and knew that in the end, faced with the blindingly bleeding obvious, Danny, even Danny, would work out what he had to do. But he also knew if he could do something, anything, that would buy himself a couple of precious minutes, he might yet escape.

"You want some, you ugly little fucker?" he said in the same menacing undertone he had used earlier.

He shifted his weight in the chair and coiled himself as if he was about to strike, and that was what did it. Danny leapt up like a scalded cat and scurried off in the direction of the door Spencer and Kirsty Black had gone through.

He looked back once and Mason heard him say, "Anyone seen, Spence?" as he disappeared through the door.

His heart thumping painfully in his chest, Mason got up, stretched extravagantly and, affecting an air of nonchalance, headed for the door that led to the toilets. The corridor outside also led to the main entrance and when he arrived there a couple of seconds later, trying to look as if he wasn't hurrying, one of the skinheads was lounging in the lobby.

Mason nodded at him. "All right, mate – anywhere in particular we're supposed to go for a smoke?"

"Wherever you like, chief, just keep the butts away from the door, Spence says."

Mason strolled through the door and began to walk along the drive that led to the gate. He passed a copse of trees and it was only when he saw that he was of sight of the house that he started to run. A moment later the gated entrance came into view and he risked a look behind him, secure in the knowledge that he was safe from pursuit.

Then, just as he was congratulating himself on having held his nerve, he heard a whirring sound and when he looked ahead, he saw to his horror that the iron gates at the end of the drive were beginning to close. He filled his lungs with air and ran for his life, but he knew in his heart he wasn't going to make it and sure enough, he was still ten yards short of the gates when they shut in front of him with a resounding clang.

The gates were attached to a high wall that Mason knew ran around the building, enclosing it completely. He shook them furiously, but the lock was large and sturdy looking, while the vertical bars were far too strong for him to break or bend. The wall was fifteen feet high and shards of broken glass were embedded in the top. If he'd had time to find a ladder or look for an overhanging tree, he might have had a chance of scaling it, but he knew that neither of those luxuries were available to him.

Although the curve in the path hid the house from view, he heard the sound of shouted imprecations and pounding footsteps, and somewhere a dog barked manically. He plunged into the undergrowth and began a desperate, scrabbling circumnavigation of the perimeter of the property, hoping against hope that a break in the wall or an overhanging branch would give him the opportunity to make his escape. A few moments later he heard a crashing in the undergrowth behind him and when he looked back, he saw tiny cylindrical beams of torchlight lighting up the sky like mini searchlights.

He stopped and dropped into a crouch and a moment later he heard the pursuit crash past him somewhere off to his left and move ahead. He waited a few seconds and then, treading with excruciating care, began to creep slowly off in the opposite direction. He was congratulating himself on having gained a few precious extra seconds when, with a crash and a snarl, a large body burst from the undergrowth and he felt a pair of teeth sinking themselves into his flesh.

At the same time, he heard the sound of the pursuit getting louder, and then, without warning, a light was suddenly shone into his face, dazzling him.

As he put a hand in front of his eyes, he heard Spencer's voice saying, "Well, well, look what we've got here!"

The dog continued to snarl and worry at his clothes until Spencer called out "Blondi," at which point it desisted abruptly, padded back to its master and sat down demurely beside him.

"Good girl," Mason heard Spencer's voice again. "Shame I can't let you rip the fucker to pieces; it would do us all a favour."

Mason felt arms dragging him to his feet and then he heard Spencer's voice once more. "Never mind, lads, never mind, just think of it as a pleasure deferred..."

XVIII

"What do you mean, she doesn't exist?" said Rees

"Just that. There's no record of a Lorraine Catherine Mary Byrne having been born or ever having existed."

"But that's…" Rees spluttered to a halt.

"Tell me about it."

"Could it be a mistake?"

"Well, after I'd done Lorraine, I entered her mother's details as well. Brenda Catherine Byrne, *nee* Reeves."

"And?"

"Nothing."

"Jesus."

"Nothing. No record of the birth of a Brenda Catherine Reeves, and no record of the marriage of a Brenda Catherine Reeves to a Mr Byrne or to anyone else. I didn't say anything when we spoke the other day because I wondered whether maybe there'd been a glitch in the system or something, so I waited twenty-four hours and entered the names on the database again."

Rees waited for him to speak and then said, "And?"

"Nothing."

They looked at each other in silence for a moment.

"Jesus Christ…" began Rees, finally, "I mean…"

"What?"

"I don't know…" he faltered.

"I don't know either, mate, except I'm starting to feel very nervous." Rees didn't reply and Archie went on. "If what we think might have happened has actually happened…"

"Go on,"

"Well, people have died because of it. I mean, people have been killed in the riots."

"I know."

"And if it is what we think it is, what do we do? I mean, I can't just go to Horace Carstairs and say, 'Look what I've found!' and expect him to give me a pat on the head and put me up for promotion. I've broken the law by hacking into a restricted database and they'd want to know how I did that, which would implicate my mate as well."

"To be honest, I think it isn't any longer about whether or not you get sacked for gross misconduct," said Rees. "As you said yourself, people have died because of all this." He thought for a moment. "I think we're in a whole new ball game."

"So, what do we do?"

"I don't know. In the normal course of events, you'd report it to Horace Carstairs, who's the nearest thing you've got to a line boss or a departmental head. But for all we know, Carstairs may be part of the…" he stopped.

"Go on, say it?"

"Say what?"

"Conspiracy. That's what you were going to say, wasn't it?"

It was indeed the word that Rees had been stumbling towards, but something had stopped him from articulating it, because if there was a conspiracy, the implications were so monumentally, mind bogglingly awful that his mind had recoiled from the whole thing.

"You're right," he said wearily. "That was the word I was going to use. And if it is a conspiracy - and I think we're going to have to face up to the fact that it probably is - we've got to get our heads around the fact that it isn't like Watergate, or… or Arms to Iraq, or any of the others, it's in a whole different league."

"So, what are we going to do?"

"The first thing we've got to do is not do *anything,* until we've had time to think. I'm not trying to be dramatic, but…" he faltered, and it was left to Shore to complete the thought.

"…our own lives could be at stake, that's what you were going to say."

"I'm not being overdramatic, am I?"

"No, I don't think you are."

"We've got to find a way to break the story, but I don't know who we can trust."

"Haven't you got contacts in the press?"

"Not anyone I'd trust with my life, not since they brought in that new Editors Law and filled the Press Council with place men. And certainly not since they put in that clause that forced editors to suppress anything 'calculated to weaken the strength of the nation abroad or at home.'"

He could feel Shore's eyes boring into him, and he shrugged. "I've got to think, Archie, I've got to think."

"Would another bottle of Becks help you with that process?"

Rees smiled wryly as his friend made his way towards the bar.

***

221

Frank Mason was sitting on a hard-backed chair in a room he hadn't visited before towards the rear of the mansion. His arms and legs were attached to the chair with plastic zip ties and a large strip of duct tape was covering his mouth. In the room with him were Mark Spencer, Kirsty Black, Danny Gates and a man whose name he couldn't, for the moment, remember.

Spencer was pacing up and down in front of him. "I told you all there was something wrong with him, I fucking told you. Didn't I say there was something wrong with him, Kirst?"

"You did say there was something you couldn't put your finger on, Spence." She was examining Mason dispassionately with her arms folded. "I'll give you that."

Danny was also walking up and down. "I knew I'd met him," he said excitedly. "I knew I'd seen him somewhere."

"Took you long enough to remember, you fucking idiot," muttered Spencer, *sotto voce,* and then raising his voice, added, "You did well, Dan, you did well."

"I knew it would come if I was patient, I knew it," Danny prattled on. "I told myself, just hang on there and it'll come. I did well, Spence, didn't I?"

"You did well, Dan, you did well."

The man whose name Mason didn't know came over and stood in front of the chair and Mason remembered he was the guy who Kirsty had jokingly threatened to have castrated. Like Briggsy, he had the unnaturally red complexion of the heavy drinker and as he squatted down so that his eyes were level with Mason's, a whiff of fried onions came off him.

"Remind me who this cunt is, again?" he said.

"Frank Mason," said Spencer. "Stepdad of the kid who got topped at the Whitewater Estate, and partner – or whatever they call it these days - of the kid's half-breed mum."

"Sat in court eyeballing me the whole time," said Danny. "Didn't frighten me, though."

He came across and squatted down in front of Mason. "You don't frighten me, mate," he quavered. "You didn't frighten me then and you don't frighten me now."

"So, what are we going to do with him, Spence?" The other guy's eyes hadn't left Mason's and he smiled an unpleasant smile."

"A very good question, Ronald," said Spencer, whose mood seemed to be oscillating between towering rage and high good humour. "A very good question. Although, of course," he looked at Mason and grinned, "it's not so much a question of *what* we're going to do, as *how* we're going to do it, and how long it's going to take."

The man who Spencer had called Ronald grabbed Mason's hair and jerked his head back. "Any time you're ready to go Spence, you just say the word."

"A word of caution, gentlemen," interjected Kirsty. "We don't know whether he's done this off his own bat or whether there are others who know he's here."

"Yeah, slow down a bit, Ron," said Spencer. "There'll be plenty of time, and there's plenty of him to go about. Kirsty's right, though, we *will* have to find out what he knows and what he doesn't. Tell you what, I can turn it into a bit of a tutorial if you like. I did a bit of what they call 'enhanced interrogation' when I was in the military and we'll all need to know the basics going forward." He pulled a pair of pliers out of his pocket and leered at Mason. "And the great thing is that you don't really need any specialist equipment, lads, if you know how to… improvise."

Ron laughed and Danny tried to join in, but his snigger turned into a gulp. Spencer continued to stare at Mason, pliers in hand, and at that moment Mason knew that in the hours ahead he was going to die a painful protracted death because Spencer's drive, his compulsive need, to kill would override all other considerations, including the need to extract information from him.

"I don't want to spoil the fun, boys but we've got quite a few things still to do tonight," said Kirsty. "Any chance all this can wait till a bit later?"

"Kirsty's right lads," said Spencer. "The pace of events is starting to accelerate, and we might need to be ready to move a bit earlier than we thought. But as I said outside; pleasure deferred, Ron, pleasure deferred."

224

He moved across to the chair and squatted down in front of Mason. "Would you mind bringing my duffle bag over, Danny?" He held the pliers up in one hand and the Japanese ice pick in the other.

"You've already seen some of the tools of my trade, Frank, but this," he fumbled in the duffle bag and brought out a small metal object with a handle at one end and a hollow circle at the other, "is my favourite, my instrument of choice if you like."

"Know what it is?" He held it inches away from Mason's face. "Seen one of these before? Of course, you can't answer, can you - how thoughtless of me - so I'll have to tell you. This, my friend, is a nutcracker."

He held it between thumb and forefinger like a hypnotist and allowed it to swing from side to side, all the while watching Mason's bulging, horrificd eyes as they followed its every move. "And it works," he looked at the clock on the wall, "as you will find out in about two hours from now."

"And you will be sure to find out exactly what he knows and whether he's working solo or there are others behind him?" said Kirsty, "Before you…"

"Business before pleasure, as always, Kirst." Spencer smiled without warmth. "Come along and watch if you like… unless you find that side of the business not to your taste."

"On the contrary," she was watching Mason the way his cat used to look at a mouse it was about to pounce on, flicking its tail lazily in anticipation of good times ahead. "I find the whole business of interrogation curiously… stimulating." She ran a hand through her hair and there was a flicker of pink as her tongue emerged to moisten an area of lip.

Spencer rubbed his hands together. "You won't be disappointed, my dear, I can assure you of that. It's a bit of an art and a bit of a science, is enhanced interrogation and I'll be interested to hear what your take on my modus operandi is afterwards. But… as you said earlier, we've got a few things we need to do first."

"Come on guys," said Kirsty, looking at the others. "Let's go."

"Is he going to be all right on his own?" asked Ron.

"Where's he going to go, Ron?" said Kirsty. "He's trussed up like a chicken and we're going to lock the door behind us. Check he's secure if you like." A moment later the door shut behind them and Mason heard the key turning in the lock.

Over the next half hour his muscles began to scream in protest, but he had few illusions that this was but a foretaste of what he would endure when Spencer returned. For he now knew that the leader of Storm Force 55 was a basket case, a fully paid-up member of the Institute of Raving Psychopaths, and that what Kirsty Black had stressed about the need to extract information would be forgotten once he got down to the pleasurable business of inflicting the maximum pain and humiliation on his victim.

And so, he sat and waited for the door to open and for what would follow. Could he have done anything differently, he wondered? And if he'd been given the time over again, would he still have taken the actions he did, knowing that they would lead to this outcome? In trying to answer these questions he recognises in himself an almost out of bodily detachment about the whole thing. It was as if the deaths of Mathew and Banca had extinguished the fire of life in him, leaving a burnt-out core, a husk of what had once been a vibrant human being.

He had known that discovering the identity of Matthew's murderer was unlikely to afford him the personal redemption he sought, so on that basis, the fact that he had ended up in his current predicament didn't really matter. And he *had* got close to finding out what had happened – only the accident of the door opening and interrupting the flow of Danny's verbal effluence had prevented him from doing so. On the basis that he'd given them a good run for his money, then, he couldn't say he'd have done anything differently.

He didn't fear death because he no longer cherished life, and while he was not looking forward to the pain - how could anyone - he had a shrewd feeling that once Spencer took of his gag, he would be able to goad him to the point where his rage would bring matters to a head. And that would be that. He would have shrugged his shoulders if he had been able to, instead he sat and ached and tried to clear his mind of thought as he waited for the door to open.

When it did slowly begin to open, less than an hour had passed but if Mason felt anything it was relief that his journey would soon be coming to an end. The figure who entered was not Spencer but Kirsty Black in the company of the man named Ron who had been in the room earlier.

"You still here, then?" grinned Ron. "Bet you'd love to be somewhere else." He squatted down so that his eyes were level with Mason's. "Anywhere else."

Kirsty had a carving knife in her hands. "Can you just check he's secure, Ron, and then take the tape off his mouth." She twirled the knife around. "And then you can leave me to it."

"Sure you don't want me to stay, Kirst?" Ron sounded disappointed.

"Sorry Ron - need to know and all that." She smiled flirtatiously and rested her hand on his arm. "You know how it is. Tell Spence to give me an hour and then it'll be over to him. You know what they say, good cop, bad cop." She winked. "Or in this case, bad cop, worse cop."

She waited until the door had shut, sat on a chair in front of Mason and regarded him silently for perhaps thirty seconds. Then she left the room, returning a few moments later pulling something big and box-like, which she left in the middle of the room. After that she crossed to where Mason was sitting and without slowing or breaking stride, swung an arm and dealt him a thunderous blow on the cheek with the open palm of her hand. She looked at him for a moment and then slapped him hard again, this time on the other cheek. After that she picked up the carving knife, slid it beneath one of the plastic tags that held Mason's legs in place, and jerked it so that the tag broke.

"Listen carefully Frank," she said in a voice that was low and urgent and completely unlike the one she'd been using when Ron was in the room. "I'm going to try and get you out of here, but I can only do that if you do exactly what I tell you. Is that clear?"

He must have been slow to respond because she repeated, "Can you hear me?" She shook him by the shoulders and hissed, "Are you listening to me, Frank?"

He nodded dumbly and she cut the last of the ties. "In here," she said in an urgent undertone, gesturing to the box, which turned out to be a large wheeled basket of the type used to store laundry. "Quick, they might be back at any moment."

He climbed into the basket and she pulled the lid down over his head. A moment later he felt the basket move as she began to manoeuvre it through the door and then he felt a smoother motion which told him they were in a corridor.

For perhaps thirty seconds he heard only the whoosh of wheels on floor tiles and then the basket slowed, and Mason heard a male voice saying, "Er… you all right, Miss?"

"Miss?" Kirsty's voice was charged with scorn. "Who do you think I am, your fucking teacher?"

"Sorry, Mi… Sorry." The anxiety in the voice was palpable.

"No worries, you just made me sound like some old spinster." Kirsty's voice now had a slightly less acerbic tone to it. "Can you open those French doors for me, I need to get this stuff out the back?"

Mason felt a bump as the wheels of the basket navigated a doorway and a moment later the rattling of his teeth told him they were travelling over a rougher surface, gravel perhaps, or concrete.

"Thanks," he heard Kirsty's voice again and then, for about twenty seconds, there was nothing but the sound of wheels turning and the squeaking of protesting woven matter. Then the basket stopped, and the lid swung open.

"Quick," He could hear urgency, and something else, fear perhaps, in Kirsty's voice, and he scrambled out of the basket and into the darkness as quickly as his protesting muscled would allow.

She pushed the basket into some bushes and grabbed his arm. "This way, run!"

A moment later they were tearing across the grass in the direction of a wall, which Mason surmised must be the one he had tried to get over earlier in the evening. Kirsty swerved off at a twenty-degree angle in the direction of a wooden door set in the wall, fumbled in her pocket and produced a key and a moment later they were

230

through, and she was shutting and locking the door behind them.

"Quick," she said. "Run."

"Where to?"

"Anywhere. Once they discover we're missing, the whole place will be crawling with them."

The door opened into an alley that had the wall of the house on one side and a hedge on the other. They hurtled down the alley and when the wall of the house began to fall away to the right, flew off in the other direction into what looked like a small park. The park emerged onto a main road and as they stood there, irresolute, a red London bus pulled up not five yards from them.

Acting purely on impulse Mason grabbed Kirsty's arm and seconds later they were sitting side by side on the top deck of the moving bus, slumped down in their seats so they couldn't be observed from below. Kirsty extracted a bobble hat from her pocket. "Put this on," she said, pulling a scarf out of her other pocket and tying it around her head.

Mason's chest was still heaving from their headlong flight and, as he sucked air desperately into his lungs, he found he couldn't speak.

"Did you see… what number bus it was?" Kirsty's voice was ragged from lack of oxygen.

"Yeah," he gasped, marvelling that some remote part of him seemed to have been detached enough to register the information. "It's the 38, going to Finsbury Park."

"Perfect!" She sank back in her seat.

"What…?" he began but she cut him off.

"Later, Frank. Later, when we've got to where we're going."

He opened his mouth to speak but something about her expression warned him against continuing, so he looked out of the window instead as the bus began its descent into Highgate. It is a spectacular view at the best of times and as the lights of London lay before him, twinkling into infinity, Mason reflected that it was a step up on the vision of a deranged Spencer, eyes alight at the prospect of torturing a fellow human being to death, he had been anticipating seeing around then.

He settled back and allowed the motion of the bus to sooth his jangling nerves. At some point they trundled past a sign welcoming them to the London Borough of Haringey and a little later, as they passed the well-known edifice of the Archway Tavern, Kirsty said, "Come on," and they began to descend the stairs. Although they did seem to be, for the present at least, clear and away, enough of the heightened adrenalin flow of the hunted remained with Mason for him to scan the road behind and ahead of them as they got off.

"Be a bloody miracle if they found us here," muttered Kirsty, "but there's definitely something about running for your life that makes you a bit jumpy. This way."

They began to walk down the Holloway Road in the direction of Highbury Corner and even though it was after eleven, the streets were full of people, and the proliferation of bars and restaurants

- Moroccan, Ethiopian, Persian, Greek – bore eloquent testimony to the noisy, bustling, life affirming buzz of this polyglot corner of North London. The crowds made Mason feel safer and the normality felt reassuring. *This is my London*, he thought to himself, as he looked around. *And it was Bianca's and Matthew's. This is what I'm fighting for, I suppose.*

After about ten minutes, they turned right and entered a short alley behind the façade of the main road. The buildings were all three storied and Kirsty led him up a flight of metal steps and into a first floor flat.

The living room was small but functional, with a bay window looking onto the Holloway Road, Mason went over to it and looked out.

"We're safe here, Frank," she said. "No one knows about this place."

He turned to her, not sure where to start. "I know I ought to thank you, it's just… I wondered…?" his words trailed off.

"Why." She finished the question for him. "You want to know why. Why I saved you, that is."

"That's as good a place to start as any, I suppose," he said.

She thought for a moment. "Do you remember the last thing I said to Ron, before I got rid of him?"

He looked blankly at her and she continued, "I was telling him I was going to interrogate you first and then hand you over to Spence. And the last thing I said was 'good cop, bad cop.' Remember?"

"I don't…?"

"Good *cop.*"

As she allowed the words to sink in Mason's face took on an expression of bewilderment that brought a smile to her face.

"You're saying…?" he stuttered.

She finished the sentence for him. "I'm saying I'm a cop."

XIX

"You're a *cop*?" He couldn't have been more surprised if she'd told him she was the Queen of Sheba.

"Or a police officer, I should say, if we don't want to sound like we're characters in a Tarantino film."

"You're a police officer?" It was if he was sounding the words out to check he hadn't misunderstood their meaning.

"Sit down, Frank," she said, "you're starting to sound like a parrot. Do you fancy a drink? You look as if you could use one."

He nodded and she left the room, returning a minute later with two clunky tumblers filled with whiskey. "No ice I'm afraid. Cheers anyway." She put the glass to her lips and drank, and wordlessly, like an automaton, Mason followed her.

They drank in silence and after a few minutes Mason began to feel seductive, glowing tendrils spreading out from his core and advancing in warm waves towards his extremities.

"Feeling better?" she asked, and he nodded.

"Ok, I'll start at the beginning. And obviously it goes without saying that what I'm going to tell you is confidential and not to be shared with anyone." She took a long pull from the glass and shuddered as the burning liquid hit her throat. "Although to be fair it's probably all academic now; I'd hazard a guess that, after tonight, my career with English Rose is over."

Mason smiled and she took a deep breath. "OK, to cut a long story short, I've been working under cover for the last three years, as part of a police initiative to try and infiltrate the far right. Have you heard of the NPOIU?"

Mason shook his head. "Or to give it its full title, the National Public Order Intelligence Unit. If you thought of it as a modern-day Special Branch with a bit of MI5 thrown in, you wouldn't be far wrong. Anyway, it was set up about twenty years ago with the idea of infiltrating extremist organisations seen as a threat to the state.

"Funnily enough in the early days the main threat was deemed to be from the hard left and the animal rights organisations – you might have read about some of the operations in the newspapers – while other officers went undercover to get dirt on football hooligans." She smiled wanly. "It seems like another age, doesn't it, and it was certainly a more innocent one.

"Anyway, fashions change, and as we know in recent years the threat to democracy has come more and more from the right. So, to cut a long story short, it was decided that I should join English Rose as a first step towards trying to infiltrate Storm Force 55.

"Strangely enough, young Matthew's death was one of the catalysts for me going undercover, but I never guessed at your identity and I was as surprised as anyone by what happened tonight. Funny, I'd seen pictures of you on TV, and I even attended the trial, but I never connected you with the bloke in court. Doesn't make me much of a copper, does it?" She smiled wryly.

"Anyway, I've spent the last three years digging and digging and getting closer and closer to the leadership of Storm Force 55." She shuddered "What a truly, truly, nasty collection of individuals they are - made me feel quite nostalgic for all those well-meaning Trots plotting world revolution from their bedsits. Well, I'd got pretty much all the evidence I needed, including a watertight case against Mark Spencer for the murder of Lenny Bryant, and the decision had been taken to pull me out, it was just a question of when. And then tonight's business kicked off and I thought I couldn't just leave you there to be tortured and killed, so…" she shrugged and took another swig from her drink.

Mason raised his own glass in a silent toast and took a long swallow. "Well, all I can say is I owe you my life."

236

"Yeah, whatever," she said. "Let's say you owe me a pint."

He offered her another toast. "Thanks Kirsty… if that's your real name, of course."

"It is," she smiled. "Not Kirsty Black of course, but it's one of the rules of our game - you'd be amazed how many people blew their cover in the early days by answering to the wrong name."

"Seriously though, if they'd caught you tonight, you'd have ended up getting the same treatment as me."

"I'm sure I would, but," she shrugged again, "it's part of the job, I guess. To be honest, I felt pretty bad about the Lenny Bryant business, even though there was nothing I could have done about it, so when it looked like your number was up, I thought I'd just bring my resignation forward a bit and kill two birds with one stone."

"I'm glad you did."

"Right," she said, "I've got to check in with my controller in the morning and see what he want me to do next. You OK to doss down on the sofa?"

"Fine," he said as she reached into a cupboard and threw a blanket at him. "But can I ask you one question before you go?"

"Shoot."

"Do you know who killed Matthew?"

"No," she said. "Like yourself I didn't want to be seen to be asking too many questions. Spencer definitely knows what happened, though, I saw him smirking a couple of times when it came up in conversation."

Mason grunted his disappointment. "Danny was that close to spilling the beans last night and then what happened? You and bloody Spencer walked in and he clammed up the moment he saw you."

"If I had to put my money on anyone it would be Spencer," she said. "You've seen yourself what a psycho he is. It's proving it, though."

"I'm not worried about needing to prove it," he grunted.

She looked at him. "Is that what the whole thing's been about?" she asked. "Finding whoever killed Matthew and…"

"Applying restorative justice, in the words of our glorious leader. Yeah, that's about the size of it."

"I don't blame you," she said. "Although of course I'm not speaking in my professional capacity when I say that."

She said goodnight and Mason stretched his length out on the sofa and within seconds had fallen into a deep and dreamless sleep. The quality of that sleep became more troubled as the night progressed, though, and he was increasingly tormented by images of death and torture. When he opened his eyes, he knew by the quality of the light that morning was well advanced and when he looked at his watch, it said 9.30. He could hear Kirsty moving about in the kitchen and then the door opened, and she came into the room looking fresh and scrubbed with a cup of coffee in each hand.

"There's a towel over there if you want a shower," she said. "I can't offer you a change of clothes, unfortunately."

"Do you think it'll be OK for me to go back to my flat in Neasden?" he asked as she handed him the coffee.

"Er…," she paused and then said, "I'm not sure."

She wore a perturbed look, and the aura of calm that usually occupied the space around her was absent. Something was clearly up.

"Everything OK?" he asked.

"Not exactly, no," she said. "I've had rather a strange message." She paused for a moment to gather her thoughts. "When you're operating in deep cover there are strict rules about how and when you contact your controller. It's all a bit cloak and dagger, I suppose, but it's intended to protect the person in the field. In my case, my controller never contacts me, and I am only supposed to contact him in an emergency. So anyway, last night I sent him a message asking where and when I should report back in, and an hour ago, I got this."

She held up her mobile phone and Mason saw on the screen a text message that read, *don't come in*

He looked at her and then back at the phone. "Is that it? he said, "'Don't come in?'"

"That's it… so far anyway."

"What does it mean?"

"That's what I've been spending the last hour trying to work out."

"Can you text back, or phone?"

"I've thought about that, but I don't want to compromise him if for some reason he can't speak freely. The brevity of the message alone suggests that might be the case." She frowned and looked at him. "I don't know what to do, to be honest."

Mason thought. "Do you trust your controller?"

"Absolutely."

"Is there another way you can reach him?"

At that moment her phone vibrated and a new text whirred in. Mason gave her time to read it and then looked enquiringly at her.

She held up the phone and he saw that the new message was considerably longer than the previous one:

Don't, repeat don't come in, officers from IOPC arrived this morning asking questions, suggest you stay out of sight for now until I can find out more. They don't currently have knowledge of this phone, but that may change so am going to destroy it once these messages are done, suggest you do the same. ID of your friend also known, and they will be checking his personal data so suggest destroying his mobile as well. Stay low, suggest GP0418. Any questions?

Mason's mind reeled and as he tried to make sense of the text a hundred questions raced through his mind.

"What's IOPC?" he finally asked.

"The Independent Office for Police Conduct. It's the unit that investigates serious complaints and allegations of misconduct against police officers."

"The body that polices the police?"

"Exactly. In the old days they investigated corruption, criminal wrongdoing, that sort of thing, but in the last few years, since they've come directly under Home Office control, it's almost like they're being used as a private army to root out officers who are, I don't know, unsound. The ones who think independently and challenge received wisdom and don't automatically accept everything they're told."

"Troublemakers, you mean?"

"That's certainly how the IOPC would class them. I've had two colleagues – good cops but the kind of blokes who ask uncomfortable questions and talk truth to power – pressured into leaving the service after being subjected to a campaign of harassment by the IOPC. It's almost like they were chosen as examples."

"To encourage the others, you mean?"

"Exactly, so if the IOPC is sniffing around asking questions about me it's not good news. And how the hell do they know about you, about your real identity I mean, and about your connection to me?"

Mason considered this. "God knows, I mean, until nine o'clock last night nobody knew what I was doing apart from me."

"Which means," she went on, "that in only," she looked at her watch, "thirteen hours, word of

241

what happened last night has somehow passed from an illegal terrorist organisation to the Home Office and/or the police body charged with investigating its own officers."

"And," said Mason as another thought struck him, "how have they managed to connect *you* with what happened last night? I mean, Spencer knew my identity, and obviously he'll have worked out that Kirsty Black helped me escape – I'd love to have seen his face, by the way – but he can't have known you were an undercover cop. He just can't?"

"But others will have known," she said thoughtfully. "Others on our side, I mean."

"How many people knew what you were doing?"

"I don't know, to be honest," she shrugged. "These kinds of operations are always conducted on a need-to-know basis. But the long and short of it is that as of last night nobody but Mark Spencer knew your real identity and no one but my controller and a few others in the police knew mine, so the fact that the IOPC are looking for both of us can only mean one thing."

"Someone from Storm Force 55 is in cahoots with someone senior in the police service."

"Which would mean…." she struggled for the right words, "… which would mean that there's a conspiracy between a domestic terrorist group and the force dedicated to preserving and defending the laws of the land. And the fact that they've been able to respond so quickly…"

"You mean the fact that they're looking for us already?"

She nodded. "… means that the conspiracy must go high; I mean, you're going to need more than a couple of dodgy DSs in your pocket to get the IOPC banging on doors so quickly."

At that moment her phone vibrated again, and she looked at the screen.

Any questions? read the message, *need to destroy this device asap*

She thought for a minute and then texted something and waited. Twenty seconds later a message came back and looking over her shoulder Mason was able to read both texts:

What about the tape? she had sent while the incoming message read:

Have been thinking about who it might be safe to take it to, suggest Matt Rees, Labour MP, impeccable credentials. Good luck.

"Right," said Kirsty and began to take the SIM card out of her phone. "I'm going to destroy this and I'm going to need to do the same with your phone." She put her hand out and he handed her his mobile. She started to take out the SIM card and then paused and appeared to come to a decision.

"I've had an idea," she said. "You definitely haven't used your phone since we got here, have you? Right, see you in half an hour or so. I'll bring back some breakfast."

With that she was gone, leaving Mason alone with his thoughts. About forty minutes later he heard a key in the door and a moment later she was in the room, baguette, cheese and milk in her arms.

"Can I ask where you went?" he said, "You had the look of a woman on a mission."

"I had a brainwave," she said. "I destroyed my own phone, but I thought I'd have a bit of fun with yours, so I nipped down to Kings Cross Station and switched it on." She looked at her watch. "It should be passing through Welwyn Garden City about now. I put it behind a radiator on the East Coast Line Inverness Express, and I'm hopeful that by this evening the Scottish Highlands will be full of police."

He laughed. "It'll be like *The Thirty-Nine Steps,* hordes of bobbies combing the moors in pursuit of a desperate fugitive."

She joined in his laughter. "Well, it'll keep the bastards occupied for a bit."

"Kirsty," he said when normal service had resumed. "Can I ask you a couple of questions?"

"Of course."

"When you texted, *what do I do with the tape*? what exactly is it? The tape, I mean."

"I'll come to that in a moment. What was the other question?"

"There were some letters and numbers your controller sent in his second text. What were they?"

"Well spotted. They are a code we agreed on in case we ever had to communicate in an emergency. GP0418. GP stands for Green Park, or rather a little pub behind it. O4 is the date, which in this case is the day after tomorrow."

"And let me guess, the 18 stands for 18.00 hours or six o'clock."

She laughed. "You've got it. That's where we'll meet, assuming all is well. If he thinks he's being followed he'll abort and come back two days later and then again two days later, and so on." She shrugged again. "It's nor perfect but it's a hell of a lot better than nothing and, in the present circumstances, it's all we've got."

"And the tape?" he asked.

"Ah yes," she said, "the tape. Come over to the table, I think you're going to need to be sitting down when I show you the tape."

XX

The Home Affairs Select Committee was about to go into session and Matt Rees was watching a recording of a press briefing President Trump had given the previous evening.

"The Homecoming is progressing very smoothly," intoned the president in the artificially high pitched, sing song tones he used when reading from a script, "and the U.S. government is carrying out the operation with full respect for the human rights of the people involved." He swivelled towards his leftward autocue as he read the final words.

Then he put his briefing paper down and switched to his normal mode of address. "More people than ever before are signing up to take part in the Homecoming, and the Homeland Security Force, which I created, is doing a sensational job. And when the Homecoming is complete our borders will be secure and we'll be safe from the bad people out there, the many bad people – terrorists, rapists, murderers, Muslims - who want to come here and destroy our beautiful, perfect country."

He stopped speaking and immediately hands went up.

"Yes, Mike," he said to the man from Breitbart News.

"Thank you, Mister President. Mister President, could you tell us about the funding of the Homecoming – who is going to be paying for it?"

"Thank you, Mike, that's a very good question. The Trump administration is meeting the full cost of the Homecoming, which means the people involved get to go on a trip to the land of their ancestors and they don't have to spend anything. They don't have to spend a cent. Can you believe that? We're taking them back to their homelands and it's all free. And the people going by sea are making the voyage on cruise ships, which means they're getting a free cruise thrown in. Can you believe that? They're going back to their homelands and they're getting a cruise as part of the deal and it's not costing them a cent? Isn't that perfect? Isn't that beautiful?"

"Mister President," a voice broke in. "How do you respond to Senator Romney's claim that you're funding the operation through the compulsory purchase, at knock down prices, of the houses of the people involved?"

The president glared in the direction of the voice. "I'm not interested in anything Romney's got to say. He's a loser - a very bad, rude person, and you're rude too for asking such a nasty question."

"Mister President…" began the reporter, but the President spoke over him, drowning out his words. "And it's not just that you're a stone-cold loser and a very bad, rude reporter; your paper's rude as well. *Fake news*!" The President glared at the reporter until he was sure his withering put down had had the desired effect, then turned to the representative of the Christian Broadcasting Network and said, "Yes?"

The man from the Christian Broadcasting Network had clearly been caught unprepared because a look of panic appeared on his face, and when he spoke, his Adam's apple wobbled and his words came out in a gabble. "Mister President, we invite you to join us in offering a prayer for the safety of these modern-day pilgrims, as they embark on their great journey? With your permission, Sir…?"

The President gave him a curt nod and the man from CBN put his hands together and intoned, "We offer our prayers for the success of these travellers as they embark on their journey, and we are sure you will agree, Mister President, that in the love of God and with the blessing of Jesus Christ, they will arrive safely at their destination."

"With the love of God, yes…," agreed the President, but then his face took on a stern expression and he shook his head. "I'm just not sure how much the blessing of Jesus Christ is worth."

Into the silence which greeted these words, the dropping of a single pin would have clanged like a thousand saucepan lids hitting a thousand concrete floors. Eyes began to turn towards the CBN man, but although his Adam's apple danced a wild fandango and his mouth opened and closed like a fish in a tank, no words came out.

Fortunately, the President came to his rescue. "I mean, they're going to need a winner on their side and, let's be honest," he spread his arms and shook his head sadly, "Jesus wasn't really a winner, was he? I mean, I've got nothing against the guy, but when it came down to it, well…he did get captured." His arms spread wider. "He got himself captured." He looked at the audience. "I mean, I'm right, aren't I?"

He paused, but the pool of silence into which his words were dripping was primordial in its stillness.

"I'm not saying Jesus was a bad person," went on the President after a few seconds. "Don't get me wrong, I'm not saying he was bad; I'm just saying maybe he wasn't very smart."

"Sir…," the CBN man words emerged as a strangled croak and looked as if he was about to be sick.

"I mean I understand God's position, don't get me wrong," the President continued. "You gotta

248

work with the people you've got around you, even the ones aren't up to the mark. I get that." He shook his head. "Believe me, nobody understands that better than me."

He leaned on the lectern and spread his palms. "Look, I'm not a priest. I'm not a pastor, OK? I'm just a guy with a very good…" he pointed to the side of his head. "I'm just saying," he spread his arms a final time, "I'm just saying, if it had been me out there, I'd have tried a bit harder not to get caught."

The only sound in the room was a succession of muffled thuds as the man from the Christian Broadcast Network fainted dead away and slid gently to the floor.

***

"Right," said Kirsty. "Sit down." She put the laptop on the table, booted it up and turned it round so that the screen was facing Mason. Then she plugged a memory stick in and clicked on a folder and a series of grainy moving images appeared on the screen. Although the film was of poor quality and had been shot in a dimly lit room, two figures could be seen, one lounging on a sofa and the other sitting in an easy chair at right angles to him.

"I do appreciate your taking the time to come and have this little chat," said the figure on the sofa and Mason recognised the distinctive locution of the nation's leader, Alexander Cadogan.

"No problem, Prime Minister," replied the figure in the chair, who looked vaguely familiar.

"Well, shall we cut to the chase, Mister Groves?" said the PM and Mason realised why the other figure had seemed familiar. "Or may I call you Vinnie?"

"Either is fine with me."

"So, Vinnie, the reason I've asked you here is to sound you out as to whether you might be interested in… joining forces - in the parliamentary sense, I mean - should certain events unfold?"

"Go on." Groves' answer was carefully neutral.

"Well," went on Cadogan, "as you know, the government doesn't currently command a majority in the House, and we've relied on support from some of the other parties, yours included. For which, by the way, we are very grateful." Groves acknowledged the tribute silently and the PM went on.

"If I say so myself, I think we've done a decent job in the circumstances, but as you can imagine, it's a time-consuming process trying to patch together a majority for every tiny piece of legislation, especially when what we really need is a sweeping programme to meet the needs of these unusual times."

Cadogan paused and appeared to choose his next words carefully. "It may be that in the future… in the not-too-distant future, people will begin to call for a different type of government, a government of many parties, a National

Government, if you like, to meet the challenge of these uniquely difficult times."

"It's an interesting notion, Prime Minister," said Groves. "But we've got our ears pretty close to the ground and we haven't heard any calls for a body like that."

"I agree that's been true up to now, but circumstances have changed."

"And what has caused these changes?"

The PM put the tips of his fingers together. "Events, dear boy."

Groves chuckled. "*Touché,* Prime Minister. Let's assume, then, that these *events* you talk about do create an atmosphere more congenial to the notion of a National Government, then what are we talking about – an electoral pact?"

"Not necessarily," said the PM, "I'm thinking more of a government put together from within the existing parliamentary representation - without the need for an election - a bit like the ones during the two world wars."

"Go on."

"It would need to be as representative a government as possible, of course, for us to implement the programme the country needs. And, well, I have to say, Vinnie that after your party's… stunning performance in the locals, we would naturally see your support as essential in giving the government the broad base it needs."

Mason dragged his eyes away from the screen. "Can you stop it for a moment, Kirsty?" he asked, and she pressed the pause button.

"When was this filmed?"

"Three days ago," she said.

"And who did the filming?"

"I did."

"Bloody hell. And did they know they were being filmed?"

"Of course they didn't, you pillock, why do you think it's so dark and grainy? It's because the camera was disguised as a little button on the front of my suit jacket. Notice the ever so gentle up and down movement? That's me breathing."

"Christ, you took a risk," he said

"No pain, no gain," she shrugged. "Shall we go on?" He nodded and she pressed the play button again.

"I mean," Cadogan was saying, "if the local elections were replicated nationally, English Rose would be the biggest party in Parliament, so wherever we're going with this process we've got a duty, considering the thumping mandate you received, to try and include you and your movement - otherwise it would simply not be fair to the English people."

"Talk about laying it on with a trowel," grunted Mason.

"You'll never get Labour MPs on board," Groves was saying, when he looked back at the screen.

"The majority of them, no, but on the other hand you'd be surprised what an appeal to…patriotism and duty can bring out in some people. And the ones who refuse to join us, well, I

252

think with what we're planning, they're going to become irrelevant anyway."

"So," said Groves, "just so I'm clear, what you envisage is a Government of National Unity formed from within the ranks of the current parliamentary membership?" He checked that Cadogan was nodding and continued, "How would that work in terms of the next election? Do you see this government as being a temporary one with a limited lifespan, or do you envisage it wanting to fight the next election on a ticket of national unity?"

"That's a very good question, Vinnie," said the PM. "And I can perhaps answer it best by referring you back to the Government of National Unity during the Second World War, which, if you remember, suspended elections for the duration of the emergency."

"Ah," Groves shifted in his chair. "I see. And in terms of the present emergency…?" he paused.

"Go on."

"Is it possible to estimate what its duration might be?"

"Well…" Cadogan spread his arms. "I mean… how long is a piece of string?"

The poor quality of the film made it difficult to interpret body language or read facial expression, but Mason could sense the atmosphere in the room change.

"An interesting proposition, Prime Minister," said Groves. "Very interesting in fact, but could I ask you how you see English Rose fitting into this coalition, if indeed you think there's a role for us?"

"Of course, I see a role for English Rose, Vinnie, of course I do. I mean I could hardly leave you out of our calculations after the bloody nose you gave us at the polls."

"And could you spell out what that role might be, in practical terms?"

"Well, high cabinet office, for one thing."

"How high and for how many?"

"That depends."

"On what?"

Cadogan sat back as if he was gathering his thoughts. "One scenario might involve the government, in addition to suspending elections, taking steps to… change the role of parliament. In this model, the government would consist of a Council of Ministers – duly appointed, of course – which would have full authority to introduce such legislation as was deemed necessary, while parliament's role would be to… advise."

"And consent?"

"Well, no, not really, just advise. The Council of Ministers would of course, be led by the Prime Minister, and would work in conjunction with the head of state to exercise executive power."

"The head of state being the current monarch?"

"Yes," Cadogan paused. "Well, yes and no, really." He paused again. "We had planned for all this to take place when a… natural vacancy for the position of head of state occurred, but the present incumbent, God bless her, is proving remarkably resilient, and it's possible that a noble and selfless

254

act of abdication may be required… in the national interest, of course."

"And the succession? Would the next in line be on board."

Cadogan chuckled. "Well, he might, and he mightn't. There are some who feel he may not have the… emotional resilience… the single mindedness… to accept what needs to be done in the national interest. Do you know what I mean?"

"You think he's a bit of a loose cannon?"

"Well, he's always been one of those, hasn't he? I suppose we worry that he might not be able to see the big picture."

"I can see your difficulty."

"However, there is someone else, someone close to the succession, someone from the same generation as the guy we've been talking about, a man who understands that life is inherently unequal and that some are born to… how shall I say, pick the fruit from the highest branches. A man unencumbered by the sort of doubts that plague the thinking of his br…, of the first in line; someone who, when we approached him with a broad outline of our plan, indicated a willingness to serve if called upon to - for the good of the nation, of course."

There was a period of silence while Groves digested this. "What about the MPs in this new set up?" he asked finally. "What would their role be? You understand I need something to take back to my members?"

"Of course, dear boy, of course. MPs would continue to serve in the House of Commons, but in an advisory capacity - with a very significant increase in salary, of course, to reflect their new duties. There would be natural wastage, of course, some would choose to… retire, while others unsuitable for such a role would need to be… removed and replaced by appointees, but the majority would remain in place. We think it's of crucial importance that the historic link between members of parliament and their constituents be maintained - after all, we are not anti-democratic."

"Of course, Prime Minister, that goes without saying. What about local government?"

"That's where we see your people, with their strong links in the community, playing a significant role," said the PM. "We will be looking to appoint commissioners at a local level to exercise the powers that councils have now and to maintain law and order on the ground."

"And what powers would these commissioners have, Prime Minister?"

"Emergency powers, dear boy, after all we are in an emergency."

Groves digested this for a moment and then said, "Going back to the high cabinet office you talked about, can you be a bit more specific…?"

"Of course, I can." Cadogan paused again and appeared to be considering his next words carefully, and if it was part of an act designed to crank up expectation, it appeared to be working because the tension in the room was palpable. "We are envisaging, Vinnie, that there will be opposition to the new set up, even public disorder, especially with the police already stretched to the limits and the military being held in reserve for other tasks. And that's where you come in."

"Go on." Groves was trying to look unconcerned, but his body language betrayed him.

"We've been impressed, Vinnie, with the qualities of leadership and the statesmanship you have shown during this difficult period. And we are also impressed with your Neighbourhood Security Force. Very impressed. A band of highly trained patriots, a citizen's army ready and willing to step forward and serve the country in its hour of need. A force able to respond to disorder but also ready and willing to go direct to its source and snuff it out there if that's what's needed. I don't need to tell you how important such a force might be in the days ahead.

"Vinnie, how would you like to be Home Secretary in the new Council of Ministers? The Neighbourhood Security Force would continue to report to you, as would the police forces of every county in the U.K. You would have full power to take the actions you deemed necessary to preserve public order, and your forces would also have unlimited powers to prevent possible *future* disorder."

Groves went through the motions of considering the offer. "I would need time to think about it, of course," he said finally. "And there would need to be positions of responsibility for colleagues as well – we have a lot of very talented people in English Rose."

"Of course, dear boy, of course," said Cadogan, waving a hand airily. "In that respect, everything's negotiable,"

"And you're confident that you can get the whole thing through Parliament?" said Groves.

"Absolutely. If I can cobble that first Government of National Unity together, the rest of the dominoes will fall into place. Once the new House of Commons sits it will immediately pass a new Emergency Powers Act extending the powers the government already has."

"You're sure about all this, Prime Minister?"

Cadogan nodded. "And wait for the next bit. It will then pass an Enabling Act abolishing itself as a legislative chamber and allowing the PM to rule by decree until the new Council of Ministers is set up."

"As simple as that?"

"Wouldn't be the first time a parliament has voted itself into oblivion, dear boy. And at the end of the day there's nothing to stop us, that's the beauty of having an unwritten constitution, if you remember your Bagehot. You can do anything you bloody well like as long as you've got the votes, not like across the pond where they've got to get two thirds Congressional approval to wipe their own arses."

There was silence for a moment and then Cadogan said, "So what about it, Vinnie, we'd love to have you on board?"

Groves said nothing for a moment and the PM looked at him.

"It's a great opportunity, you've got to admit, Vinnie. Home Secretary with full power on all matters relating to domestic security."

"It's very tempting Prime Minister, but if I could make so bold, there are other areas where English Rose could be of equal assistance. I'm talking specifically about the need to re-educate our population." Groves leaned forward in his seat. "Prime Minister, we have a once in a lifetime chance to change this country fundamentally for the better, but we need to rewrite the National Curriculum in schools so that coming generations understand the world in a way that will make some of the things we are going to have to do explicable to them.

"So, we'll need to teach history in a totally different way, and the social sciences, and science itself. And most importantly, our citizens' understanding of human biology will have to be radically different if they are going to make sense of the new world we're heading towards. Given all that, English Rose would want representation at the DfE and a significant input in the planning of the new curriculum."

Cadogan sat back and put the tips of his fingers together like a ham actor playing Sherlock Holmes.

"I can give you more than an input, Vinnie," he finally said. "Supposing we were to bring education under the aegis of the Home Office? That would give you overall authority to determine education policy, and it goes without saying I'd be happy to delegate the relevant ministerial appointments to yourself."

The silence grew and eventually it was the Prime Minister who spoke again.

"So, what about it, Vinnie? Home Secretary with full power on all matters relating to domestic security, plus the authority to develop a blueprint for education that will shape the minds of generations of future citizens. And remember in the new set up you could plan for the long term, secure in the knowledge that your position was not subject to the whim of the electorate."

"It's a very tempting offer, Prime Minister."

"Full power to shape the future of the country for as long as the emergency lasts."

"And remind me how long you said the emergency might last, Prime Minister."

"Well, as to that, dear boy, I mean to say, how long is a piece of string?"

XXI

The film finished there and Kirsty said, "That's where it ended, the memory was full, I think."

Mason was still staring at the screen and she waved a hand in front of his face. "Hello!"

He turned in slow motion. "But that's incredible," he stuttered. "I've never heard anything like it. I mean, they're plotting a… a…"

"A coup," she said.

"Jesus! When did you say this conversation took place?"

"Earlier in the week, Tuesday," she said.

"And there's no time frame for when it might happen?"

"No, at least not one they talked about. I think the original idea was for it to happen during the accession of a new monarch, but the present incumbent is a tough old bird, isn't she, and it looks like she's not ready to go anywhere just yet."

Mason grunted. "Her mother lived to be over a hundred, if I remember rightly."

"But I did get the impression that the clock might be ticking a bit faster."

"How did you happen to be at the meeting?"

"In my capacity as an English Rose official, so that I could corroborate Vinnie's version of events. One of the PM's posh boys was in the room as well, but he was out of shot."

"I bet you couldn't believe what you were hearing."

"That's putting it mildly. My brief was to infiltrate Storm Force and see if there were links between them and English Rose. But this? This is the story of the bloody century."

"So, what are we going to do?"

"Good question. I emailed the film to my controller and he told me to sit tight while he took advice. And now he's telling me not to come in and to destroy my mobile."

"Not great, is it?"

"I mean, basically he's telling me I'm a fugitive. And that you are too, Frank. And, as we said earlier, that's where it gets properly murky, because how come the police know your identity this morning when at nine o'clock last night Mark Spencer had only just found it out himself? It looks like there's a conspiracy out there, and if I know anything about conspiracies, it's a fucking great big one with a three-litre engine, fuel injection and alloy wheels."

"So, what do we do now?" he returned to his earlier question.

"I'll come to that in a minute. First I want to show you something else." She started to fiddle with the laptop. "One night a few months ago Vinnie got really pissed and took this bit of paper out of his pocket and started waving it about and going on about being able to see into the future. He wouldn't let the rest of us see it, just kept winking and tapping his nose and mumbling something about 'Area 51.' Anyway, he put it back into his jacket and later when he went for a piss, I took it out and photographed it on my mobile."

"Bloody, hell, that was brave," said Mason

"That's what I was there for, Frank," she shrugged. "Anyway, have a look at it." She turned the computer screen towards him, and he saw what appeared to be a black and white aerial shot, very grainy, of a cuboid shaped hole in the ground. The ground itself was so flat and featureless that it was impossible to hazard any guess as to scale.

"So, what is it?" he asked.

262

"What does it look like to you?"

"A hole."

She rolled her eyes. "No shit, Sherlock!"

"OK," he inspected the photo minutely. "Well, it's definitely a hole in the ground, and it's regular, and about twice as long as it's wide. Impossible to say how deep it is because you can't see the bottom." He considered it further. "Looks like it's in a desert, or some similar environment, and because it's so barren and featureless, it's hard to say how big it is because there's nothing to compare it with." He thought again for a moment. "You said Groves mentioned Area 51, isn't that the place where the US government is supposed to have some kind of secret facility, out in New Mexico or Arizona or somewhere?"

"Nevada," she said.

"OK, Nevada." He turned the screen away from him. "Right, it's hole in the ground, maybe in Nevada, that's the best I can do."

She minimized the photo and brought up another one, almost identical except that a small section in the bottom left corner had been magnified. "What do you see now?"

The magnified section was so pixelated that it was hard to make out anything other than a blurry 3D shape. He screwed his eyes up and moved his head to give him a different perspective but was eventually forced to shake his head. "No idea."

"Our lab kept magnifying it until they were able to see what the dot was."

"And?"

"It's a digger."

"A digger?"

"Or to be more precise, an excavator. Or to be completely accurate, it's a CAT 6090, the world's biggest excavator, so big it's normally only used in mining, so big it's bucket is over 50 metres long."

"That dot?"

"That dot."

"But that would mean…" he began.

"That would mean," she said, "that the hole in the ground is a big one. A very big one."

"How big?"

"Well," she said. "Using the excavator for scale our lab was able to calculate the dimensions of the hole. And according to them the hole is three miles long by a mile and a half wide… give or take a few hundred yards."

"Three miles?"

"Give or take."

"Jesus."

"They can't estimate the depth of the hole because the bottom isn't visible in the photo, but you can see for yourself how deep it must be."

Mason tried to take in the scale of it all. "Why?" he said eventually, stumbling over his words. "Why would someone want to build a massive hole - a hole three miles long - in the middle of nowhere?"

"And why," asked Kirsty, "would a hole in the desert five thousand miles away cause Vinnie

Groves to nearly wet himself with excitement and talk about seeing into the future?"

There was an interminable silence and then Mason said, "I don't even want to go there."

"Me neither. The main thing is to get the film and the photo into the hands of the right people."

"But who? Who are the right people? I mean, who could we trust not to simply bury whatever we gave them?"

"Good question. We already know the Met has been compromised, which probably means the Home Office has been as well."

"The newspapers?" he suggested.

"You're having a laugh, aren't you? With a few honourable exceptions they've all gone down the trail News International blazed for them years ago, and for those that haven't, the new Editors Law doesn't leave them any wriggle room."

"What about the BBC?"

"Same thing really. Depending who you approached you might be lucky, or… on the other hand…" her voice trailed off. "Be a bit like playing Russian roulette, wouldn't it?"

"When you say *a bit like* Russian roulette, it's more than that for or us, isn't it?"

"You're absolutely right Frank. It's a life and death decision for us, and maybe for the country as well.

"I'm more worried about us than the country at the moment, if I'm honest."

She chuckled. "You and me both, mate, so we'd just better make sure, for our sakes and the country's – in that order if you like – that we get it right."

"What about the Labour MP - Matt Rees was it - that your controller talked about in his final text?"

"Yeah, I've been thinking about that. I've seen him on TV, and he comes across as a decent, straight talking guy, the sort of MP who's there because he wants to represent his constituents rather than just climb the greasy pole to power. I can't think of anyone else, can you?"

Racking his brains Mason suddenly thought of Raj Kumar. "Do you remember the night I knifed that Asian bloke after the meeting in Bayswater?" he said and proceeded to fill Kirsty in on the Indian blogger and how he had put his own safety at risk to aid Mason's undercover infiltration.

"Well, you're a dark horse, Frank Brown, or Mason, or whatever your name is," she laughed. "We're the ones who're supposed to pull stunts like that. If we get out of this alive, I'll recommend you for undercover work with the NPOIU."

"All right, but only if it's something less dangerous than this, like Columbian drug cartels."

She laughed. "No harm in calling this Kumar up, I suppose. Have you got a phone number for him?"

He nodded and she pulled a cheap mobile out of her pocket. "I got one of these for each of us when I was out - pay as you go so no contract and therefore no trail." As she handed it to him their hands touched for a second and he noticed how long and slender her fingers were.

He put the SIM card in, dialled and a moment later he heard Kumar's voice on the line.

"Raj, it's Frank," he said. "Frank Mason. Listen I'm going to get straight to the point; I'm in a bit of a tricky situation and I would appreciate any advice you might be able to give me. Just wondered whether you might be free to meet up today?"

"On the mezzanine floor?"

"Perfect."

"What time?"

Mason looked at his watch. "About an hour?"

"No worries. See you there, and listen mate, don't worry, whatever it is, I'm sure if we put our heads together, we can sort it out."

Putting the phone down, Mason felt a surge of relief. He had forgotten how much he had come to rely on Kumar, and the simple common sense of his words left him with a renewed feeling of optimism.

"He's going to meet me at Euston Station in an hour. We've met there before and it's a pretty safe rendezvous, I'd say."

"Keep your bobble hat on," she said. "Just in case CCTV has been alerted. And wear these," she pulled a pair of Dierdre Barlow style glasses out of a drawer. "They're plain glass so they won't interfere with your vision."

He put them on, and she looked at him appraisingly. "They might interfere with your pulling power, though."

He laughed and looked at his watch. "I've just got time to finish that baguette and then I'll be off."

***

The Home Affairs Select Committee had taken more evidence from Horace Carstairs, and the civil servant had treated the exercise as a minor inconvenience, swatting away the questions with the disdain a magistrate in a remote corner of India might have reserved for some persistent flies. Rees had hoped that Archie Shore might have been able to suggest some new lines he could pursue, but he hadn't heard from him by the time the committee met and, in the end, Carstairs had fielded his questions with ease. It was afterwards that Rees had got a message from Archie suggesting they meet and by early afternoon they were sitting in their usual seats in The Buckingham Arms.

"Sorry I couldn't get anything to you earlier," said Archie over the first bottle of Becks. "But with the old buffer out of the way there was a chance for me and my mate to do some digging."

"What's he like, Carstairs – to work for, I mean?"

Shore thought for a minute and took a swig of Becks. "Well, I suppose he's living proof that Wodehouse drew from life; Bertie Wooster would have described him as a 'downy old bird.'"

He took another drink. "Wears tweeds and brogues, walks about carrying a stick with a bone handle, and talks with a silly ass accent, but he's as sharp as a tack and doesn't miss a trick. There's something about him though, that's always made me feel uneasy; sort of bloke you could imagine defiling a housemaid or horsewhipping a groom."

"Not the kind of man to whistle blow out of a sense of duty and fair play, then?"

"No, I think his type usually contrive to swim in whichever direction the tide happens to be going."

"What's it like over there? Still got that feeling there's something funny going on?"

"All those new guys from the MOD haven't gone anywhere, and, as I said, there's a feeling around that some people have access to an inner circle of knowledge that the rest of us aren't privy to."

"What was it that you wanted to tell me about?"

"Well," Shore took a sip of his beer. "Me and my mate were surfing around in some areas of the system we're not supposed to have access to, and we came across something really odd. There's this tract of land on Salisbury Plain - you know where the MOD has its restricted facilities – that's been transferred over to Home Office control. Nothing sinister about that except that for some reason the record of the transfer has been placed in the restricted area of the system.

"And then, in the same part of the network, we found a proposal to build a major spur from the main railway line into the area, with compulsory purchases approved and properties appropriated and all the rest of it. And there were plans to build what looked like huts or barracks, hundreds of them."

Rees whistled. "That lot would cost a pretty penny."

"And that's not all," said Archie. "In the same folder there were what looked like train timetables. Detailed ones. And when I say detailed, I mean incredibly detailed, there were pages and pages of them. They weren't dated, but they seemed to show, in minute detail, the movement of hundreds of thousands, perhaps millions, of what were referred to as "units" into the area."

Rees had been giving his undivided attention to the story and now he took a sip from his Becks and said, "Interesting that it all seems to have been hidden from view."

"Isn't it!"

"I'm sure it's occurred to you already, Archie," Rees spoke slowly. "But didn't the government talk about… facilities, where the OCCD's, the poor bastards scheduled for repatriation, were going to be housed ahead of the deportations?"

"That was my initial thought, yes."

"And I suppose they've got to house them somewhere. I mean, they've not tried to hide the fact that that's what they're planning to do."

"That's all fine, but there's two things that don't add up. If this is just going to be a temporary holding facility for people on their way out of the county, I mean."

"Go on."

"In the first place, there are thousands, maybe millions more people scheduled to come into the area than there is accommodation for them, even if all the huts detailed in the plans were built before anyone arrived."

Rees raised his eyebrows carefully. "And what's the other thing?"

"The timetables."

"What about them?"

"They've got something missing."

"What?"

"They only go one way."

"Sorry, Archie," said Rees, "I'm not sure what you mean?"

Shore took a deep breath. "They only go in one direction, Matt. All those *units,* hundreds of thousands, perhaps millions of them, far too many to be housed in the space available, go in."

He paused and exhaled slowly. "But nothing goes the other way. Nothing goes out."

XXII

Mason left for his appointment with Raj with time to spare. Kirsty had given him a peck on the cheek as he left and told him to be careful.

"What are you going to do while I'm gone?" he asked.

"Nothing much I can do except keep my head down and wait for you to come back. We have no idea how far this conspiracy extends, and London may be crawling with coppers on the lookout for us, not to mention every right-wing fanatic in the capital."

"And we're definitely safe here?

"Absolutely – a friend of mine asked me to look after it for her while she went travelling for a year, and nobody else knows about it. But there will be people looking for us out there, so, keep your head down and don't do anything to draw attention to yourself."

"At least we've got the mobiles," he said. "I'll give you a ring afterwards to let you know what Raj says."

In the end he took the Piccadilly line from Holloway Road to Kings Cross and walked down the Euston Road, arriving at Euston Station five minutes ahead of the meeting time. He took his seat at the café, expecting the usual delay before Raj appeared, but in only a couple of minutes he saw a familiar figure approaching.

They shook hands and Mason filled his friend in on the events leading up to his capture.

"Shit," said Raj when he had finished. "What were the odds of Danny turning up in the very room you were in?"

"I nearly got away with it. He knew he recognised me from somewhere and you could almost see his brain frying as he tried to work it out."

Raj laughed. "Not the brightest, is he, our Danny?"

"I feel a bit sorry for him, to be honest," said Mason. "He's desperate to be part of something and to be accepted by the people he sees as authority figures; in another life he might have made a good sea scout."

When he came to the bit about how he had escaped, Mason swore Raj to secrecy, especially in relation to Kirsty's real identity. "Bloody hell, she's a brave one and no mistake," the blogger whistled when he'd finished.

"She certainly is. I owe my life to her. But it's all going to count for nothing if we end up getting wasted by Storm Force or renegade coppers."

"Absolutely," said Raj.

"So, what do you think we should do?"

"Well, I've been thinking about that." He paused for a moment. "I'd be happy to break the story on my blog, but to be really effective it's got to be broadcast on a platform that reaches as wide an audience as possible. And that's where I think your girl's handler is bang on the money. Matt Rees has impeccable credentials in terms of his decency and integrity, and if he broke the story, it would carry much more weight than if it was broadcast by people who are unknown to the public or by an obscure blogger like me."

"I wonder how we can get to him?" mused Mason.

"Well, I just might be able to help you there," said Kumar. "I've met him a few times – you'd be surprised how small the world of London

273

progressive politics is – and I've got his mobile number."

"That's brilliant," said Mason. "I was wondering how we'd get to him if we did decide he was the guy for us; I imagine the average MP must be on the end of a lot of unsolicited traffic from cranks of one kind or another."

"Leave it to me," said Kumar. "I'll try and set up a meet as soon as possible."

"Cheers mate, I can't thank you enough."

"No problem."

"The one thing we've got to be careful about," said Mason, "is where we meet him. Anywhere around Westminster will be crawling with people, and that's without the ones who'll already be looking for us."

"You're absolutely right," said Kumar. He considered for a minute and said, "A relative of mine has got a house that's empty in a village on the edge of London. It's a sleepy little place not far from where the M25 and M40 intersect and would be perfect for the kind of meet we're looking at. When would be a good time for you guys?"

"Funnily enough, we haven't got a lot on at the moment," said Mason. "The sooner the better, to be honest – tomorrow if it's doable."

"I'll get on the case and try and set it up for tomorrow afternoon," said Kumar. "Give me a ring at about seven o'clock. Right, I'll go first and then you follow in five minutes." He jumped up, shook hands and was gone, and a moment later Mason was watching him weave through the throng of travellers on the concourse below.

On exiting the tube at Holloway Road, Mason passed under a large advertising hoarding, on which a gleaming new poster had just been pasted. Its headline screamed: YOUR FACE IS YOUR PASSPORT, and under the text was a head and shoulder shot in soft focus of a smiling young woman with milky white skin and cheeks of burnished pink. It was an image straight from an advertising campaign of the nineteen fifties and the only thing missing was the mug of Ovaltine. Below the picture was some text: *If you are an OCCD (Overseas Citizen currently Domiciled) you must register with your local authority by June 30th or you will be arrested, interned and deported. By order of Her Majesty's Government*. There were details of how to register at the bottom of the page.

He returned to the flat and filled Kirsty in on the meeting, and with several hours to spare before he was due to call Raj, they decided to open a bottle of wine.

"Have you worked out what we're going to say to this Rees bloke?" Mason asked once they were settled, Kirsty on the sofa and he at the table.

"Well, we've got the film, that should be enough on its own. And don't forget the photo of the hole in the desert. And we've got the fact that Vinnie Groves is mobilising a secret army equipped with thousands of semi-automatic assault weapons from North Korea to go out and kill people."

Mason smiled. "Put like that, I can see why it might make him sit up."

"And that our democratically elected Prime Minister," went on Kirsty who had evidently built up a head of steam, "is planning to suspend parliament and turn the country into a fascist dictatorship based on the kind of crude, racially driven pseudo-science that inspired the Nazis."

"All right, all right, you've convinced me," said Mason, hands up in a gesture of surrender. "And I'm sure you'll convince him. I didn't realize you felt quite so passionately about it."

"Three years undercover, Frank," she said. "Three years having to listen people like Vinnie Groves and Mark Spencer, pretending to laugh at their jokes and agree with the disgusting things they said, pretending I was as disgusting as them. It made me feel physically unclean in the end. Sometimes I used to feel so dirty I'd try to wash it off - actually wash it off, in the shower - but I never could. Didn't you feel the same, I mean you were working undercover as well?"

"I did," he said, and in truth there had been times when he felt he was in danger of drowning in the cesspit he had immersed himself in. "I didn't have to do it for as long as you did, though, so I don't blame you for sounding off."

"Mark Spencer was the worst," she shuddered as she spoke. "I mean, don't get me wrong, there was a lot of competition, but he was out there on his own. Sometimes when I sat next to him, I could feel my flesh actually crawling."

"He's clinically mad, if you ask me. Were you there the night be beat some bloke half to death because the guy made a comment about him being gay?"

"No, but I heard about it. I think he's got a problem with his sexual identity." She paused and thought for a moment. "Not that it can be easy being gay in an organisation like Storm Force."

Mason had been thinking the same thing himself. In the steadily darkening, increasingly illiberal world they lived in, sexual identity was one area where society appeared to be continuing to move into the light. Mason remembered overhearing Matthew and some of his friends having a discussion one afternoon - it turned out that one of them had an older brother who was gay and another a sister - and the way the kids had talked about the whole thing so matter-of-factly, with none of the baggage that previous generations would have brought to the conversation, had been genuinely heartening.

None of that would have applied to Storm Force, though. It was an organisation in which the attitudes and prejudices of the previous century were deeply rooted, and Mason had heard discriminatory language about sexuality used as casually and with as much frequency as it was about race and colour. For someone like Spencer, whose sense of himself was likely to have been bound up in traditional notions of masculinity and male strength, being gay couldn't have been easy.

"Yeah," nodded Kirsty when he shared this thought with her. "He's got this thing about having to appear macho, about being a hard man. Everyone knew about his sexual orientation, but apart from Vinnie, no one ever dared bring it up. Vinnie used to tease him about it, in a gentle way, and Spencer would take it from him, after a fashion. 'I'm not gay, though, Vin, I'm not *gay*,' he'd say - it was if he had a horror of what "gayness" in its wider sense - as a lifestyle choice, I mean - might insinuate about him.

"He had this thing about the books that would come out in the future, the ones that would tell the story of the movement and celebrate the lives of its leaders. He wanted to be sure his place in the pantheon of heroes was secure. 'When those books are written, Vin,' he'd say when he was pissed, 'when those books are written, I want them to say, *Frank Spencer was a heterosexual who happened to sleep with men.*'"

"Bloody hell!" said Mason

"Vinnie was always good with him. He'd sooth his ego, 'Yes, Spence, of course, Spence,' but I don't know how he kept a straight face. Well, I do, I suppose, if I'm honest; like the rest of us he knew he was dealing with a psychopath and that one wrong word - malign or innocent, it didn't matter which - might tip him over the edge, and then we'd all have been in trouble."

"Did you ever find out who the Chameleon was?" asked Mason, remembering the conversation in the house in Highgate.

"No, they were both very secretive about his identity, Groves and Spencer, I mean. The only thing they'd say was that there was another big beast of the movement out there somewhere and that he'd emerge from the shadows at a time of his own choosing."

"Anyway, let's hope we've seen the last of them," said Mason.

"Like you, I wouldn't lose any sleep if I never clapped eyes on any of them again. But if we did," she started to rummage in a box, "it would be no harm to have something to fight back with, something that might give us an edge."

She held up what looked like a black torch, about eight or nine inches in length. "Any idea what this is?"

Mason inspected it for a moment. "It looks a bit like a torch to me, Kirst."

"It does look a bit like a torch, Frank," she said. "Congratulations on your powers of observation."

She continued to twirl it around in her fingers until eventually he shrugged and said, "What are you planning to do, shine it in their eyes and hope they suddenly see the light?"

She laughed and Mason noticed for the first time how small, white and even her teeth were.

"As I said, it does look like a torch," she said, "but it's actually something quite different."

"All right," he held up his hands in mock surrender. "If it's not a torch, what is it?"

"This little device, innocent as it looks, delivers an electrical charge powerful enough to totally immobilize – maybe even kill - a fourteen stone man."

He looked at it for a moment. "Like a taser?"

"Almost exactly like a taser." She passed it across to him and as he examined it, she began to explain.

"One of the problems when you go undercover is that if you carry a weapon, all it takes is for someone to discover it and your cover's blown. And," she went on, "depending on where you are, that could be enough to cost you your life. But at the same time when you're working undercover, you're desperate - psychologically if for no other reason - to have something up your sleeve that the opposition doesn't know about, something you can use if you're in real trouble. So, with that in mind, one of my colleagues in the NPOIU started to think, and then he went way and did a bit of tinkering - all unofficially like – and eventually he came back gave me a couple of these."

She reached out her hand and Mason passed the device back to her. "It works on the same principal as a taser, but someone working undercover carrying a taser would be putting themselves at much at risk as if they were concealing a gun, so, what my clever colleague – a bit like 'C' in the James Bond movies, only he does it in his spare time – came up with was this.

"It looks like a simple torch but has the power of a taser. He got the idea from one of the stun guns they have in America; they're designed for use against muggers and one of them is called a Sabre and looks exactly like a torch. Now, normal stun guns don't work in the same way as a taser; they don't transmit a current along wires, but need to be applied directly onto the body, and they haven't got as much stopping power.

"A taser, as I said, operates in a different way; when it's fired two thin wires carry the current at high speed towards the victim and embed themselves in his body. That's why, unlike a stun gun, a taser can be fired from several feet away and why it delivers a much more powerful current. And this is what my clever colleague came up with for me." She held the device up. "A taser and stun gun hybrid that combines the best features of both. Isn't it beautiful, a unique, completely bespoke weapon that I can carry about without it raising the slightest suspicion?"

"Very ingenious," said Mason.

"And that's not all," she said. "He did something to the battery that enabled it to carry a much higher charge than normal tasers. He said the science was complicated, but that if I thought of it as being like fitting a Saturn V rocket engine into a Mini Cooper chassis, I wouldn't be far wrong."

"So, the punch it packs is greater than a normal taser." said Mason. "How much greater?"

"Well," she said, "we never actually fired it into anything living, but he estimated that it would

281

incapacitate the average adult completely and might even prove fatal."

"Did you want it to be fatal?"

"That's what I asked him, and he said, with the kind of people I was dealing with, he presumed I would."

"Yeah," said Mason. "Good point."

She laughed. "So, we left it at that."

At seven o'clock Mason phoned Kumar and a moment later he heard the familiar voice.

"Hi Raj, it's Frank," he said

"Hi mate," came the reply. "I spoke to Rees today."

"What did you tell him?"

"I told him that you and Kirsty had been working undercover inside English Rose but that you'd been rumbled. I also told him you had reason to believe that elements within the police force and possibly within the Home Office were involved in some sort of conspiracy and that they were looking for you and that consequently you were now in fear of your lives."

"And what did he say to that?"

"Something to the effect that anyone who was at war with Vinny Groves could count on his support; *my enemy's enemy is my friend* was I think the phrase he used."

"And did you mention the film."

"I told him you were sitting on the story of the century and when he asked me to elaborate, I said that you had proof - incontrovertible proof – that Cadogan and Vinnie Groves were involved in a conspiracy to bring down Parliament and turn the country into a police state."

"And what did he say to that."

"To say he was interested was putting it mildly - I could almost hear him rubbing his hands."

"And did he agree to meet us?"

"Yeah, it's all set for three o'clock tomorrow afternoon."

"Brilliant." Mason quickly relayed the information to Kirsty and then asked, "Where?"

"A little place called Denham, on the Middlesex / Bucks border, just off the M40, so dead easy to get to. Will you be driving? No? Get the train from Marylebone, then, it takes about half an hour. It's a quiet little place with lots of big houses set back from the road. I'll meet you there and let you in and then I'll let you get on with it." He gave Mason the address and ended the call.

XXIII

Mason spent another night on Kirsty's sofa and this time his sleep was more restful. He awoke to the reflection that while the prospect of death by slow torture undoubtedly left the psyche a bit skittery, time was a great healer. On this comforting note he greeted Kirsty warmly when she emerged, tousle haired, from the shower room.

"You sound a bit chirpier this morning," she said.

"Might be something to do with the fact that I didn't spend the whole night dreaming about Mark Spencer and his nutcracker."

She laughed. "Yeah, I had a better night as well."

She spent the morning working on her computer while he read, and after finishing off the baguette from the day before they started to think about the upcoming meeting.

"I'll take my PC so that we can play Rees the film," she said, "And I've got another copy for him on a memory stick.

"What about the, er... torches?" he asked.

She picked one of the devices up. "My colleague said that if I needed to use it in a hurry, there probably wouldn't be time to get it out of a bag or a pocket or whatever, so I should deploy it like this." She rolled the sleeve of her suit jacket up and laid the torch against the skin on the underside of her right forearm.

"You attach it with tape and then you can "aim" your arm in any direction you like. To fire it you release the safety catch," she showed him, "and then if you bring your other hand across and press the button - you can even do it through cloth – off go the wires.

"The one thing you've got to remember is to make sure the hand of the arm it's strapped to isn't in the path of the wires when you press the button, otherwise you'll be firing a potentially lethal dose of electricity into yourself from about an inch away - not wise. So just make sure you lift the palm of your hand out of the way – think of those camp little Nazi salutes Hitler used to give when he was reviewing troops. Quite appropriate really."

Mason marched around the room lifting his hand up and down and it was comically reminiscent of the Fuhrer strutting self-importantly around a parade ground. "Just as well Mark Spencer can't see me now," he said.

She laughed. "If he never sees us again it'll still be too soon for me."

At three o'clock they headed off down the Holloway Road, Mason with his bobble hat pulled own over his eyes and Kirsty with her scarf strategically positioned. Instead of getting a tube at Holloway Road Station they continued southwards towards Highbury Corner, passing on their way several more billboards that proclaimed, YOUR FACE IS YOUR PASSPORT.

Under one of the billboards a news vendor was selling copies of *The Sun*. The front page contained an artist's impression of sinister looking Asiatic types with sharp, pointed teeth swimming towards an outline of the English coast, while above it a headline screamed, THEY'RE COMING!

They caught a Victoria Line tube from Highbury and Islington, and eventually took an overground train from Marylebone to Denham. The part of the village that Raj had directed them to - main street with combined post office / general store, village green with thousand-year-old oak tree and mock rustic pub - was a picture postcard representation of England straight from the Vinnie Groves school of ersatz nostalgia.

The house, when they found it, was called The Gables and stood in its own grounds, with the doorway set well back from the street. As they walked up the path the door opened and Raj beckoned them inside, directing them down a wide carpeted corridor into a room straight from the pages of *Country Life*. The stocky, balding man with thick rimmed spectacles who turned to face them appeared to be in his forties and an air of restless, tightly coiled energy seemed to cloak him.

"Matt Rees, meet Kirsty Black and Frank Mason," said Raj and a moment later Mason's hand was seized in a grip of iron and he found himself the object of a piercing, unflinching gaze.

"Pleased to meet you," said Rees. "By the sounds of it, you've been through the mill," he included them both in his words, "and that's putting it mildly."

"I'll let you guys get on," said Kumar.

"Sure you don't want to stay, Raj?" asked Rees.

Kumar shook his head. "Probably best to keep things on a need-to-know basis for the time being. I've got a few things to do in the locality, so if one of you gives me a ring on my mobile when you're finished, I'll come back and lock up."

He left and Kirsty got straight down to business. "I think the best thing we can do is play you what we've got," she said, pointing to the computer. "Anyone see a socket?"

She plugged the laptop in, and Rees started to watch the film. After a couple of minutes, he pressed the pause button, looked up and said tersely, "When did this meeting take place?"

"Last Tuesday," answered Kirsty.

"And who was doing the filming?"

"Me with a concealed camera."

"And apart from you was there anyone else in the room?"

"Someone from Cadogan's office. I don't know his name."

Rees returned to his scrutiny of the film and watched the rest of it in silence. At the end he sat for a few moments with a hand cradling his forehead and then stood up and started to pace around the room. "How many people know about this film?" he asked eventually.

"Just the two of us," said Kirsty. "And my controller at the NPOIU. And of course, Raj knows about it, but he hasn't watched it yet."

Rees continued to pace. "I'm trying to decide how best we might use the film. In the old days it wouldn't have been a problem, I could have run it around to the nearest BBC office, or to ITN news, or Channel Four, or any of the national dailies or a hundred other news agencies, and that would have been that. Resignation of both parties followed by prosecution on conspiracy charges, certain disgrace, probable imprisonment and end of career for both men. But," he searched for the right words. "we don't live in straightforward times anymore, do we?"

"But isn't it blindingly obvious they're planning a coup?" said Kirsty. "I mean, they're condemned by their own words, surely?"

"Well, again, I'd have said 'Yes' in any other times than the ones we live in now. But the truth has become such a… a moveable feast these days that we can't be sure about anything anymore."

"But," said Kirsty, "to go back to what I said, don't their own words condemn them so absolutely that if the meeting was broadcast, they wouldn't have a leg to stand on?"

"Up to a point," answered Rees. "I agree that if the film went out without them having time to rebut it, the effect would be devastating for them. But anything less than that and they'd probably be able to muddy the waters enough to get away with it. I know what you're going to say," he looked at Kirsty. "That they've condemned themselves out of their own mouths and that there's no room for doubt. And I would have agreed with you in the old days, but we're not in the old days anymore, not since Trump.

"The first thing they'd do is question the authenticity of the film; they'd say it was fake – *fake news!* – and that it was cobbled together by corrupt elements within the news media. Then they'd say it was entrapment, that they were led into saying things they didn't really believe in, and then they'd find some obscure law that suggests their rights were being infringed by illegal filming, and after that they'd say that their words were being deliberately taken out of context. And then they'd wrap the whole thing up by reminding us, if we'd forgotten, that you can't trust the liberal media and that even if it did look damning, the whole thing was probably a hoax carried out by the same people who forged Obama's U.S. passport and faked the moon landings."

"Even though we have the whole thing on film in their own words?"

"Even though we have the whole thing on film in their own words. Just take your mind back to Trump; how many times did we have it all in *his* own words? How many times did he say ridiculous things in interviews and in press briefings, outright lies that were broadcast directly to millions of people without any kind of media filter, and yet his people were able to muddy the waters so successfully afterwards that we all began to doubt the evidence of our own eyes and ears?"

"What about using the internet?" asked Mason. "To get the story out, I mean. No one controls that, do they?"

"The internet, in my opinion, is an overrated medium," grunted Rees. "Certainly in terms of it being a trusty sword with which a lone seeker after truth can change the world."

"But there isn't a way government can censor it, am I right?" asked Mason

"That is still just about true, as we speak," said Rees, "but our government is looking very closely at a piece of legislation that was passed in Singapore years ago called The Prevention of Falsehood and Manipulation Act, which allowed the government to take action against anything that they felt challenged their policies. It gave them carte blanche to close sites they didn't like and governments around the world have been watching them and taking note ever since."

He stopped for a moment and gathered his thoughts. "Think of the impact of the internet as a bit like the arrival of print. When Gutenberg produced his first printing press, the Establishment, or whatever it called itself back then, was terrified that cheap printed matter would stir up the masses and unleash a revolution that would destroy the established order. And I'm not saying it had no effect – the Reformation probably wouldn't have happened the way it did without the new technology – but once things had settled down, who were the people who generated most of the printed material and benefited most from it? The people who already had power and had the money to afford the expenditure.

"And I think you'll find the internet will develop in the same way. Yes, we can all tweet our opinions or post our little clips on YouTube, but the weight of material generated by the people with power and money will always swamp the stuff produced by the little man. I mean, governments and big corporations are already producing algorithms that target specific messages at individual users, and they're probably doing other stuff so complicated that we wouldn't understand it even if they explained it to us."

"I'm starting to see what you mean," said Mason.

"And if the high-tech stuff doesn't work you can simply go back to boots on the ground. They say the Chinese government employs millions of its own citizens to post material on the internet supporting state policy, and that for each item posted individuals receive a tiny payment. They call them the fifty-cent army."

Mason and Kirsty exchanged looks of frustration.

"Sorry to bang on," said Rees, "but we've got to get this right and I think the internet on its own is too risky."

"What then," said Kirsty.

"I don't know." Rees recommenced his relentless pacing. "And whatever we do decide to do, time is of the essence, because once the coup has actually happened, we can probably forget the whole thing."

They looked expectantly at him and he smiled. "You look exactly like a couple of kids who've got themselves into a scrape and are handing the whole thing over to Daddy, secure in the knowledge that he'll sort it out for them."

Mason chuckled and Rees gave him a wry smile and said, "I wish I shared your confidence in me." He bowed his head in thought once more. "I do have a contact at the BBC," he said, eventually, breaking the silence. "You know, one of those old-school Reithian types…"

He broke off as they heard the sound of the front door closing.

"That'll be Raj," said Mason.

At that moment the door of the room opened, and into the room walked not Raj Kumar but Ron the Storm Force skinhead, carrying a gun in one hand and a length of rope in the other.

And before they'd had a chance to process, or even properly register this, another man walked in behind him and they saw that it was Mark Spencer and that he was cradling a North Korean assault rifle in his arms.

XXIV

The first emotion Mason registered was surprise - that mild sense of dislocation one experiences when a familiar person like a work colleague is chanced upon in an unfamiliar setting like the supermarket - and his lips were already forming the words, "Hello Mark," when the reality of what he was seeing crashed in on him. Perhaps it was the smile on Spencer's face as he said, "Well, isn't this nice," perhaps it was the snicker that issued from Ron in response, or maybe it was Kirsty's stifled scream, but the spell was suddenly well and truly broken.

It was Rees whose reaction was the most natural. "Sorry, who…?" he began but he didn't have a chance to finish his words.

"Shut the fuck up, Trotsky," said Spencer and jabbed him hard in the chest with the assault rifle.

As he did so Ron covered the others with his pistol. "Hello Kirsty," he said with a wink. "Been hoping we'd have a chance to catch up."

"Ron was a bit disappointed with you the other night." Spencer had moved into Kirsty's intimate personal space and his face was only inches from hers. "And I've given him permission to administer whatever… punishment he sees fit. Quite inventive is our Ron, but I won't spoil the surprise."

"Always did have a soft spot for you, Kirst." Ron winked again and licked his lips. "And I'm going to enjoy showing you the error of your ways."

"How did you find us?" she said dully.

"Doesn't matter how we found you," Spencer laughed. "Wasn't hard though – bunch of fucking amateurs."

He moved towards Mason until he was up close and personal. "You've gone a bit quiet, Frank, what's up, cat got your tongue?" he said, and Mason felt a spray of warm spittle hit his chin. "A bit like Ron, I've been thinking about what methods of correction I might employ, and I've quite enjoyed the process, to be honest."

As Spencer leaned closer, Mason noticed a small badge on the lapel of his jacket and inspecting it from a few inches away he saw that it was a circular metallic disc with the inscription, *West Ham United: The Irons*, running around the edge. An earlier conversation niggled at his memory and then he remembered the message that had been left on Mathew's body and Raj's suggestion that there might be a link with the West Ham Inter City Firm. His eyes travelled slowly up until they were looking straight into Spencer's and at that moment, in a blinding moment of revelation, he realised that it must have been Spencer who had murdered Mathew.

Rees hadn't spoken since he'd been poked in the chest with the rifle. "Who are these people?" he asked finally.

"Who are these people?" mimicked Spencer in a high falsetto. "You'll find out soon enough, you Marxist cunt."

"I'll tell you who they are, Matt." Mason, the blood pounding in his ears, turned to Rees. "That one over there," he pointed at Ron, "he's just pondlife, so no need to worry about him. But this one, the one in front of me, well, he's a suitable case for treatment if there ever was one. Hard to know where to start, really. He's a bully and a braggart," he began to check the points off on his finger, "and he's got an obsession with big guns, probably to compensate for the guilt he feels about his own masculinity, or lack of it. And the guilt that's eating way at him is all down to the fact that he's gay but can't square it with his own notion of what manliness should be. *'Remember, Vin,'* he mimicked in a camp voice, looking straight into Spencer's eyes, *'when those books are written, I want them to say, Mark Spencer was a heterosexual who just happened to take it up the chuff.'"*

294

Spencer started to say something, but Mason raised his voice, drowning the words out. "Who knows what events in his sad life turned him into the basket case he is today? But that's what he is, a nutter, a pathetic, deluded psychopath and a figure of fun to everyone around him. Mark Spencer?" he laughed into the other man's face. "More like Frank Spencer."

It was clear from his bulging eyes and the vein pulsing rhythmically on his temple that Spencer was fighting a battle with himself not to simply kill Mason on the spot and have done with it. And a remote, semi-detached part of Mason recognised that he was trying to goad Spencer into killing him straight away so that he wouldn't have to face the unspeakable acts the other man was planning to carry out on him.

"What's the matter, *Spence*?" he said. "Come on, what's stopping you, or are you not man enough for it?"

Spencer almost executed him there and then but, with a visible effort, he managed to restrain himself and the arm holding the rifle dropped to his side. "Oh, no, *Frank*," he replied, "don't think you're going to get off that lightly. And I promise you that by the time I've finished, you'll be singing from a very different hymn sheet."

Another remote sensor now offered Mason the thought that with Spencer in no hurry to bring things to a head, and with Raj presumably somewhere in the vicinity, there might be a tiny window of hope for them, and he realised he was no longer in the high arousal state he had entered into when he had seen the West Ham badge, and that he was once more capable of coherent thought.

"Oh, no." Spencer was now speaking in a playful, high-pitched voice that was far more terrifying than his usual menacing monotone. "We're going to have some fun before we're done."

He pointed at Rees. "I've no particular truck with you, Trotsky, so I'm going to make it easy for you. Ron here will take you out first - nice clean head shot - you OK with that, Ron?"

"Your wish is my command, Spence." Ron bowed.

"Ron is proud of his accuracy and his efficiency, aren't you Ron? Funny how we're all different in that respect. I'm a bit more artistic, myself." He giggled. "After that, it'll be over to Ron and Kirsty for a little floor show, and then it's me and you, Frank. Want to tell Kirsty what you've got in mind for her, Ron?"

"You know what I've got in mind for her, Spence, I told you on the way down. I'm going to rape her senseless."

Spencer tutted. "Don't tell me, Ron. Be a gentleman and tell her."

Ron turned to Kirsty and smiled. "I'm going to fuck you bandy, Kirst," he said, "and, to be honest, the more it hurts you and the more you scream, the more I'll enjoy it."

He winked at her. "Never been much of a one for foreplay, me. On the other hand, the one thing I am is thorough."

He ran his eyes up and down her body and chuckled. "Very thorough indeed. Bit of an obsession with me, to be honest. Not one to leave any avenue unexplored, if you get my drift."

He winked at her again and although she stared stonily back at him, the colour had drained from her face and she looked as if she might be about to faint.

"And then," said Spencer, "it'll be over to you and me, Frank, for a little floor show of our own. Right, Ronald," he rubbed his hands. "Do the honours with the bald fucker and then we can get down to business."

Ron was fitting what looked like a silencer onto the end of his pistol when the door behind him opened and Mason saw something scuttle across the floor, keeping close to the wainscoting the way a rodent does. And then he went blind. One minute he was standing in a room full of people and the next, it was as if a photographer had set off a huge flash right in front of him, imprinting a blinding white light directly onto his retina.

At the same time his senses were assailed by a wall of sound so powerful it sent him staggering. A wave of nausea coursed through him and he felt his body connect with something hard and unyielding that knocked the wind out of him and completed the process of disorientation. Blind and deaf, he waited, helpless as a child, until eventually, with agonizing slowness, his thoughts began to unscramble. He wondered, in a detached, almost out of body way, whether the impact he had felt had been his body hitting the ground, and when he explored around him with trembling fingers, he found that he did appear to be lying on the floor.

Presently the profound deafness gave way to a yammering, ringing sound in his ears and shapes began to dance around on the inside of his eyelids. He opened an eye cautiously and the view – an expanse of carpet with the sole of a foot sticking up inches from his eyes – confirmed that he did indeed seem to be lying on his side on the floor. He tried to focus on the foot, but the image looked all wrong - like the negative of a photograph - so he closed his eye again.

Then another wave of dizziness and nausea coursed through him and he thought he was going to be sick. He tried to grab hold of something to stop the yawing, seesawing sensation, and his hands scrabbled about on the carpet but couldn't find a purchase. And then gradually the world seemed to settle back onto its axis, the pounding in his ears gave way to something less insistent and when he opened his eyes, he found that he could, after a fashion, see.

During his period of disorientation, Mason had been aware that some kind of commotion was going on around him, but the whole thing had had a muffled, unreal quality to it, as if it was taking place in a distant part of the house. Moving gingerly, he managed to prop himself up on one elbow and the first thing he saw was Kirsty on her hands and knees, gasping and retching and choking and gulping in great gobbets of air.

He turned his head and the sole of a shoe that was resting on the floor perhaps eighteen inches from him filled his view. He concentrated all his attention on the shoe and noticed two things; the first was that it was attached to the body Mark Spencer and the second was that the hilt of a knife was protruding from the body's stomach. Which meant that unless his eyes were playing tricks with him, Mark Spencer was dead, or if not dead, very, very unwell.

As he was trying to make sense of all this, a head attached to a pair of shoulders swam into his field of vision and he recognised it as belonging to Matt Rees. The head's lips began to move and, as Mason concentrated on trying to understand what they were saying to him, random sounds began to coalesce into recognisable words.

"Frank! It's me, Matt!" He now realized what Rees was saying. "Frank! Can you hear me?"

Aware that Ron might still be in the vicinity, he tried to jump up but was immediately hit by another wave of nausea.

"It's all right, Frank," he heard Rees's voice again. "Relax, it's all over." He sank back to the floor, grateful for the opportunity to allow his thoughts to unscramble fully.

When he looked up again, Spencer's body was still on the floor and Kirsty was sitting up, wan and pale but obviously with her wits about her. On the other side of the room a man he didn't know was leaning over an inert figure on the ground who he took to be Ron and, as he watched, the man looked across and gave a thumbs up to Rees.

"You OK now?" Rees asked Mason and he nodded.

After a couple of seconds Kirsty asked, "What happened?" in an unsteady voice.

"May I introduce Mr Archie Shore, from the Home Office," said Rees and the figure in the corner rose to its feet and moved towards them.

"Er… pleased to meet you," he said. He was thin and balding, with wispy strands of hair that floated, Bobby Charlton style, above his head. He held out a hand, realized it was covered in blood, and withdrew it quickly.

"What happened?" asked Kirsty again.

"Well," said Rees, "Archie created a bit of diversion and then…. we did what we had to do."

"Who are you?" asked Mason after a moment.

"You know who we are," answered Rees. "I'm Matt Rees, M.P. and this is Archie Shore from the Home Office."

"But how…?" began Kirsty.

"As we're not likely to be interrupted," said Rees, looking down at the bodies, "I'll start at the beginning." He paused to gather his thoughts. "Like many others, yourselves included, Archie and I have become very concerned about what's happening in Parliament, in the Home Office and in the country. Anyway, when Raj set up the meeting, we thought it might make sense, given the kind of people who seem to be involved in this business, to have a bit of backup available in case things went wrong."

"So, I followed Matt down to Denham," Shore took up the story, "at a discreet distance, of course, and took up a watching brief outside the house. Well, it wasn't long before these two charmers," he gestured dismissively at the bodies, "turned up. Anyway, I gave them a few minutes to go in and then I followed them inside and had a listen at the door. And when I heard what they were planning to do to you guys, I whipped a stun grenade into the room and, well, the rest was plain sailing."

Mason looked at the bodies, one crumpled on its side in the corner, the other lying on its back with a knife sticking out of it. "When you say, plain sailing…" he began.

"Plain sailing is probably a bit of an exaggeration, Archie," Rees agreed. "We're no James Bonds, but what we do have is several years active service in the T.A."

"The T.A.?" said Mason. "Remind me…"

"The Territorial Army; a much-maligned organisation with a membership frequently derided as a bunch of weekend soldiers." He pointed to the bodies on the floor. "But as you can see, when push comes to shove, the training pays off."

"But they were armed," said Mason, "and you…"

"We had the Fairbairn-Sykes fighting knife," said Rees, pointing to the wicked looking handle sticking out of Spencer's stomach. "Beloved of

British commandos from time immemorial; I was carrying one strapped to my leg, and as soon as the grenade went off, I whipped it out."

"But still…," said Mason.

"Never underestimate the power of surprise," went on Rees. "When I saw the grenade rolling across the floor, I knew that if I just squeezed my eyes tight shut for a second, they'd be blind while we'd be able to see." He shrugged his shoulders, "After that it was just a question of us deciding which one we were going to, er… pair off with."

"It's a tidy little grenade is the M84," said Shore. "Delivers a flash of a million candela and a bang of 180 decibels, inducing disorientation and confusion in anyone within a radius of twenty feet. The loss of balance is caused by a spike in pressure which disturbs the fluid in the ear canals, so don't be surprised if you feel a bit nauseous for a while."

"Shouldn't we be getting the hell out of here?" Kirsty was looking nervously towards the door. "In case there are more of them."

"I watched them arrive," said Shore. "And I checked to see whether there was anything that might suggest they had back up. I'm happy they came alone."

"Listen guys," said Mason as he climbed uncertainly to his feet. "We can't thank you enough…"

"All in a day's work," said Shore, lightly. He looked around, scanned the room as if he was looking for something, then took several steps in the direction of the door and vomited into a wastepaper basket. "Apologies for that," he said a moment later, wiping a hand across his mouth. "It's not actually something I've…"

He broke off and Rees continued, "What Archie is saying is that this kind of thing isn't really our bread and butter it's probably not surprising if it causes a… reaction."

"Are you OK yourself, Matt?" Kirsty asked tentatively.

"I'm fine, funnily enough," he said. "I've never killed before, and like most people I've always wondered whether I'd actually be able to go through with it - taking someone's life, I mean - when the time came. But do you know what," he looked down at the bodies, "once I'd seen those two in action, it didn't feel any different from squashing a couple of bluebottles with a piece of rolled up newspaper."

"Would this be a good time to contact Raj?" said Mason, after a moment. "Although what he'll say when he sees this lot…?"

"Good idea." Rees said.

Mason texted, *unexpected developments here, can you come straight away?* and almost immediately got a reply that read, *on my way*

Rees crouched down beside Spencer's inert body and stretched a tentative hand towards the handle of the knife. "They say if you want to avoid a blood spurt, not to withdraw it for a bit. What do you think Archie?"

Shore was leaning over Ron and Mason noticed a hilt protruding from the dead man's stomach.

"You both went for the same spot," Mason said. "With the knives I mean."

"It's the training. You're supposed to slide it in under the ribs and up it goes straight into the heart. Our RSM used to say that if you got it right it was so smooth it was like slipping your…" he stopped and cleared his throat. "Sorry, ladies present…"

"Don't worry," said Kirsty. "After what I've had to listen to over the last couple of years..."

"Here goes," said Rees taking hold of the hilt of the knife and withdrawing it carefully. Thankfully, his action produced no jet of arterial blood and Rees cleaned the blade with a piece of rag he had taken from his pocket.

Mason looked down at Spencer's face and was amazed at how different it looked in death. The angry lines were gone, and his facial muscles had relaxed so that he appeared to be in repose.

Kirsty had come and stood next to him. "Looks almost human, doesn't he?"

Mason grunted. "He looks human because he's dead, and that's the best place for him."

"No regrets?"

"You're joking! I mean, who'd have any regrets about the putting down of a mad, rabid dog? I've got a tiny bit of… not sympathy exactly, compassion perhaps, for the likes of Ron over there, despite what he was planning to do to you. Blokes like him spend their lives in an environment where violence is the norm, and don't know any other way to behave. But that bastard?" He looked down at Spencer. "I'm only sorry I wasn't able to execute him myself."

He felt her eyes on him. "If I sound a bit rabid myself, it's probably because I found out it was Spencer who killed Mathew." He filled her in on Raj's theory about the West Ham connection. "That's probably why I went into one and started insulting him; I think the red mist descended big time."

"You should have seen his face," she said. "If I hadn't been scared half out of my wits I would have laughed." She gave his arm a squeeze. "It's something, isn't it? Knowing who killed Mathew, I mean. It won't bring either of them back, but it must bring you some... solace, to know their deaths have been avenged.

"Even if I didn't avenge them myself? Personally, I mean."

She smiled at him. "Even if you didn't avenge them yourself."

At that moment they heard the front door opening. Rees grabbed his knife, but they heard Raj's voice saying, "Only me," and then the door opened, and he was gazing in astonishment at the sight that met his eyes.

"What...?" he began and then stopped, speechless, his eyes moving around the room in slow-motion as he surveyed the carnage.

"There's been a bit of... bother," said Rees.

"A bit of bother? It looks more like World War Three." He moved towards the centre of the room and looked at the bodies.

"Raj Kumar, meet Mark Spencer," said Mason. "And the one over there's called Ron – you remember me telling you about him – I don't know his second name."

"And they're both…?"

"They're both dead." Rees grunted.

"I wonder how they knew?" mused Mason. "Where to find us, I mean."

"Could have been any number of ways," shrugged Kirsty. "We have no idea how big this conspiracy is or what technology is being employed. That's one of the problems – we've never known exactly who or what we're up against at any given time."

"That's true enough." Raj opened his mouth to continue and his mobile rang. He took the call, listened, said one terse word, "OK," then sent a brief text and let the phone fall to his side.

"I'm afraid we're too late," he said. "It's just been announced."

"What's been announced?"

"The coup."

"Shit!" exploded Rees.

"Apparently TV and radio stopped broadcasting suddenly and a message was read out. Government of National Unity, temporary state of emergency, suspension of right of assembly, night-time curfew, blah, blah, blah. It finished with an appeal for calm, a quote from Churchill about us all going forward together, and the playing of the National Anthem."

"Shit," said Rees again. "Well, that makes the whole thing a hundred times harder."

"A thousand times," said Shore.

There was silence for a moment and then, looking at Rees, Kirsty asked, "What are we going to do?"

"I'm trying to think," he answered tersely.

Raj stooped down and picked up the assault rifle that had fallen from Spencer's hand. "We're going to need to tidy up here, somehow, before we do anything," he said as he retrieved Ron's handgun from the area of floor it had skittered into.

"We need to get back to London," said Archie, "Particularly if there's going to be a curfew."

Raj came forward and stood in the centre of the room. "Do me a favour, Matt and Archie," he said, "and pop those knives of yours onto the floor for me."

"Sorry?" said Rees, and Shore looked up in surprise.

"You heard me. Put the knives onto the floor and go and sit down against the wall." Kumar spoke with deceptive mildness but the way he was waving the barrel of the Type 88 around belied the words.

"Would you mind doing the same, Frank and Kirsty?" He gestured towards the wall with the assault rifle. "I'm afraid things aren't quite what they seem."

XXV

Rees watched him for a moment and then slipped the knife out from his trouser leg and put it on the floor. "I hope you've got an explanation for this," he growled.

"All will be revealed in a few moments, Matt. Archie?" Kumar gestured with the barrel of the gun and a moment later there were two knives on the floor and four people sitting in a row against the wall.

"What's going on Raj?" asked Mason, by now thoroughly confused

"I do owe you an explanation, Frank," said Raj. He considered for a moment and then said, "I'm afraid there's someone here who isn't quite what they seem to be."

He waited and the others exchanged looks that held, as far as Mason could tell, nothing but surprise and consternation. Kumar looked at each of them in turn as if he was hoping to learn something.

"Perhaps the easiest way to come at the whole thing is by reference to Kirsty," he said finally.

"Kirsty?" Mason was completely at sea. He looked to Kirsty for help, but she only shrugged.

"What would you say is the central factor in what Kirsty has been doing, the key to understanding her role."

"The fact that it *was* a role, I suppose," said Mason after a few second's thought. "I mean the fact that she was working undercover."

"Precisely. You were doing the same thing yourself to a certain extent, Frank, but Kirsty was doing it for real. False identity, false past, the whole deal."

"And?" Mason couldn't see where all this might be heading.

"Well, supposing I was to tell you that there's someone else here who's been doing the same thing, taking on a false identity, playing a part, acting out a role."

Mason looked at Kirsty, who stared back at him incredulously. Then he looked at Matt and Archie and their faces seemed to reflect the same bewilderment.

"Who...?" he began, but Kumar interrupted him.

"Someone who's been stringing everyone along, playing the part of a good guy when all along they've been batting for the other side. What would you say to that, Frank?"

Mason looked at Kirsty, who had risked her own life to save his and all he could see in her face was shock and bewilderment. He looked at Matt Rees and Archie Shore, who had, not ten minutes earlier, unless he was going completely mad, terminated the lives of evil human beings in the cause of freedom and justice. Was Raj suggesting that one of them was an imposter? Surely not -

every fibre of his being rejected such a notion as ridiculous.

He turned back to Kumar. "I don't understand, Raj…?" he began and then stopped. Kumar was regarding him with an inscrutable expression on his face but behind it Mason could see something else, the hint of a twinkle that suggested he might be enjoying himself.

His mind reeled as he fought to make sense of the other man's words. Was he implying… but surely it couldn't be? This was Raj Kumar, rock of dependability, the one person he'd been able to confide in when he'd felt in danger of drowning in the rank, foetid swamp that was white supremacy.

"What are you saying, Raj?" He had to force the words out.

Instead of answering directly, Kumar smiled and said, "Do you remember which of us contacted the other first?"

Mason thought for a moment. "It was me," he said. "I wanted to find out about the far right and your name kept coming up as a committed fighter against racism."

"And the rest, as they say, is history."

"What exactly are you saying, Raj?" Mason was growing tired of the other man's circumlocution. "Why don't you get to the point instead of talking in fucking riddles."

"Pity, I was rather hoping you'd get there yourself." Kumar waited, his face wearing the same expression, as if he was party to a private joke that no one else knew about. "But if you're sure…"

310

Mason's head, already woozy from the effects of the concussion, was spinning. What exactly was Raj hinting at and why was he wearing that supercilious smile and looking so pleased with himself? He tried to work out the answer to those questions, but he had a splitting headache and couldn't think straight, and in the end, he couldn't think what to do other than to continue to stare stonily at the other man.

"OK, Frank," said Raj eventually, "I'll cut to the chase." He folded his arms as if he was about to deliver a bedtime story to a bunch of children. "What would you say if I told you that Raj Kumar, anti-racist blogger and fighter for the rights of minorities, doesn't really exist." He was watching Mason intently. "Other than as a figment of someone's rather overactive imagination, I mean?"

"But…" Mason's mind was reeling. "I mean… you've been blogging for years. I've checked it out."

"I've been blogging for years, for sure…. in the role of Raj Kumar."

"Are you saying Raj Kumar's not your name?"

"I think the penny's finally starting to drop, Frank. I'd clap my hands, only, judging by the expression on your faces, I'm probably going to need to keep this gun handy. Think about me as a kind of Kirsty in reverse, working undercover to get inside information on the opposition"

"The opposition? I don't understand."

"Come on, Frank, do you want me to spell it out for you?"

"Are you saying," said Mason, hardly daring to breathe, "that you're… part of…?"

"You're getting there, Frank."

"But you're Raj Kumar," interjected Rees. "I've read your blogs, I've talked to you on the phone, I've even attended conferences with you. You're Raj Kumar."

"It's a nice name, isn't it, if I say so myself."

"You're saying it's not your real name?"

"I'm saying it's not my real name."

"Then who are you?"

"Well, I'll start by telling you who I'm not. I'm not an anti-racist and I'm certainly not an Indian blogger called Raj Kumar. I'll let you into a secret…" He leaned forward like a comedian about to deliver a punchline. " …I'm not even Indian."

"You're not…?" Mason's mind was still reeling.

"A naturally dark complexion topped up with a hint of something that alters the pigmentation and, well…," he spread his arms out and chuckled, "Bob, or perhaps I should say, Babu's your uncle."

Mason could see his own incomprehension reflected in the faces of his companions.

"Don't look so surprised. It wouldn't be the first time it's been done, and I thought I did a convincing job of it, if I say so myself. A better one than Spike Milligan or Peter Sellers ever managed, anyway." He pasted a silly grin onto his face, waggled his head and chanted, *"Goodness, gracious me!"*

"But why…?" Mason started to formulate a question, didn't quite know what he wanted to say, and spluttered into silence.

"Why did I do it all, you mean?" Kumar looked at his watch. "Well, we do seem to have a bit of time. Some colleagues of mine - in the movement, I mean - are on their way down to help me tidy this lot up, but they're coming on the A40 in the rush hour, so they're probably still half an hour away." He looked at his watch again. "In the meantime, I'm happy to help you fill in the gaps in the story."

To say Mason was stunned would have been the understatement of the millennium. Of all the people he had met since he had set out to avenge Mathew's death, Kumar was the one he had come to trust the most. He had seemed straightforward and honourable; in fact he had radiated decency and Mason had quickly grown to feel he could trust him with knowledge that would cost him his life if it fell into the wrong hands. But more than all that, on an instinctive level he had *liked* the man.

Raj had been watching him closely and must have seen the hurt in his eyes because he said, "I've disappointed you, haven't I, Frank."

Determined not to give the other man anything, Mason just shrugged, but in truth, he was just about played out. Having been delivered out of the jaws of death firstly by Kirsty's brave decision to rescue him, then by Archie Shore's timely intervention, he was now facing execution for a third time, for he had little doubt that that would be their fate once Kumar had finished with them. He knew in his heart that he had used up all his luck on the first two occasions and that if it was going to be third time lucky for anyone, it was going to be for the people who wanted him dead.

Putting a hand on the floor to shift position, he felt a lump under his arm, and as he realized he was armed with a turbo charged taser, a rush of adrenalin jolted along his veins. He tried to make eye contact with Kirsty without it appearing too obvious; he knew she would be thinking the same thing as him, which was that the tasers gave them a chance – admittedly not much of a chance against a man armed with an automatic weapon that discharged dozens of rounds per second - but a chance all the same of turning the tables on Kumar if they could only persuade him to halve the physical distance between him and them.

He was also starting to realize that Kumar, or whatever his name really was, was one of those types who craves an audience to whom he can show off, and that if they could just keep him talking, his egocentricity might cause him to lower his guard enough to give them a chance.

"So," said Kumar, and there was just a hint of impatience in his voice. "Do you want to hear what I've got to say, or what?"

"Well, Raj." He shrugged elaborately. "There's not a lot else we can do - I mean, we're the original captive audience, aren't we?"

314

"That's better, Frank," said Kumar, a smile spreading across his face. "It's always better when we try to resolve these situations in a civilised way." He chuckled. "A captive audience, I like that. Who wants to go first?"

Mason risked a glance in Kirsty's direction and his ears registered the merest hint of the word, "Wait," as it ghosted from her lips.

"So, who are you, then?" He turned back to Raj. "If you don't mind me going back to my original question?"

"My name isn't important," said Kumar, "and you wouldn't know it anyway. Suffice to say it's as English as any of yours and that Vinnie Groves and I go back a long way, longer than anyone else in the movement, even Mark Spencer; and that what's happening in the country now is the result of years, decades even, of planning."

He settled back in the manner of a professor about to explain a complex theorem to a class of dull-witted freshmen. "At a certain point, it was decided that I might best help the movement by going underground, a bit like you Kirsty – pleased to meet you, by the way, I've heard a lot about you - so that's what I did. I became an Indian blogger committed to anti-racism, but I also did stuff for English Rose and for Storm Force, liaising with like-minded organisations ahead of the day when we could all come out into the open.

"Quite a few people in the movement knew there was a big fish, other than Vinnie and Spence, working in the background, but only those two

315

knew what my new identity was. It was a clever idea, if I say so myself, and I was able to keep my ear close to the ground as Raj Kumar and tip off Vinnie about a lot of useful stuff.

"I got the idea from a book I read when I was at university. It was written by a white American called John Howard Griffin who took some stuff to darken his skin and travelled around the southern states of the US during the civil rights era to see what the "negro" experience was. It was called *Black Like Me* and it caused quite a stir.

"Its main conclusion was that the Darkies were having a tough time of it in the South, which was pretty bleeding obvious really, the silly sod could have saved himself all that bother. But the central conceit of the book – a white man pretending to be a black man and getting away with it - intrigued me, so that's what I decided to do. And I think I can say in all modesty that I did it quite successfully - successfully enough to fool you lot, anyway."

Mason risked another glance in Kirsty's direction, and fancied he detected a millimetric shake of her head.

"I did hear quite a lot about you, Kirsty," Kumar was now saying, "Vinnie was very impressed with you, kept saying we needed more people like you in the movement."

She grunted. "I obviously didn't get close enough to him or I'd have found out about you."

"He's far too fly to have let something like that slip," said Kumar, "but he must have talked about a mysterious figure working undercover who was going to emerge into the open when the time was right. They all did."

"The Chameleon, you mean? I figured that was just a Storm Force urban myth." She stopped speaking and looked at him. "You're not saying you're the Chameleon?"

"Think about it, Kirsty?" Kumar was really enjoying himself now. "What is it that's special about a chameleon – I mean, what is it that it does to avoid detection?"

"A chameleon?" she said. "That's obvious, it changes c…" she stopped abruptly, covered her face with her hands and said, "Oh, God!"

"Let me finish it for you," said Kumar. "It changes colour."

Kirsty's head was still in her hands.

"I came up with the name myself; quite clever, don't you think, in view of what I was doing? I usually think people who invent those kinds of names for themselves are a bit ridiculous but…"

He let the words trail off and there was a silence. After a few moments he said rather irritably, "I do think my disclosure might have provoked a bit more of a reaction…"

"Sorry Raj," Kirsty broke in and Mason noticed that her voice had suddenly gone all fluttery. "You're absolutely right. You don't mind me calling you Raj, do you, I mean we haven't been properly introduced…?"

He smiled modestly and said, "Raj is fine."

"It's just that the whole thing's taken my breath away a bit, to be honest. But there are a few things I'd like to ask you; a few things I haven't been able to make sense of that you might be able to throw a light on…"

Kumar looked at his watch. "Well, we've got a good… twenty minutes before my associates arrive, so go ahead."

"It's a bit hard to hear you properly from over there," said Kirsty. "Any chance you could come a bit closer?"

"Unfortunately, not, my dear. You see, there are four of you and you are, not to put too fine a point on it, desperate - Matt there is crouching like a tiger about to spring. So, I'm happy to talk, but only from these respective positions. And please don't be in any doubt that if you were thinking of rushing me - and I'm looking at you again, Matt – I could cut the four of you down with one burst before you'd gone a quarter of the way.

Mason tried to think of a something, anything, he could do that might cause Kumar to drop his guard, but it was Kirsty, finally, who broke the silence.

"What I don't understand, Raj," she said, "is why you brought us here in the first place? I mean, you could have told Spencer where we were once Frank had called, or you could have had us picked up on our way down here. You could have got to us in any number of ways and yet you brought us all the way down here for a meeting you knew wasn't going to lead to anything. Why?"

"Do you know, my dear, I do regret that we're not going to have the chance to work together," said Raj, "because that is a really intelligent question." He considered for a few moments. "If you thought of the whole thing as an internal matter - a little, local difficulty, to coin a phrase - a problem within the movement that I felt needed solving, you wouldn't be too far off the mark."

He leaned back against the table. "How can I best describe the problem? Well, if you take a look at the lump of meat over there that used to be Mark Spencer, you'll have got to the nub of it." He stopped for a moment and considered. "Now don't get me wrong, Mark did a hell of a lot in the early days, no one did more, but we're at a stage in the journey now where there simply isn't room for someone like him in the leadership of the movement."

He paused again. "You remember Ernst Röhm, don't you, Kirsty?" She nodded. "Well, Mark Spencer had become our Röhm, a loose cannon who was damaging the credibility of the movement and someone whose behaviour we simply couldn't tolerate any longer."

He turned to the others. "Röhm was one of Hitler's earliest supporters and he was also the leader of the Sturmabteilung, better known over here as the Brownshirts. He played a big part in helping Hitler to gain power - no one has ever denied that - but once the new Germany began to take shape, to say he became a liability would have been putting it mildly.

"I mean, there they were, all those strapping, clean limbed young Aryan boys, pride of the Fatherland, jumping up and down in fields in their shorts and singlets, and the moment they left the Hitler Youth and joined the SA, Röhm and his mates started syphoning off the pretty ones so they could creep into their tents in the middle of the night and bum them.

"Not the sort of behaviour that reflected well on the new Germany, was it really, and the Fuhrer needed to be protected from that, so Goering and Goebbels got together and worked on Hitler and in the end, they convinced him that Röhm was a liability and had to go. It took a lot of doing though, because Hitler felt a great sense of loyalty towards Röhm, but he finally gave permission for the SA to be purged and its leaders were dragged out of their beds and executed on the spot. Hitler apparently gave the order that Röhm be provided with a revolver so he could do the honourable thing – for old time's sake, you understand – but Röhm refused to use it and, in the end, they had to shoot him like a dog."

"So, you're saying Mark Spencer was your movement's Ernst Röhm?" Kirsty had leaned forward, and Mason noticed that her right arm was resting on her thigh.

"Exactly. His behaviour was an embarrassment and a threat to everything we hoped to achieve; it was just so… undignified. Not that

I've got a problem with undignified behaviour, you understand. In fact, at the lower levels of the movement, the more undignified the behaviour is, the better - it teaches the citizenry a bit of respect. But not at the top, and especially not at a time like this."

"I understand what you've told us, Raj," said Kirsty, "but what I don't understand is how it led to this?" She gestured around her.

"Now, that's the really clever part," said Kumar, "if I say so myself."

In his enthusiasm to complete the story he moved a couple of paces forward, but he was still a fifteen-foot putt away from his captives. Mason racked his brain to try and remember what Kirsty had said the effective range of the tasers was, but he couldn't recall, other than that it wasn't very far.

He also knew that the improvised weapons offered them but a single chance and that if they failed to take it there wouldn't be a second one. He risked another look and wasn't sure whether the tiny, almost imperceptible shake of Kirst's head was real or the product of his imagination.

"Go on, Raj." Kirsty's smile was warm and inviting and Kumar smiled back at her.

"You could have knocked me down with a feather when Frank contacted me and told me he was trying to infiltrate Storm Force. Anyway, I decided to point him in the direction of Spence and see how close he could get to him; it was amazing really, like having your own drone and being able to fly it closer and closer to the target and knowing you could weaponize it at any time.

"So," he went on, "I knew that Spence needed to go, but I also knew that Vinnie, who is incredibly loyal – that's one of the things that makes him a great man – would be highly resistant to the idea. I also knew I wouldn't be needing my alias for much longer, so when you phoned me out of the blue the other day, Frank, I couldn't believe my luck.

"I mean what an opportunity to demonstrate Spence's incompetence to the boss, and you've got to admit it *is* amazingly incompetent to let two people like you slip out of his grasp at such a sensitive time. My first thought was to… neutralize you myself, and in the process point out to Vinnie how close Spence had come to blowing everything. And then I had a brainwave…"

Kirsty leaned towards him encouragingly, and, in his excitement, Kumar took another step forward.

"I got word to Spence - as a friend, you understand - that you were on your way down here and that he had a chance to dig himself out of the hole he was in, but that he needed to be discreet and only bring one or two people with him. I knew he wouldn't be satisfied with just… nullifying you and that he'd want to have some fun first, that's why I chose this place. There are hidden cameras in all the rooms that would have recorded what he did, not in glorious technicolour you understand - in fact it's an old-fashioned system that records onto videotape -

but enough for anyone watching to be able to see exactly what was going on."

Rees looked around him. "Hidden cameras, bloody hell, who owns his place?"

Kumar smiled. "Let's just say, a supporter - and you'll be amazed at how many supporters are going to crawl out of the woodwork in the days ahead. Anyway, where was I? Ah yes, Spence and the little entertainment he had planned for the two of you. I knew that a recording of what he was planning to do - especially to you, Frank – would finish him with Vinnie. I mean we're none of us squeamish, but Spence had taken the business of enhanced interrogation to a whole new level, and I knew Vinnie would realize that in his position – especially from now on – there would need to be protective layers, layers of deniability, between himself and that sort of thing.

"And that would be the end of Spence, especially if I struck quickly and denied him a chance to defend himself once I'd denounced him. And the fact that a well-known MP had become part of the carnage at such a sensitive time would have further demonstrated Spence's recklessness and unfitness for high office."

He beamed at them and took another step forward. "And do you know what the beauty of the whole thing was? If by any chance you managed to turn the tables on him – for which congratulations by the way – he'd have been out of the way for good, anyway."

He extended his arms, palms up. "I mean, If I say so myself, it was beautiful. Heads I won, tails he lost. And nobody knew about the whole thing but me; even the guys on their way down now only know that I need them to do a bit of mopping up for me."

He smiled ruefully. "A bit cloak and dagger, the whole thing, I know, but," he shrugged and smiled again, "I suppose I must have got used to working alone."

"Weren't you worried about Spencer recognising you when we staged that knife attack?" asked Mason.

"No. My face was well concealed by that hoodie and I'm pretty good at disguising my voice." He smiled modestly. "I mean, they don't call me the Chameleon for nothing."

"You really have managed the thing incredibly well," said Kirsty. "I mean you've been way ahead of us the whole time, haven't you? So, what's next - for you, I mean?" She gave Kumar a flirtatious smile. "Where do see yourself in five years?"

"I hope I'll be marching at Vinnie's side as he leads the country back to greatness."

"He's not leading anything at the moment, though, is he?" growled Rees.

"Not yet. But who's going to stop him. Alexander Cadogan? Do me a favour! *'Oh, Zander,'* he said in an exaggerated public-school accent. "We'll ease him out soon enough when the time is right, don't worry about that. Wouldn't even need to do that if it was like it is across the pond where, as long as they tell their guy he's a genius and give him shiny things to play with, they can do whatever they like.

"But to get back to your question about the future," he was talking to Kirsty again now, "my principal role will be to protect Vinnie and to keep him safe. Do you know, Hitler never visited a concentration camp, or went to a slave labour site, or witnessed a public execution? He was shielded from all that by the people around him, for reasons of plausible deniability, of course, but equally to protect him from the squalor of the whole thing, to keep his greatness from being tainted by the unpleasantness of it all."

He stretched out a foot and scuffed the surface of the carpet with his toe. *Just come a tiny bit closer*, *please just come a couple of steps closer,* Mason willed him silently, but Kumar remained tantalisingly and frustratingly just out of reach.

"You've seen Vinnie, Kirsty," went on Kumar, "You've worked with him. Surely you can see his greatness?"

"I suppose all that sort of thing will be judged in retrospect. I mean, it will depend on what he does with the power he's given."

"Have you heard him talk about what the country's going to be like when this is all over? Makes the hairs on your neck stand up, it does. Wait till we've had a couple of generations of the new history curriculum, he says. We'll leave a few of the battles in, of course, especially the ones against foreigners, but the rest of it - the past, I mean - will disappear. Can you believe that? Eight hundred years of history, all gone. And better than that, *it never happened.*

"Magna Carta? Never happened. The Bill of Rights? What was that? All those Reform Acts widening the franchise; none of them ever happened. Minority rights? What the fuck are they? And in place of all that old bollocks, a lean, hard country, where the strong rule for everyone and the weak are happy to be led, the way it used to be and the way it was always meant to be."

Kumar wiped a hand across his mouth and then, to Mason's utter dismay, he half turned and began to head back towards the table.

"Raj," he said. *"Raj!"* Anything to gain the other man's attention. Kumar stopped and looked at him and Mason, desperate to say anything that would keep him where he was, started speaking without knowing what he was going to say.

"When you say you're Vinnie's protector, Raj, who do you see yourself as then, Goering or Goebbels?" Without waiting for Kumar to reply he went on, "I mean, are you Goering, the obese, narcissistic druggie …?"

Kumar stopped abruptly and stared at him.

"Or are you more like Goebbels, the socially inept cripple with an inferiority complex?"

Kumar looked at him as if he couldn't believe his ears,

"So, which one are you then, Raj?" he went on. "The fat junkie or the social inadequate?"

326

Kumar took a step towards them and Mason saw Kirsty's left hand begin to slide across her body.

"By the way Frank," Raj had now recovered himself and he was smiling at Mason. "You know you've been trying to work out who killed the kid; well maybe I could help you there."

"It was Spencer." Mason spoke mechanically.

"Spencer? Did he tell you it was him, then?"

"No, I worked it out."

Kumar smiled. "Fell for my little West Ham story, did you?"

Mason stared at him but didn't speak.

"Ah, that got your attention." Kumar's smile broadened. "What do I need to say to convince you, Frank? Supposing I was to tell you I *know* Mark Spencer didn't kill little Mathew, and the reason I know *he* didn't was because I know who did."

Several seconds elapsed during which the two men continued to look at each other. "Just waiting for the tumblers to click, Frank, just waiting for the penny to drop."

He watched Mason's eyes widen. "Ah, you're finally getting there, Frank. Ironic really isn't it, you seeking me out and asking me to help you find the killer while all along... I mean, you couldn't make it up really, could you?"

He smiled again and, in a blinding flash, Mason knew it was true, knew it wasn't just another mind game, knew that it was Raj Kumar himself who had killed Matthew.

"Funny old world, isn't it?" Kumar took another step forward and looked into Mason's eyes. "I remember the expression on his little Jungle Bunny face as if it was yesterday. When he saw the baseball bat in my hand, he wet himself, and then, when he saw the piss running down his leg, he was embarrassed - no, more than that, ashamed."

He took another step forward and leaned forward so that his eyes were level with Mason's. "Embarrassment and shame; those were the last emotions the poor little fucker experienced. And do you know what....?"

He didn't finish the sentence because at that moment Mason heard a sound somewhere between a clunk and a whoosh, and Kumar's body jerked. In a flash he moved his right hand out of the way and pressed the taser button with his left and after a millimetric pause there was a small explosion and he felt the release of the wires as they leapt from the end of the device, sped through the air and hit Kumar in the midriff.

The impact caused Raj's body, already jerking around from the impact of Kirsty's wires, to spasm further and he heard Kirsty's voice, low and urgent. "Keep the button down, Frank, keep the button down."

Kumar was dancing like a marionette on steroids and although he still seemed to be conscious, it was clear he had lost control of his bodily movements. The barrel of the assault weapon swung past them and they all ducked and then its arc changed and a moment later it emptied its magazine into the ceiling.

Plaster and other material began to descend from the ceiling and Mason heard Kirsty's voice repeating, "Keep the button down, Frank!" while through the debris Kumar continued to dance a demented, spastic jig.

There was a crackling, sizzling sound, and an aroma redolent of frying onions wafted towards them, and then smoke started to appear and a moment later there was a soft popping sound and Mason watched transfixed as one of Kumar's eyes jumped out of its socket and, still on its stalk, began to yo-yo gently up and down in front of his face.

He heard Kirsty's voice shouting, "OK, Frank, you can stop now," and as he took his finger off the button, Kumar's body slumped to the floor and there was sudden, blessed calm.

XXVI

After a moment the stunned silence was broken by Archie's faltering voice. "What was…?"

"Never mind," Rees broke in tersely. "We need to get out of here before his mates arrive."

Wordlessly they grabbed the things that they had brought with them and headed for the door. "Everyone OK?" asked Rees. "Then let's go."

"Hang on," said Kirsty, "We don't know who's going to be investigating this, so we need to get rid of any fingerprints."

As Mason and Rees began wiping surfaces and door handles Kirsty pointed to the wastepaper basket. "Sorry Archie, you're going to have to take that with you."

He gave her a look and she shrugged. "There's a hell of a lot of DNA in human puke, I'm afraid. Come on, you can chuck it away later."

He picked up the basket, then put it down again and hurried over to a bag that was propped against the wall.

"I've had a thought," he said as he took a device about the size of an iPad out of the bag and plugged it into a wall socket. "Remember, he said there would be cameras recording what was going on?" He began to play with some of the dials and buttons on the console.

"This little device – another innovation from my hacker mate – will fry the insides of anything here that's electrically powered, including film recordings."

"Well done, Archie," said Rees and Kirsty shook her head and said, "Christ, I hadn't thought of that."

As they passed the still smouldering body she stopped and looked at it. "I wonder who he was?"

"Don't suppose we'll ever know," answered Mason. "The funny thing was, I really did like him, and I'd have trusted him with my life."

"Probably one of the reasons he was so good at what he did," she grunted. "Getting people to trust him, I mean."

They hurried down the corridor and as they got to the end Rees said tersely, "Straight through, Archie. Don't worry about checking if there's anyone out there – if there is, we're fucked anyway."

Without further ado they bolted through the door and raced down the drive. "You guys got a car?" gasped Mason

"In the road," said Rees, pointing and they all piled into a BMW parked a few yards from the gate. Moments later they were flying through the centre of Denham Village at a speed likely to attract the attention of the local constabulary.

"Slow down a bit, Arch," said Rees, who was sitting in the passenger seat

Shore reduced his speed and their progress became more sedate. "Sorry guys," he said ruefully, "must be adrenalin, or something."

A couple of minutes later they were climbing the slip road that led onto the M4O, while at the same time, on the other side of the carriageway, a minivan with blacked out windows began to descend onto the road that led into Denham. As they joined the dual carriageway, Shore turned the radio on, and it was immediately clear that Kumar had been telling the truth about the coup because they heard a sonorous voice relaying information about curfews and the temporary suspension of liberties.

Rees turned around in his seat. "You two, OK?" he asked, and they nodded. "What the hell was that stunt you pulled in there?" he said, adding after a moment, "if you don't mind me asking?"

Kirsty explained and when she had finished Rees shook his head. "Couldn't believe it when he started jerking around, I thought I was having hallucinations."

Shore chuckled. "Well, if we've got your guy from the Bond movies to thank for our deliverance, I'll drink a pint to him as soon as we get to a pub. Seriously though," he looked at Rees. "What are we going to do? I mean, what are you and I going to do in light of recent events, and what are we going to do with these two?"

"That's a good question." Rees turned in his seat and looked at the passengers in the back. "I've been thinking about nothing else since we got free, and I've come to the conclusion that we might actually have a little window of time before we need to start doing anything."

He continued to look at Mason and Kirsty. "Let me just run my thinking past you. Apart from Spencer and the other guy - Ron, was it? - no one in Storm Force knew about our meeting, Kumar made sure of that by telling them to keep it secret. And Kumar was playing a lone game too, wasn't he? So, I think it's safe to assume that we're in the clear in terms of anyone knowing we were down here – anyone who's still alive, that is. Are you with me so far - in terms of my reasoning, I mean?"

"What about whoever owns the house," asked Mason. "This 'supporter,' whoever he or she is?"

"Yeah, I've been thinking about that as well, and the place didn't have the look of somewhere that's been temporarily vacated for a meeting, did it? I mean, somewhere that's lived in on a day-to-day basis. My guess is that Kumar had access to it when he needed it but didn't need to ask permission to use it, which would have suited him down to the ground, we know what a secretive bastard he was."

"Can't fault your logic so far, Matt."

"Which means, Archie," he looked at the driver, "that there isn't a connection between the two of us and what's just happened, I mean, at least not for the time being."

He turned to Mason and Kirsty. "You two, however, are a different kettle of fish. Kirsty, your cover is well and truly blown, and you can't go home to the NPOIU because the Met itself may have been compromised, while you, Frank, are still on a Storm Force death list for daring to infiltrate them. "And," he paused, "on top of that you're both still being hunted by whoever else is involved in the conspiracy, and that could be a lot of people from a lot of organisations."

"Well, thanks for painting such a rosy picture of the future for us, Matt," said Kirsty. "I mean, I was just starting to relax, there."

"I *have* got a plan, actually," Rees grinned. "You obviously can't carry on with your old identities. "But," he paused, "you could always take on new ones."

"And how are we going to do that?" asked Kirsty, wearily. "I mean, who's going to give us new identities, our fairy godmothers?"

Rees chuckled. "Archie, how is that magic wand of yours?"

"Birth certificates, passports, identity cards, national insurance cards," Shore recited the names like a sales rep, "you name it, me and my mate can hack into the relevant database. I can build each of you a completely bespoke new identity in a couple of days."

Mason and Kirsty looked at each other and then back at Shore. "Some of us have seen this coming for a long time," said Rees finally, "which means we've been organising for a long time. We've built up a network of people we can trust, which also takes time, because in this life you can never be completely sure who you can or can't trust, can you?

"There are a number of us in the House of Commons, not a majority certainly, but a growing number of members, from all sides of the house, who've seen the way things are going and feel they've got a duty above and beyond just slavishly adhering to the clique that's currently working the levers of power. And as I said, that doesn't just apply to Labour, there are Lib Dems, Nationalists, and Conservatives too. Made me question my own prejudices, to be honest, when I saw how many Tories there are who are prepared to put country before party – Pringle for one (he named the Grand Old Man), and Kent, and Curran and quite a few others. And there's a network of likeminded people in the civil service too, isn't there Archie?"

"There certainly is."

334

"And there are a number of senior people in the military who are uneasy about the way things are heading - not enough of them I'll grant you - but principled people who aren't just willing to stand by while the country they love sleepwalks into tyranny."

He paused. "Wish I could say the same for the higher reaches of the judiciary, but," he winced, "I suppose a high court judge is always going to be a high court judge at the end of the day.

"I'm not saying it isn't going to be difficult, especially now the National Government is in place, but we do have an organisation out there and it's a growing one. In some ways today's news might actually make it easier for us to gain recruits – it will present people with a stark choice - my country's future liberty or my own selfish agenda. And for all the ones whose heads will be turned by the promise of a job with a posh title or a uniform with shiny buttons they can polish, there are others who'll continue to believe in something greater than themselves.

"And there are more of us every day. I've been reading about the *Maquis,* the French Resistance group that operated against the Nazis during World War Two. They used to appear out of nowhere to carry out their attacks before melting away into the background, and their name apparently derived from the undergrowth they hid themselves in. Well, our undergrowth is the Establishment and there's room for an awful lot of people to hide there until they're needed."

He looked at Kirsty and then at Mason. "Want to join us?"

They exchanged looks. "We'd be delighted to join you, Matt," said Mason, and Kirsty added, "Not that we've got much choice, when it comes down to it."

"What about your controller, Kirsty?" asked Rees. "The guy you're supposed to be meeting in Green Park."

"What about him?"

"Do you trust him?"

"Implicitly."

"Then meet him and bring him on board."

"I might just do that."

"And don't forget there's the film," said Rees. "Although I'm still not sure what to do with it. As I said earlier, we can't trust any outlet in the UK not to simply bury it – and us shortly afterwards."

"Abroad?" said Kirsty.

"That's what I've been thinking, but where? America? Waste of time. France? Not with the advances the far right has made there."

"Germany?" she said.

"Yeah," he said slowly. "You might be on to something there. The Germans have managed this whole series of crises better than anyone else, like a mature democracy rather than a rabble. So maybe you're right, Kirsty, maybe Germany's the place to go to with the film."

"Funny," said Kirsty.

"What?"

336

"Well, right wing dictatorships taking control all over Europe, with Germany the last hope for liberal democracy."

He laughed. "Maybe it's *because* of Germany's past that they've reacted to all this in a different way to the rest of us," said Rees. "Merkel grew up in the old East Germany, so she'll have had first-hand experience of that form of totalitarianism, and the whole country will know what happened in the thirties and forties with Hitler. Maybe," he said, thinking aloud, "maybe there's less likelihood of a country sleepwalking into tyranny if it's been there before and got the album, so to speak."

A silence descended on the car as it headed back towards London. In all the excitement Mason hadn't really had a chance to process Kumar's revelation that it had been he who had murdered Mathew, but now he realized that, in killing the man who had killed Mathew, he had completed the task he'd set himself.

He allowed himself to think of Matthew and Bianca and at that moment he sensed, in some way he couldn't define, that they were near to him. He felt their essence in the air around him - the smell of Matthew's freshly washed hair, the tantalising scent of Bianca's perfume - and he allowed it to enter him and pass into the centre of his being and possess him in a way it hadn't been able to for a long time.

He knew he would miss them forever, knew the sadness would always be there, but also felt that he had, in some way, begun to atone for the part he had played in their deaths. He drew their spirits into the core of his being for what he knew would be the last time, then consciously and deliberately, he let them go and, in that moment, they left him - he felt the weight of them leaving him. He waited a few moments and then very slowly his lips formed the words, *Goodbye, I'll never forget you.*

He rotated his head and his neck moved with a freedom it hadn't known for as long as he could remember, and he felt a lightening of the weight of his thoughts and the weight of his body that was palpable.

Incongruously he recalled some lines from the Greek poet Aeschylus that he had read somewhere and remembered:

> *He who learns must suffer.*
> *And even in our sleep pain that cannot forget*
> *Falls drop by drop upon the heart*
> *And in our own despair, against our will*
> *Comes wisdom to us by the awful grace of God*

He looked around and saw Kirsty regarding him gravely. "Are you all right, Frank?" she said.

"I'm fine…" he said and at that moment a wave of sadness and hope and renewal rushed through him and his throat constricted, and the words wouldn't come. Ignoring the tears stinging the corners of his eyes, he gathered himself, took a deep breath and tried again. "It's just…" he began, but once more the words clotted in his throat and he couldn't continue.

"It's OK, Frank," she said, and he felt her hand slip into his. "It's nothing to worry about, I think you're just coming back to life."

He looked into her eyes and deep within him a sense memory relating to physical passion stirred and sent a tentative signal in the direction of his brain. He smiled at her and she smiled back at him.

Shortly after the A40 passes under the Hangar Lane underpass it rises on giant struts onto a stretch of road called the Westway, and much of central London is laid out before it.

As he looked ahead Mason felt another wave of emotion course through his body. *Goodbye*, he breathed, *I'll never forget you, but now it's time for me to move on and make you proud.*

He considered the predicament he was in - hunted by unknown enemies in a society on the road to totalitarian tyranny and as likely as not to end up dead in a ditch with a bullet in the back of his head - and yet he felt as alive as he had ever done in his life.

He looked at his companions; Kirsty next to him, with a twinkle in her eye and the hint of a promise in her smile, Archie Shore in the driver's seat, willing to storm a room full of armed fanatics and do murder to rescue people he'd never met, and next to him, Rees, solid and reassuring and forensically intelligent, with decency and integrity oozing from every pore of his body.

It could be worse, he thought to himself. To be allied with such people, to work with and share a common purpose with people who were decent and honourable and who believed in something greater than themselves - freedom, or the rule of law, or liberal democracy, everyone would have a different name for it but it came down to the same thing – this was not a prospect to be feared.

And even though he knew that for every person willing to fight for justice, there are many more who will make their peace with any tyranny that brings them gain, he was ready for the fight.

Printed in Great Britain
by Amazon